The Ancient Allan

The Ancient Allan

H. Rider Haggard

MINT EDITIONS

The Ancient Allan was first published in 1920.

This edition published by Mint Editions 2021.

ISBN 9781513277639 | E-ISBN 9781513278049

Published by Mint Editions®

 MINT
EDITIONS

minteditionbooks.com

Publishing Director: Jennifer Newens
Design & Production: Rachel Lopez Metzger
Project Manager: Micaela Clark
Typesetting: Westchester Publishing Services

Contents

I

An Old Friend

Now I, Allan Quatermain, come to the weirdest (with one or two exceptions perhaps) of all the experiences which it has amused me to employ my idle hours in recording here in a strange land, for after all England is strange to me. I grow elderly. I have, as I suppose, passed the period of enterprise and adventure and I should be well satisfied with the lot that Fate has given to my unworthy self.

To begin with, I am still alive and in health when by all the rules I should have been dead many times over. I suppose I ought to be thankful for that but, before expressing an opinion on the point, I should have to be quite sure whether it is better to be alive or dead. The religious plump for the latter, though I have never observed that the religious are more eager to die than the rest of us poor mortals.

For instance, if they are told that their holy hearts are wrong, they spend time and much money in rushing to a place called Nauheim in Germany, to put them right by means of water-drinking, thereby shortening their hours of heavenly bliss and depriving their heirs of a certain amount of cash. The same thing applies to Buxton in my own neighbourhood and gout, especially when it threatens the stomach or the throat. Even archbishops will do these things, to say nothing of such small fry as deans, or stout and prominent lay figures of the Church.

From common sinners like myself such conduct might be expected, but in the case of those who are obviously poised on the topmost rungs of the Jacobean—I mean, the heavenly—ladder, it is legitimate to inquire why they show such reluctance in jumping off. As a matter of fact the only persons that, individually, I have seen quite willing to die, except now and again to save somebody else whom they were so foolish as to care for more than they did for themselves, have been not those "upon whom the light has shined" to quote an earnest paper I chanced to read this morning, but, to quote again, "the sinful heathen wandering in their native blackness," by which I understand the writer to refer to their moral state and not to their sable skins wherein for the most part they are also condemned to wander, that is if they happen to have been born south of a certain degree of latitude.

To come to facts, the staff of Faith which each must shape for himself, is often hewn from unsuitable kinds of wood, yes, even by the very best among us. Willow, for instance, is pretty and easy to cut, but try to support yourself with it on the edge of a precipice and see where you are. Then of a truth you will long for ironbark, or even homely oak. I might carry my parable further, some allusions to the proper material of which to fashion the helmet of Salvation suggest themselves to me for example, but I won't.

The truth is that we fear to die because all the religions are full of uncomfortable hints as to what may happen to us afterwards as a reward for our deviations from their laws and we half believe in something, whereas often the savage, not being troubled with religion, fears less, because he half believes in nothing. For very few inhabitants of this earth can attain either to complete belief or to its absolute opposite. They can seldom lay their hands upon their hearts, and say they *know* that they will live for ever, or sleep for ever; there remains in the case of most honest men an element of doubt in either hypothesis.

That is what makes this story of mine so interesting, at any rate to me, since it does seem to suggest that whether or no I have a future, as personally I hold to be the case and not altogether without evidence, certainly I have had a past, though, so far as I know, in this world only; a fact, if it be a fact, from which can be deduced all kinds of arguments according to the taste of the reasoner.

And now for my experience, which it is only fair to add, may after all have been no more than a long and connected dream. Yet how was I to dream of lands, events and people where of I have only the vaguest knowledge, or none at all, unless indeed, as some say, being a part of this world, we have hidden away somewhere in ourselves an acquaintance with everything that has ever happened in the world. However, it does not much matter and it is useless to discuss that which we cannot prove.

Here at any rate is the story.

IN A BOOK OR A record which I have written down and put away with others under the title of "The Ivory Child," I have told the tale of a certain expedition I made in company with Lord Ragnall. Its object was to search for his wife who was stolen away while travelling in Egypt in a state of mental incapacity resulting from shock caused by the loss of her child under tragic and terrible circumstances. The thieves were the priests of a certain bastard Arab tribe who, on account of a birthmark shaped like the young moon which was visible above her breast, believed her to be the priestess or oracle of their worship. This worship evidently had its origin in Ancient Egypt since, although they did not seem to know it, the priestess was nothing less than a personification of the great goddess Isis, and the Ivory Child, their fetish, was a statue of the infant Horus, the fabled son of Isis and Osiris whom the Egyptians looked upon as the overcomer of Set or the Devil, the murderer of Osiris before his resurrection and ascent to Heaven to be the god of the dead.

I need not set down afresh all that happened to us on this remarkable adventure. Suffice it to say that in the end we recovered the lady and that her mind was restored to her. Before she left the Kendah country, however, the priesthood presented her with two ancient rolls of papyrus, also with a quantity of a certain herb, not unlike tobacco in appearance, which by the Kendah was called *Taduki*. Once, before we took our great homeward journey across the desert, Lady Ragnall and I had a curious conversation about this herb whereof the property is to cause the person who inhales its fumes to become clairvoyant, or to dream dreams, whichever the truth may be. It was used for this purpose in the mystical ceremonies of the Kendah religion when under its influence the priestess or oracle of the Ivory Child was wont to announce divine revelations. During her tenure of this office Lady Ragnall was frequently subjected to the spell of the *Taduki* vapour, and said strange things, some of which I heard with my own ears. Also myself once I experienced its effects and saw a curious vision, whereof many of the particulars were afterwards translated into facts.

Now the conversation which I have mentioned was shortly to the effect, that she, Lady Ragnall, believed a time would come when she or I or both of us, were destined to imbibe these *Taduki* fumes and see wonderful pictures of some past or future existence in which we were both concerned. This knowledge, she declared, had come to her while she was officiating in an apparently mindless condition as the priestess of the Kendah god called the Ivory Child.

At the time I did not think it wise to pursue so exciting a subject with a woman whose mind had been recently unbalanced, and afterwards in the stress of new experiences, I forgot all about the matter, or at any rate only thought of it very rarely.

Once, however, it did recur to me with some force. Shortly after I came to England to spend my remaining days far from the temptations of adventure, I was beguiled into becoming a steward of a Charity dinner and, what was worse, into attending the said dinner. Although its objects were admirable, it proved one of the most dreadful functions in which I was ever called upon to share. There was a vast number of people, some of them highly distinguished, who had come to support the Charity or to show off their Orders, I don't know which, and others like myself, not at all distinguished, just common subscribers, who had no Orders and stood about the crowded room like waiters looking for a job.

At the dinner, which was very bad, I sat at a table so remote that I could hear but little of the interminable speeches, which was perhaps fortunate for me. In these circumstances I drifted into conversation with my neighbour, a queer, wizened, black-bearded man who somehow or other had found out that I was acquainted with the wilder parts of Africa. He proved to be a wealthy scientist whose passion it was to study the properties of herbs, especially of such as grow in the interior of South America where he had been travelling for some years.

Presently he mentioned a root named Yagé, known to the Indians which, when pounded up into a paste and taken in the form of pills, had the effect of enabling the patient to see events that were passing at a distance. Indeed he alleged that a vision thus produced had caused him to return home, since in it he saw that some relative of his, I think a twin-sister, was dangerously ill. In fact, however, he might as well have stayed away, as he only arrived in London on the day after her funeral.

As I saw that he was really interested in the subject and observed that he was a very temperate man who did not seem to be romancing, I told him something of my experiences with *Taduki*, to which he listened with a kind of rapt but suppressed excitement. When I affected disbelief in the whole business, he differed from me almost rudely, asking why I rejected phenomena simply because I was too dense to understand them. I answered perhaps because such phenomena were inconvenient and upset one's ideas. To this he replied that all progress involved the upsetting of existent ideas. Moreover he implored me, if the chance should ever come my way, to pursue experiments with *Taduki* fumes and let him know the results.

Here our conversation came to an end for suddenly a band that was braying near by, struck up "God save the Queen," and we hastily exchanged cards and parted. I only mention it because, had it not

H. RIDER HAGGARD

occurred, I think it probable that I should never have been in a position to write this history.

The remarks of my acquaintance remained in my mind and influenced it so much that when the occasion came, I did as a kind of duty what, however much I was pressed, I am almost sure I should never have done for any other reason, just because I thought that I ought to take an opportunity of trying to discover what was the truth of the matter. As it chanced it was quick in coming.

Here I should explain that I attended the dinner of which I have spoken not very long after a very lengthy absence from England, whither I had come to live when King Solomon's Mines had made me rich. Therefore it happened that between the conclusion of my Kendah adventure some years before and this time I saw nothing and heard little of Lord and Lady Ragnall. Once a rumour did reach me, however, I think through Sir Henry Curtis or Captain Good, that the former had died as a result of an accident. What the accident was my informant did not know and as I was just starting on a far journey at the time, I had no opportunity of making inquiries. My talk with the botanical scientist determined me to do so; indeed a few days later I discovered from a book of reference that Lord Ragnall was dead, leaving no heir; also that his wife survived him.

I was working myself up to write to her when one morning the postman brought me here at the Grange a letter which had "Ragnall Castle" printed on the flap of the envelope. I did not know the writing which was very clear and firm, for as it chanced, to the best of my recollection, I had never seen that of Lady Ragnall. Here is a copy of the letter it contained:

My dear Mr. Quatermain,

Very strangely I have just seen at a meeting of the Horticultural Society, a gentleman who declares that a few days ago he sat next to you at some public dinner. Indeed I do not think there can be any doubt for he showed me your card which he had in his purse with a Yorkshire address upon it.

"A dispute had arisen as to whether a certain variety of Crinum lily was first found in Africa, or Southern America. This gentleman, an authority upon South American flora, made a speech saying that he had never met with it there, but that an acquaintance of his, Mr. Quatermain, to whom he had spoken on the subject, said that he had seen something of the sort in the interior of Africa." (This was quite true for I remembered the incident.) "At the tea which followed the meeting I spoke to this gentleman whose name I never caught, and to my astonishment learnt that he must have been referring to you whom I believed to be dead, for so we were told a long time ago. This seemed certain, for in addition to the evidence of the name, he described your personal appearance and told me that you had come to live in England.

"My dear friend, I can assure you it is long since I heard anything which rejoiced me so much. Oh! as I write all the past comes back, flowing in upon me like a pent-up flood of water, but I trust that of this I shall soon have an opportunity of talking to you. So let it be for a while.

"Alas! my friend, since we parted on the shores of the Red Sea, tragedy has pursued me. As you will know, for both my husband and I wrote to you, although you did not answer the letters" (I never received them), "we reached England safely and took up our old life again, though to tell you the truth, after my African experiences things could never be quite the same to me, or for the matter of that to George either. To a great extent he changed his pursuits and certain political ambitions which he once cherished, seemed no longer to appeal to him. He became a student of past history and especially of Egyptology, which under all the circumstances you may think strange, as I did. However it suited me well enough, since I also have tastes that way. So we worked together and I can now read hieroglyphics as well as most people. One year he said that he would like to go to Egypt again, if I were not afraid. I answered that it had not been a very lucky place for us, but that personally I was not in the least afraid and longed to return there. For as you know, I have, or think I have, ties with Egypt and indeed with all Africa. Well, we went and had a very happy time, although I was always expecting to see old Harût come round the corner.

"After this it became a custom with us who, since George practically gave up shooting and attending the House of

Lords, had nothing to keep us in England, to winter in Egypt. We did this for five years in succession, living in a bungalow which we built at a place in the desert, not far from the banks of the Nile, about half way between Luxor which was the ancient Thebes, and Assouan. George took a great fancy to this spot when first he saw it, and so in truth did I, for, like Memphis, it attracted me so much that I used to laugh and say I believed that once I had something to do with it.

"Now near to our villa that we called 'Ragnall' after this house, are the remains of a temple which were almost buried in the sand. This temple George obtained permission to excavate. It proved to be a long and costly business, but as he did not mind spending the money, that was no obstacle. For four winters we worked at it, employing several hundred men. As we went on we discovered that although not one of the largest, the temple, owing to its having been buried by the sand during, or shortly after the Roman epoch, remained much more perfect than we had expected, because the early Christians had never got at it with their chisels and hammers. Before long I hope to show you pictures and photographs of the various courts, etc., so I will not attempt to describe them now.

"It is a temple to Isis—built, or rather rebuilt over the remains of an older temple on a site that seems to have been called Amada, at any rate in the later days, and so named after a city in Nubia, apparently by one of the Amen-hetep Pharaohs who had conquered it. Its style is beautiful, being of the best period of the Egyptian Renaissance under the last native dynasties.

"At the beginning of the fifth winter, at length we approached the sanctuary, a difficult business because of the retaining walls that had to be built to keep the sand from flowing down as fast as it was removed, and the great quantities of stuff that must be carried off by the tramway. In so doing we came upon a shallow grave which appeared to have been hastily filled in and roughly covered over with paving stones like the rest of the court, as though to conceal its existence. In this grave lay the skeleton of a large man, together with the rusted blade of an iron sword and some fragments of armour. Evidently he had never been mummified, for there were no wrappings, canopic jars, *ushapti* figures or funeral offerings. The state of the bones showed us why, for the right forearm was cut through and the skull smashed in; also an iron arrow-head lay among the ribs. The man had been buried hurriedly after a battle in which he had met his death. Searching in the dust beneath the bones we found a gold ring still on one of the fingers. On its bezel was engraved the cartouche of 'Peroa, beloved of Ra.' Now Peroa probably means Pharaoh and perhaps he was Khabasha who revolted against the Persians and ruled for a year or two, after which he is supposed to have been defeated and killed, though of his end and place of burial there is no record. Whether these were the remnants of Khabasha himself, or of one of his high ministers or generals who wore the King's cartouche upon his ring in token of his office, of course I cannot say.

"When George had read the cartouche he handed me the ring which I slipped upon the first finger of my left hand, where I still wear it. Then leaving the grave open for further examination, we went on with the work, for we were greatly excited. At length, this was towards evening, we had cleared enough of the sanctuary, which was small, to uncover the shrine that, if not a monolith, was made of four pieces of granite so wonderfully put together that one could not see the joints. On the curved architrave as I think it is called, was carved the symbol of a winged disc, and beneath in hieroglyphics as fresh as though they had only been cut yesterday, an inscription to the effect that Peroa, Royal Son of the Sun, gave this shrine as an 'excellent eternal work,' together with the statues of the Holy Mother and the Holy Child to the 'emanations of the great Goddess Isis and the god Horus,' Amada, Royal Lady, being votaress or high-priestess.

"We only read the hieroglyphics very hurriedly, being anxious to see what was within the shrine that, the cedar door having rotted away, was filled with fine, drifted sand. Basketful by basketful we got it out and then, my friend, there appeared the most beautiful life-sized statue of Isis carved in alabaster that ever I have seen. She was seated on a throne-like chair and wore the vulture cap on which traces of colour remained. Her arms were held forward as though to support a child, which perhaps she was suckling as one of the breasts was bare. But if so, the child had gone. The execution of the statue was exquisite and its tender and mystic face extraordinarily beautiful, so life-like also that I think it must have been copied from a living model. Oh! my friend, when I looked upon it, which we did by the light of the candles, for the sun was sinking and shadows gathered in that excavated hole, I felt—never mind what I felt—perhaps *you* can guess who know my history.

"While we stared and stared, I longing to go upon my knees, I knew not why, suddenly I felt a faint trembling of the ground. At the same moment, the head overseer of the works, a man called Achmet, rushed up to us, shouting out—'Back! Back! The wall has burst. The sand runs!'

"He seized me by the arm and dragged me away beside of and behind the grave, George turning to follow. Next instant I saw a kind of wave of sand, on the crest of which appeared the stones of the wall, curl over and break. It struck the shrine, overturned and shattered it, which makes me think it was made of four pieces, and shattered also the alabaster statue within, for I saw its head strike George upon the back and throw him forward. He reeled and fell into the open grave which in another moment was filled and covered with the débris that seemed to grip me to my middle in its flow. After this I remembered nothing more until hours later I found myself lying in our house.

"Achmet and his Egyptians had done nothing; indeed none of them could be persuaded to approach the place till the sun rose because, as they said, the old gods of the land whom they looked upon as devils, were angry at being disturbed and would kill them as they had killed the Bey, meaning George. Then, distracted as I was, I went myself for there was no other European there, to find that the whole site of the sanctuary was buried beneath hundreds of tons of sand, that, beginning at the gap in the broken wall, had flowed from every side. Indeed it would have taken weeks to dig it out, since to sink a shaft was impracticable and so dangerous that the local officials refused to allow it to be attempted. The end of it was that an English bishop came up from Cairo and consecrated the ground by special arrangement with the Government, which of course makes it impossible that this part of the temple should be further disturbed. After this he read the Burial Service over my dear husband.

"So there is the end of a very terrible story which I have written down because I do not wish to have to talk about it more than is necessary when we meet. For, dear Mr. Quatermain, we shall meet, as I always knew that we should—yes, even after I heard that you were dead. You will remember that I told you so years ago in Kendah Land and that it would happen after a great change in my life, though what that change might be I could not say. . ."

This is the end of the letter except for certain suggested dates for the visit which she took for granted I should make to Ragnall.

II

RAGNALL CASTLE

When I had finished reading this amazing document I lit my pipe and set to work to think it over. The hypothetical inquirer might ask why I thought it amazing. There was nothing odd in a dilettante Englishman of highly cultivated mind taking to Egyptology and, being, as it chanced, one of the richest men in the kingdom, spending a fraction of his wealth in excavating temples. Nor was it strange that he should have happened to die by accident when engaged in that pursuit, which I can imagine to be very fascinating in the delightful winter climate of Egypt. He was not the first person to be buried by a fall of sand. Why, only a little while ago the same fate overtook a nursery-governess and the child in her charge who were trying to dig out a martin's nest in a pit in this very parish. Their operations brought down a huge mass of the overhanging bank beneath which the sand-vein had been hollowed by workmen who deserted the pit when they saw that it had become unsafe. Next day I and my gardeners helped to recover their bodies, for their whereabouts was not discovered until the following morning, and a sad business it was.

Yet, taken in conjunction with the history of this couple, the whole Ragnall affair was very strange. When but a child Lady Ragnall, then the Hon. Miss Holmes, had been identified by the priests of a remote African tribe as the oracle of their peculiar faith, which we afterwards proved to be derived from old Egypt, in short the worship of Isis and Horus. Subsequently they tried to steal her away and through the accident of my intervention, failed. Later on, after her marriage when shock had deprived her of her mind, these priests renewed the attempt, this time in Egypt, and succeeded. In the end we rescued her in Central Africa, where she was playing the part of the Mother-goddess Isis and even wearing her ancient robes. Next she and her husband came home with their minds turned towards a branch of study that took them back to Egypt. Here they devote themselves to unearthing a temple and find out that among all the gods of Egypt, who seem to have been extremely numerous, it was dedicated to Isis and Horus, the very divinities with whom they recently they had been so intimately concerned if in traditional and degenerate forms.

Moreover that was not the finish of it. They come to the sanctuary. They discover the statue of the goddess with the child gone, as their child was gone. A disaster occurs and both destroys and buries Ragnall so effectually that nothing of him is ever seen again: he just vanishes into another man's grave and remains there.

A common sort of catastrophe enough, it is true, though people of superstitious mind might have thought that it looked as though the goddess, or whatever force was behind the goddess, was working vengeance on the man who desecrated her ancient shrine. And, by the way, though I cannot remember whether or no I mentioned it in "The Ivory Child," I recall that the old priest of the Kendah, Harût, once told me he was sure Ragnall would meet with a violent death. This seemed likely enough in that country under our circumstances there, still I asked him why. He answered,

"Because he has laid hands on that which is holy and not meant for man," and he looked at Lady Ragnall.

I remarked that all women were holy, whereon he replied that he did not think so and changed the subject.

Well, Ragnall, who had married the lady who once served as the last priestess of Isis upon earth, was killed, whereas she, the priestess, was almost miraculously preserved from harm. And—oh! the whole story was deuced odd and that is all. Poor Ragnall! He was a great English gentleman and one whom when first I knew him, I held to be the most fortunate person I ever met, endowed as he was with every advantage of mind, body and estate. Yet in the end this did not prove to be the case. Well, while he lived he was a good friend and a good fellow and none can hope for a better epitaph in a world where all things are soon forgotten.

And now, what was I to do? To tell the truth I did not altogether desire to reopen this chapter in past history, or to have to listen to painful reminiscences from the lips of a bereaved woman. Moreover, beautiful as she had been, for doubtless she was *passée* now, and charming as of course she remained—I do not think I ever knew anyone who was quite so charming—there was something about Lady Ragnall which alarmed me. She did not resemble any other woman. Of course no woman is ever quite like another, but in her case the separateness, if I may so call it, was very marked. It was as though she had walked out of a different age, or even world, and been but superficially clothed with the attributes of our own. I felt that from the first moment I set eyes upon her and while reading her letter the sensation returned with added force.

Also for me she had a peculiar attraction and not one of the ordinary kind. It is curious to find oneself strangely intimate with a person of whom after all one does not know much, just as if one really knew a great deal that was shut off by a thin but quite impassable door. If so, I did not want to open that door for who could tell what might be on the other side of it? And intimate conversations with a lady in whose company one has shared very strange experiences, not infrequently lead to the opening of every kind of door.

Further I had made up my mind some time ago to have no more friendships with women who are so full of surprises, but to live out the rest of my life in a kind of monastery of men who have few surprises, being creatures whose thoughts are nearly always open and whose actions can always be foretold.

Lastly there was that *Taduki* business. Well, there at any rate I was clear and decided. No earthly power would induce me to have anything more to do with *Taduki* smoke. Of course I remembered that Lady Ragnall once told me kindly but firmly that I would if she wished. But that was just where she made a mistake. For the rest it seemed unkind to refuse her invitation now when she was in trouble, especially as I had once promised that if ever I could be of help, she had only to command me. No, I must go. But if that word—*Taduki*—were so much as mentioned I would leave again in a hurry. Moreover it would not be, for doubtless she had forgotten all about the stuff by now, even if it were not lost.

The end of it was that as I did not wish to write a long letter entering into all that Lady Ragnall had told me, I sent her a telegram, saying that if convenient to her, I would arrive at the Castle on the following Saturday evening and adding that I must be back here on the Tuesday afternoon, as I had guests coming to stay with me on that day. This was perfectly true as the season was mid-November and I was to begin shooting my coverts on the Wednesday morning, a function that once fixed, cannot be postponed.

In due course an answer arrived—"Delighted, but hoped that you would have been able to stay longer."

Behold me then about six o'clock on the said Saturday evening being once more whirled by a splendid pair of horses through the gateway arch of Ragnall Castle. The carriage stopped beneath the portico, the great doors flew open revealing the glow of the hall fire and lights within, the footman sprang down from the box and two other footmen descended the steps to assist me and my belongings out of the carriage. These, I remember, consisted of a handbag with my dress clothes and a yellow-backed novel.

So one of them took the handbag and the other had to content himself with the novel, which made me wish I had brought a portmanteau as well, if only for the look of the thing. The pair thus burdened, escorted me up the steps and delivered me over to the butler who scanned me with a critical eye. I scanned him also and perceived that he was a very fine specimen of his class. Indeed his stately presence so overcame me that I remarked nervously, as he helped me off with my coat, that when last I was here another had filled his office.

"Indeed, Sir," he said, "and what was his name, Sir?"

"Savage," I replied.

"And where might he be now, Sir?"

"Inside a snake!" I answered. "At least he was inside a snake but now I hope he is waiting upon his master in Heaven."

The man recoiled a little, pulling off my coat with a jerk. Then he coughed, rubbed his bald head, stared and recovering himself with an effort, said,

"Indeed, Sir! I only came to this place after the death of his late lordship, when her ladyship changed all the household. Alfred, show this gentleman up to her ladyship's boudoir, and William, take his—baggage—to the blue room. Her ladyship wishes to see you at once, Sir, before the others come."

So I went up the big staircase to a part of the Castle that I did not remember, wondering who "the others" might be. Almost could I have sworn that the shade of Savage accompanied me up those stairs; I could feel him at my side.

Presently a door was thrown open and I was ushered into a room somewhat dimly lit and full of the scent of flowers. By the fire near a tea-table, stood a lady clad in some dark dress with the light glinting on her rich-hued hair. She turned and I saw that she still wore the necklace of red stones, and beneath it on her breast a single red flower. For this was Lady Ragnall; about that there was no doubt at all, so little doubt indeed that I was amazed. I had expected to see a stout, elderly woman whom I should only know by the colour of her eyes and her voice, and perhaps certain tricks of manner. But, this was the mischief of it, I could not perceive any change, at any rate in that light. She was just the same! Perhaps a little fuller in figure, which was an advantage; perhaps a little more considered in her movements, perhaps a little taller or at any rate more stately, and that was all.

These things I learned in a flash. Then with a murmured "Mr. Quatermain, my Lady," the footman closed the door and she saw me.

Moving quickly towards me with both her hands outstretched, she exclaimed in that honey-soft voice of hers,

"Oh! my dear friend—" stopped and added, "Why, you haven't changed a bit."

"Fossils wear well," I replied, "but that is just what I was thinking of you."

"Then it is very rude of you to call me a fossil when I am only approaching that stage. Oh! I am glad to see you. I *am* glad!" and she gave me both the outstretched hands.

Upon my word I felt inclined to kiss her and have wondered ever since if she would have been very angry. I am not certain that she did not divine the inclination. At any rate after a little pause she dropped my hands and laughed. Then she said,

"I must tell you at once. A most terrible catastrophe has happened—"

Instantly it occurred to me that she had forgotten having informed me by letter of all the details of her husband's death. Such things chance to people who have once lost their memory. So I tried to look as sympathetic as I felt, sighed and waited.

"It's not so bad as all that," she said with a little shake of her head, reading my thought as she always had the power to do from the first moment we met. "We can talk about *that* afterwards. It's only that I hoped we were going to have a quiet two days, and now the Atterby-Smiths are coming, yes, in half an hour. Five of them!"

"The Atterby-Smiths!" I exclaimed, for somehow I too felt disappointed. "Who are the Atterby-Smiths?"

"Cousins of George's, his nearest relatives. They think he ought to have left them everything. But he didn't, because he could never bear the sight of them. You see his property was unentailed and he left it all to me. Now the entire family is advancing to suggest that I should leave it to them, as perhaps I might have done if they had not chosen to come just now."

"Why didn't you put them off?" I asked.

"Because I couldn't," she answered with a little stamp of her foot, "otherwise do you suppose they would have been here? They were far too clever. They telegraphed after lunch giving the train by which they were to arrive, but no address save Charing Cross. I thought of moving up to the Berkeley Square house, but it was impossible in the time, also I didn't know how to catch you. Oh! it's *most* vexatious."

"Perhaps they are very nice," I suggested feebly.

"Nice! Wait till you have seen them. Besides if they had been angels I did not want them just now. But how selfish I am! Come and have some tea. And you can stop longer, that is if you live through the Atterby-Smiths who are worse than both the Kendah tribes put together. Indeed I wish old Harût were coming instead. I should like to see Harût again, wouldn't you?" and suddenly the mystical look I knew so well, gathered on her face.

"Yes, perhaps I should," I replied doubtfully. "But I must leave by the first train on Tuesday morning; it goes at eight o'clock. I looked it up."

"Then the Atterby-Smiths leave on Monday if I have to turn them out of the house. So we shall get one evening clear at any rate. Stop a minute," and she rang the bell.

The footman appeared as suddenly as though he had been listening at the door.

"Alfred," she said, "tell Moxley" (he, I discovered, was the butler) "that when Mr. and Mrs. Atterby-Smith, the two Misses Atterby-Smith and the young Mr. Atterby-Smith arrive, they are to be shown to their rooms. Tell the cook also to put off dinner till half-past eight, and if Mr. and Mrs. Scroope arrive earlier, tell Moxley to tell them that I am sorry to be a little late, but that I was delayed by some parish business. Now do you understand?"

"Yes, my Lady," said Alfred and vanished.

"He doesn't understand in the least," remarked Lady Ragnall, "but so long as he doesn't show the Atterby-Smiths up here, in which case he can go away with them on Monday, I don't care. It will all work out somehow. Now sit down by the fire and let's talk. We've got nearly an hour and twenty minutes and you can smoke if you like. I learnt to in Egypt," and she took a cigarette from the mantelpiece and lit it.

That hour and twenty minutes went like a flash, for we had so much to say to each other that we never even got to the things we wanted to

H. RIDER HAGGARD

say. For instance, I began to tell her about King Solomon's Mines, which was a long story; and she to tell me what happened after we parted on the shores of the Red Sea. At least the first hour and a quarter went, when suddenly the door opened and Alfred in a somewhat frightened voice announced—"Mr. and Mrs. Atterby-Smith, the Misses Atterby-Smith and Mr. Atterby-Smith junior."

Then he caught sight of his mistress's eye and fled.

I looked and felt inclined to do likewise if only there had been another door. But there wasn't and that which existed was quite full. In the forefront came A.-S. senior, like a bull leading the herd. Indeed his appearance was bull-like as my eye, travelling from the expanse of white shirt-front (they were all dressed for dinner) to his red and massive countenance surmounted by two horn-like tufts of carroty hair, informed me at a glance. Followed Mrs. A.-S., the British matron incarnate. Literally there seemed to be acres of her; black silk below and white skin above on which set in filigree floated big green stones, like islands in an ocean. Her countenance too, though stupid was very stern and frightened me. Followed the progeny of this formidable pair. They were tall and thin, also red haired. The girls, whose age I could not guess in the least, were exactly like each other, which was not strange as afterwards I discovered that they were twins. They had pale blue eyes and somehow reminded me of fish. Both of them were dressed in green and wore topaz necklaces. The young man who seemed to be about one or two and twenty, had also pale blue eyes, in one of which he wore an eye-glass, but his hair was sandy as though it had been bleached, parted in the middle and oiled down flat.

For a moment there was a silence which I felt to be dreadful. Then in a big, pompous voice A.-S. *père* said,

"How do you do, my dear Luna? As I ascertained from the footman that you had not yet gone to dress, I insisted upon his leading us here for a little private conversation after we have been parted for so many years. We wished to offer you our condolences in person on your and our still recent loss."

"Thank you," said Lady Ragnall, "but I think we have corresponded on the subject which is painful to me."

"I fear that we are interrupting a smoking party, Thomas," said Mrs. A.-S. in a cold voice, sniffing at the air for all the world like a suspicious animal, whereon the five of them stared at Lady Ragnall's cigarette which she held between her fingers.

"Yes," said Lady Ragnall. "Won't you have one? Mr. Quatermain, hand Mrs. Smith the box, please."

I obeyed automatically, proffering it to the lady who nearly withered me with a glance, and then to each to each in turn. To my relief the young man took one.

"Archibald," said his mother, "you are surely not going to make your sisters' dresses smell of tobacco just before dinner."

Archibald sniggered and replied,

"A little more smoke will not make any difference in this room, Ma."

"That is true, darling," said Mrs. A.-S. and was straightway seized with a fit of asthma.

After this I am sure I don't know what happened, for muttering something about its being time to dress, I rushed from the room and wandered about until I could find someone to conduct me to my own where I lingered until I heard the dinner-bell ring. But even this retreat was not without disaster, for in my hurry I trod upon one of the young lady's dresses; I don't know whether it was Dolly's or Polly's (they were named Dolly and Polly) and heard a dreadful crack about her middle as though she were breaking in two. Thereon Archibald giggled again and Dolly and Polly remarked with one voice—they always spoke together,

"Oh! clumsy!"

To complete my misfortunes I missed my way going downstairs and strayed to and fro like a lost lamb until I found myself confronted by a green baize door which reminded me of something. I stood staring at it till suddenly a vision arose before me of myself following a bell wire through that very door in the darkness of the night when in search for the late Mr. Savage upon a certain urgent occasion. Yes, there could be no doubt about it, for look! there was the wire, and strange it seemed to me that I should live to behold it again. Curiosity led me to push the door open just to ascertain if my memory served me aright about the exact locality of the room. Next moment I regretted it for I fell straight into the arms of either Polly or Dolly.

"Oh!" said she, "I've just been sewn up."

I reflected that this was my case also in another sense, but asked feebly if she knew the way downstairs.

She didn't; neither of us did, till at length we met Mrs. Smith coming to look for her.

If I had been a burglar she could not have regarded me with graver suspicions. But at any rate *she* knew the way downstairs. And there to my joy I found my old friend Scroope and his wife, both of them grown stout and elderly, but as jolly as ever, after which the Smith family ceased to trouble me.

Also there was the rector of the parish, Dr. Jeffreys and an absurdly young wife whom he had recently married, a fluffy-headed little thing with round eyes and a cheerful, perky manner. The two of them together looked exactly like a turkey-cock and a chicken. I remembered him well enough and to my astonishment he remembered me, perhaps because Lady Ragnall, when she had hastily invited him to meet the Smith family, mentioned that I was coming. Lastly there was the curate, a dark, young man who seemed to be always brooding over the secrets of time and eternity, though perhaps he was only thinking about his dinner or the next day's services.

Well, there we stood in that well-remembered drawing-room in which first I had made the acquaintance of Harût and Marût; also of the beautiful Miss Holmes as Lady Ragnall was then called. The Scroopes, the Jeffreys and I gathered in one group and the Atterby-Smiths in another like a force about to attack, while between the two, brooding and indeterminate, stood the curate, a neutral observer.

Presently Lady Ragnall arrived, apologizing for being late. For some reason best known to herself she had chosen to dress as though for a great party. I believe it was out of mischief and in order to show Mrs. Atterby-Smith some of the diamonds she was firmly determined that family should never inherit. At any rate there she stood glittering and lovely, and smiled upon us.

Then came dinner and once more I marched to the great hall in her company; Dr. Jeffreys got Mrs. Smith; Papa Smith got Mrs. Jeffreys who looked like a Grecian maiden walking into dinner with the Minotaur; Scroope got one of the Miss Smiths, she who wore a pink bow, the gloomy curate got the other with a blue bow, and Archibald got Mrs. Scroope who departed making faces at us over his shoulder.

"You look very grand and nice," I said to Lady Ragnall as we followed the others at a discreet distance.

"I am glad," she answered, "as to the nice, I mean. As for the grand, that dreadful woman is always writing to me about the Ragnall diamonds, so I thought that she should see some of them for the first and last time. Do you know I haven't worn these things since George and I went to Court together, and I daresay shall never wear them again, for there is only one ornament I care for and I have got *that* on under my dress."

I stared and her and with a laugh said that she was very mischievous.

"I suppose so," she replied, "but I detest those people who are pompous and rude and have spoiled my party. Do you know I had half a mind to come down in the dress that I wore as Isis in Kendah Land. I have got it upstairs and you shall see me in it before you go, for old time's sake. Only it occurred to me that they might think me mad, so I didn't. Dr. Jeffreys, will you say grace, please?"

Well, it was a most agreeable dinner so far as I was concerned, for I sat between my hostess and Mrs. Scroope and the rest were too far off for conversation. Moreover as Archibald developed an unexpected quantity of small talk, and Scroope on the other side amused himself by filling pink-bow Miss Smith's innocent mind with preposterous stories about Africa, as had happened to me once before at this table, Lady Ragnall and I were practically left undisturbed.

"Isn't it strange that we should find ourselves sitting here again after all these years, except that you are in my poor mother's place? Oh! when that scientific gentleman convinced me the other day that you whom I had heard were dead, were not only alive and well but actually in England, really I could have embraced him."

I thought of an answer but did not make it, though as usual she read my mind for I saw her smile.

"The truth is," she went on, "I am an only child and really have no friends, though of course being—well, you know," and she glanced at the jewels on her breast, "I have plenty of acquaintances."

"And suitors," I suggested.

"Yes," she replied blushing, "as many as Penelope, not one of whom cares twopence about me any more than I care for them. The truth is, Mr. Quatermain, that nobody and nothing interest me, except a spot in the churchyard yonder and another amid ruins in Egypt."

"You have had sad bereavements," I said looking the other way.

"Very sad and they have left life empty. Still I should not complain for I have had my share of good. Also it isn't true to say that nothing interests me. Egypt interests me, though after what has happened I do not feel as though I could return there. All Africa interests me and," she added dropping her voice, "I can say it because I know you will not misunderstand, you interest me, as you have always done since the first moment I saw you."

"*I!*" I exclaimed, staring at my own reflection in a silver plate which made me look—well, more unattractive than usual. "It's very kind of you to say so, but I can't understand why I should. You have seen very little of me, Lady Ragnall, except in that long journey across the desert when we did not talk much, since you were otherwise engaged."

"I know. That's the odd part of it, for I feel as though I had seen you for years and years and knew everything about you that one human being can know of another. Of course, too, I do know a good lot of your life through George and Harût."

"Harût was a great liar," I said uneasily.

"Was he? I always thought him painfully truthful, though how he got at the truth I do not know. Anyhow," she added with meaning, "don't suppose I think the worse of you because others have thought so well. Women who seem to be all different, generally, I notice, have this in common. If one or two of them like a man, the rest like him also because something in him appeals to the universal feminine instinct, and the same applies to their dislike. Now men, I think, are different in that respect."

"Perhaps because they are more catholic and charitable," I suggested, "or perhaps because they like those who like them."

She laughed in her charming way, and said,

"However these remarks do not apply to you and me, for as I think I told you once before in that cedar wood in Kendah Land where you feared lest I should catch a chill, or become—odd again, it is another you with whom something in me seems to be so intimate."

"That's fortunate for your sake," I muttered, still staring at and pointing to the silver plate.

Again she laughed. "Do you remember the *Taduki* herb?" she asked. "I have plenty of it safe upstairs, and not long ago I took a whiff of it, only a whiff because you know it had to be saved."

"And what did you see?"

"Never mind. The question is what shall we *both* see?"

"Nothing," I said firmly. "No earthly power will make me breathe that unholy drug again."

"Except me," she murmured with sweet decision. "No, don't think about leaving the house. You can't, there are no Sunday trains. Besides you won't if I ask you not."

"'In vain is the net spread in the sight of any bird,'" I replied, firm as a mountain.

"Is it? Then why are so many caught?"

At that moment the Bull of Bashan—I mean Smith, began to bellow something at his hostess from the other end of the table and our conversation came to an end.

"I say, old chap," whispered Scroope in my ear when we stood up to see the ladies out. "I suppose you are thinking of marrying again. Well, you might do worse," and he glanced at the glittering form of Lady Ragnall vanishing through the doorway behind her guests.

"Shut up, you idiot!" I replied indignantly.

"Why?" he asked with innocence. "Marriage is an honourable estate, especially when there is lots of the latter. I remember saying something of the sort to you years ago and at this table, when as it happened you also took in her ladyship. Only there was George in the wind then; now it has carried him away."

Without deigning any reply I seized my glass and went to sit down between the canon and the Bull of Bashan.

III

ALLAN GIVES HIS WORD

M r. Atterby-Smith proved on acquaintance to be even worse than unfond fancy painted him. He was a gentleman in a way and of good family whereof the real name was Atterby, the Smith having been added to secure a moderate fortune left to him on that condition. His connection with Lord Ragnall was not close and through the mother's side. For the rest he lived in some south-coast watering-place and fancied himself a sportsman because he had on various occasions hired a Scottish moor or deer forest. Evidently he had never done anything nor earned a shilling during all his life and was bringing his family up to follow in his useless footsteps. The chief note of his character was that intolerable vanity which so often marks men who have nothing whatsoever about which to be vain. Also he had a great idea of his rights and what was due to him, which he appeared to consider included, upon what ground I could not in the least understand, the reversal of all the Ragnall properties and wealth. I do not think I need say any more about him, except that he bored me to extinction, especially after his fourth glass of port.

Perhaps, however, the son was worse, for he asked questions without number and when at last I was reduced to silence, lectured me about shooting. Yes, this callow youth who was at Sandhurst, instructed me, Allan Quatermain, how to kill elephants, he who had never seen an elephant except when he fed it with buns at the Zoo. At last Mr. Smith, who to Scroope's great amusement had taken the end of the table and assumed the position of host, gave the signal to move and we adjourned to the drawing-room.

I don't know what had happened but there we found the atmosphere distinctly stormy. The ample Mrs. Smith sat in a chair fanning herself, which caused the barbaric ornaments she wore to clank upon her fat arm. Upon either side of her, pale and indeterminate, stood Polly and Dolly each pretending to read a book. Somehow the three of them reminded me of a coat-of-arms seen in a nightmare, British Matron *sejant* with Modesty and Virtue as supporters. Opposite, on the other side of the fire and evidently very angry, stood Lady Ragnall, *regardant*.

"Do I understand you to say, Luna," I heard Mrs. A.-S. ask in resonant tones as I entered the room, "that you actually played the part of a heathen goddess among these savages, clad in a transparent bed-robe?"

"Yes, Mrs. Atterby-Smith," replied Lady Ragnall, "and a nightcap of feathers. I will put it on for you if you won't be shocked. Or perhaps one of your daughters——"

"Oh!" said both the young ladies together, "please be quiet. Here come the gentlemen."

After this there was a heavy silence broken only by the stifled giggles in the background of Mrs. Scroope and the canon's fluffy-headed wife, who to do her justice had some fun in her. Thank goodness the evening, or rather that part of it did not last long, since presently Mrs. Atterby-Smith, after studying me for a long while with a cold eye, rose majestically and swept off to bed followed by her offspring.

Afterwards I ascertained from Mrs. Scroope that Lady Ragnall had been amusing herself by taking away my character in every possible manner for the benefit of her connections, who were left with a general impression that I was the chief of a native tribe somewhere in Central Africa where I dwelt in light attire surrounded by the usual accessories. No wonder, therefore, that Mrs. A.-S. thought it best to remove her "Twin Pets," as she called them, out of my ravening reach.

Then the Scroopes went away, having arranged for me to lunch with them on the morrow, an invitation that I hastily accepted, though I heard Lady Ragnall mutter—"Mean!" beneath her breath. With them departed the canon and his wife and the curate, being, as they said, "early birds with duties to perform." After this Lady Ragnall paid me out by going to bed, having instructed Moxley to show us to the smoking room, "where," she whispered as she said good night, "I hope you will enjoy yourself."

Over the rest of the night I draw a veil. For a solid hour and three-quarters did I sit in that room between this dreadful pair, being alternately questioned and lectured. At length I could stand it no longer and while pretending to help myself to whiskey and soda, slipped through the door and fled upstairs.

I arrived late to breakfast purposely and found that I was wise, for Lady Ragnall was absent upstairs, recovering from "a headache." Mr. A.-Smith was also suffering from a headache downstairs, the result of champagne, port and whisky mixed, and all his family seemed to have pains in their tempers. Having ascertained that they were going to the church in the park, I departed to one two miles away and thence walked straight on to the Scroopes' where I had a very pleasant time, remaining till five in the afternoon. I returned to tea at the Castle where I found Lady Ragnall so cross that I went to church again, to the six o'clock service this time, only getting back in time to dress for dinner. Here I was paid out for I had to take in Mrs. Atterby-Smith. Oh! what a meal was that. We sat for the most part in solemn silence broken only by requests to pass the salt. I observed with satisfaction, however, that things were growing lively at the other end of the table where A.-Smith *père* was drinking a good deal too much wine. At last I heard him say,

"We had hoped to spend a few days with you, my dear Luna. But as you tell us that your engagements make this impossible"—and he paused to drink some port, whereon Lady Ragnall remarked inconsequently,

"I assure you the ten o'clock train is far the best and I have ordered the carriage at half-past nine, which is not very early."

"As your engagements make this impossible," he repeated, "we would ask for the opportunity of a little family conclave with you to-night."

Here all of them turned and glowered at me.

"Certainly," said Lady Ragnall, "'the sooner 'tis over the sooner to sleep.' Mr. Quatermain, I am sure, will excuse us, will you not? I have had the museum lit up for you, Mr. Quatermain. You may find some Egyptian things there that will interest you."

"Oh, with pleasure!" I murmured, and fled away.

I spent a very instructive two hours in the museum, studying various Egyptian antiquities including a couple of mummies which rather terrified me. They looked so very corpse-like standing there in their wrappings. One was that of a lady who was a "Singer of Amen," I remember. I wondered where she was singing now and what song. Presently I came to a glass case which riveted my attention, for above it was a label bearing the following words: "Two Papyri given to Lady Ragnall by the priests of the Kendah Tribe in Africa." Within were the papyri unrolled and beneath each of the documents, its translation, so far as they could be translated for they were somewhat broken. No. 1, which was dated, "In the first year of Peroa," appeared to be the official appointment of the Royal Lady Amada, to be the prophetess to the temple of Isis and Horus the Child, which was also called Amada, and situated on the east bank of the Nile above Thebes. Evidently this was the same temple of which Lady Ragnall had written to me in her letter, where her husband had met his death by accident, a coincidence which made me start when I remembered how and where the document had come into her hands and what kind of office she filled at the time.

The second papyrus, or rather its translation, contained a most comprehensive curse upon any man who ventured to interfere with the personal sanctity of this same Royal Lady of Amada, who, apparently in virtue of her office, was doomed to perpetual celibacy like the vestal virgins. I do not remember all the terms of the curse, but I know that it invoked the vengeance of Isis the Mother, Lady of the Moon, and Horus the Child upon anyone who should dare such a desecration, and in so many words doomed him to death by violence "far from his own country where first he had looked on Ra," (i.e. the sun) and also to certain spiritual sufferings afterwards.

The document gave me the idea that it was composed in troubled days to protect that particularly sacred person, the Prophetess of Isis whose cult, as I have since learned, was rising in Egypt at the time, from threatened danger, perhaps at the hands of some foreign man. It occurred to me even that this Princess, for evidently she was a descendant of kings, had been appointed to a most sacred office for that very purpose. Men who shrink from little will often fear to incur the direct curse of widely venerated gods in order to obtain their desires, even if they be not their own gods. Such were my conclusions about this curious and ancient writing which I regret I cannot give in full as I neglected to copy it at the time.

I may add that it seemed extremely strange to me that it and the other which dealt with a particular temple in Egypt should have passed into Lady Ragnall's hands over two thousand years later in a distant part of Africa, and that subsequently her husband should have been killed in her presence whilst excavating the very temple to which they referred, whence too in all probability they were taken. Moreover, oddly enough Lady Ragnall had herself for a while filled the rôle of Isis in a shrine whereof these two papyri had been part of the sacred appurtenances for unknown ages, and one of her official titles there was Prophetess and Lady of the Moon, whose symbol she wore upon her breast.

Although I have always recognized that there are a great many more things in the world than are dreamt of in our philosophy, I say with truth and confidence that I am not a superstitious man. Yet I confess that these papers and the circumstances connected with them, made me feel afraid.

H. RIDER HAGGARD

Also they made me wish that I had not come to Ragnall Castle.

Well, the Atterby-Smiths had so far effectually put a stop to any talk of such matters and even if Lady Ragnall should succeed in getting rid of them by that morning train, as to which I was doubtful, there remained but a single day of my visit during which it ought not to be hard to stave off the subject. Thus I reflected, standing face to face with those mummies, till presently I observed that the Singer of Amen who wore a staring, gold mask, seemed to be watching me with her oblong painted eyes. To my fancy a sardonic smile gathered in them and spread to the mouth.

"That's what *you* think," this smile seemed to say, "as once before you thought that Fate could be escaped. Wait and see, my friend. Wait and see!"

"Not in this room any way," I remarked aloud, and departed in a hurry down the passage which led to the main staircase.

Before I reached its end a remarkable sight caused me to halt in the shadow. The Atterby-Smith family were going to bed *en bloc*. They marched in single file up the great stair, each of them carrying a hand candle. Papa led and young Hopeful brought up the rear. Their countenances were full of war, even the twins looked like angry lambs, but something written on them informed me that they had suffered defeat recent and grievous. So they vanished up the stairway and out of my ken for ever.

When they had gone I started again and ran straight into Lady Ragnall. If her guests had been angry, it was clear that *she* was furious, almost weeping with rage, indeed. Moreover, she turned and rent me.

"You are a wretch," she said, "to run away and leave me all day long with those horrible people. Well, they will never come here again, for I have told them that if they do the servants have orders to shut the door in their faces."

Not knowing what to say I remarked that I had spent a most instructive evening in the museum, which seemed to make her angrier than ever. At any rate she whisked off without even saying "good night" and left me standing there. Afterwards I learned that the A.-S.'s had calmly informed Lady Ragnall that she had stolen their property and demanded that "as an act of justice" she should make a will leaving everything she possessed to them, and meanwhile furnish them with an allowance of £4,000 a year. What I did not learn were the exact terms of her answer.

Next morning Alfred, when he called me, brought me a note from his mistress which I fully expected would contain a request that I should depart by the same train as her other guests. Its real contents, however, were very different.

> "My dear Friend," it ran, "I am so ashamed of myself and so sorry for my rudeness last night, for which I deeply apologise. If you knew all that I had gone through at the hands of those dreadful mendicants, you would forgive me.
>
> L.R.

> "P.S.—I have ordered breakfast at 10. Don't go down much before, for your own sake."

Somewhat relieved in my mind, for I thought she was really angry with me, not altogether without cause, I rose, dressed and set to work to write some letters. While I was doing so I heard the wheels of a carriage beneath and opening my window, saw the Atterby-Smith family in the act of departing in the Castle bus. Smith himself seemed to be still enraged, but the others looked depressed. Indeed I heard the wife of his bosom say to him,

"Calm yourself, my dear. Remember that Providence knows what is best for us and that beggars on horseback are always unjust and ungrateful."

To which her spouse replied,

"Hold your infernal tongue, will you," and then began to rate the servants about the luggage.

Well, off they went. Glaring through the door of the bus, Mr. Smith caught sight of me leaning out of the window, seeing which I waved my hand to him in adieu. His only reply to this courtesy was to shake his fist, though whether at me or at the Castle and its inhabitants in general, I neither know nor care.

When I was quite sure that they had gone and were not coming back again to find something they had forgotten, I went downstairs and surprised a conclave between the butler, Moxley, and his satellites, reinforced by Lady Ragnall's maid and two other female servants.

"Gratuities!" Moxley was exclaiming, which I thought a fine word for tips, "not a smell of them! His gratuities were—'Damn your eyes, you fat bottle-washer,' being his name for butler. *My* eyes, mind you,

Ann, not Alfred's or William's, and that because he had tumbled over his own rugs. Gentleman! Why, I name him a hog with his litter."

"Hogs don't have litters, Mr. Moxley," observed Ann smartly.

"Well, young woman, if there weren't no hogs, there'd be no litters, so there! However, he won't root about in this castle no more, for I happened to catch a word or two of what passed between him and her Ladyship last night. He said straight out that she was making love to that little Mr. Quatermain who wanted her money, and probably not for the first time as they had forgathered in Africa. A gentleman, mind you, Ann, who although peculiar, I like, and who, the keeper Charles tells me, is the best shot in the whole world."

"And what did she say to that?" asked Ann.

"What did she say? What didn't she say, that's the question. It was just as though all the furniture in the room got up and went for them Smiths. Well, having heard enough, and more than I wanted, I stepped off with the tray and next minute out they all come and grab the bedroom candlesticks. That's all and there's her Ladyship's bell. Alfred, don't stand gaping there but go and light the hot-plates."

So they melted away and I descended from the landing, indignant but laughing. No wonder that Lady Ragnall lost her temper!

Ten minutes later she arrived in the dining-room, waving a lighted ribbon that disseminated perfume.

"What on earth are you doing?" I asked.

"Fumigating the house," she said. "It is unnecessary as I don't think they were infectious, but the ceremony has a moral significance—like incense. Anyway it relieves my feelings."

Then she laughed and threw the remains of the ribbon into the fire, adding,

"If you say a word about those people I'll leave the room."

I think we had one of the jolliest breakfasts I ever remember. To begin with we were both hungry since our miseries of the night before had prevented us from eating any dinner. Indeed she swore that she had scarcely tasted food since Saturday. Then we had such a lot to talk about. With short intervals we talked all that day, either in the house or while walking through the gardens and grounds. Passing through the latter I came to the spot on the back drive where once I had saved her from being abducted by Harût and Marût, and as I recognized it, uttered an exclamation. She asked me why and the end of it was that I told her all that story which to this moment she had never heard, for Ragnall had thought well to keep it from her.

She listened intently, then said,

"So I owe you more than I knew. Yet, I'm not sure, for you see I was abducted after all. Also if I had been taken there, probably George would never have married me or seen me again, and that might have been better for him."

"Why?" I asked. "You were all the world to him."

"Is any woman ever all the world to a man, Mr. Quatermain?"

I hesitated, expecting some attack.

"Don't answer," she went on, "it would be too long and you wouldn't convince me who have been in the East. However, he was all the world to me. Therefore his welfare was what I wished and wish, and I think he would have had more of it if he had never married me."

"Why?" I asked again.

"Because I brought him no good luck, did I? I needn't go through all the story as you know it. And in the end it was through me that he was killed in Egypt."

"Or through the goddess Isis," I broke in rather nervously.

"Yes, the goddess Isis, a part I have played in my time, or something like it. And he was killed in the temple of the goddess Isis. And those papyri of which you read the translations in the museum, which were given to me in Kendah Land, seem to have come from that same temple. And—how about the Ivory Child? Isis in the temple evidently held a child in her arms, but when we found her it had gone. Supposing this child was the same as that of which I was guardian! It might have been, since the papyri came from that temple. What do you think?"

"I don't think anything," I answered, "except that it is all very odd. I don't even understand what Isis and the child Horus represent. They were not mere images either in Egypt or Kendah Land. There must be an idea behind them somewhere."

"Oh! there was. Isis was the universal Mother, Nature herself with all the powers, seen and unseen, that are hidden in Nature; Love personified also, although not actually the queen of Love like Hathor, her sister goddess. The Horus child, whom the old Egyptians called Heru-Hennu, signified eternal regeneration, eternal youth, eternal strength and beauty. Also he was the Avenger who overthrew Set, the Prince of Darkness, and thus in a way opened the Door of Life to men."

"It seems to me that all religions have much in common," I said.

"Yes, a great deal. It was easy for the old Egyptians to become Christian, since for many of them it only meant worshipping Isis and Horus under new and holier names. But come in, it grows cold."

We had tea in Lady Ragnall's boudoir and after it had been taken away our conversation died. She sat there on the other side of the fire with a cigarette between her lips, looking at me through the perfumed smoke till I began to grow uncomfortable and to feel that a crisis of some sort was at hand. This proved perfectly correct, for it was. Presently she said,

"We took a long journey once together, Mr. Quatermain, did we not?"

"Undoubtedly," I answered, and began to talk of it until she cut me short with a wave of her hand, and went on,

"Well, we are going to take a longer one together after dinner to-night."

"What! Where! How!" I exclaimed much alarmed.

"I don't know where, but as for how—look in that box," and she pointed to a little carved Eastern chest made of rose or sandal wood, that stood upon a table between us.

With a groan I rose and opened it. Inside was another box made of silver. This I opened also and perceived that within lay bundles of dried leaves that looked like tobacco, from which floated an enervating and well-remembered scent that clouded my brain for a moment. Then I shut down the lids and returned to my seat.

"*Taduki*," I murmured.

"Yes, *Taduki*, and I believe in perfect order with all its virtue intact."

"Virtue!" I exclaimed. "I don't think there is any virtue about that hateful and magical herb which I believe grew in the devil's garden. Moreover, Lady Ragnall, although there are few things in the world that I would refuse you, I tell you at once that nothing will induce me to have anything more to do with it."

She laughed softly and asked why not.

"Because I find life so full of perplexities and memories that I have no wish to make acquaintance with any more, such as I am sure lie hid by the thousand in that box."

"If so, don't you think that they might clear up some of those which surround you to-day?"

"No, for in such things there is no finality, since whatever one saw would also require explanation."

"Don't let us argue," she replied. "It is tiring and I daresay we shall need all our strength to-night."

I looked at her speechless. Why could she not take No for an answer? As usual she read my thought and replied to it.

"Why did not Adam refuse the apple that Eve offered him?" she inquired musingly. "Or rather why did he eat it after many refusals and learn the secret of good and evil, to the great gain of the world which thenceforward became acquainted with the dignity of labour?"

"Because the woman tempted him," I snapped.

"Quite so. It has always been her business in life and always will be. Well, I am tempting you now, and not in vain."

"Do you remember who was tempting the woman?"

"Certainly. Also that he was a good school-master since he caused the thirst for knowledge to overcome fear and thus laid the foundation-stone of all human progress. That allegory may be read two ways, as one of a rise from ignorance instead of a fall from innocence."

"You are too clever for me with your perverted notions. Also, you said we were not to argue. I have therefore only to repeat that I will not eat your apple, or rather, breathe your *Taduki*."

"Adam over again," she replied, shaking her head. "The same old beginning and the same old end, because you see at last you will do exactly what Adam did."

Here she rose and standing over me, looked me straight in the eyes with the curious result that all my will power seemed to evaporate. Then she sat down again, laughing softly, and remarked as though to herself,

"Who would have thought that Allan Quatermain was a moral coward!"

"Coward," I repeated. "Coward!"

"Yes, that's the right word. At least you were a minute ago. Now courage has come back to you. Why, it's almost time to dress for dinner, but before you go, listen. I have some power over you, my friend, as you have some power over me, for I tell you frankly if you wished me very much to do anything, I should have to do it; and the same applies conversely. Now, to-night we are, as I believe, going to open a great gate and to see wonderful things, glorious things that will thrill us for the rest of our lives, and perhaps suggest to us what is coming after death. You will not fail me, will you?" she continued in a pleading voice. "If you do I must try alone since no one else will serve, and then I *know*—how I cannot say—that I shall be exposed to great danger. Yes, I think that I shall lose my mind once more and never find it again this side the grave. You would not have that happen to me, would you, just because you shrink from digging up old memories?"

"Of course not," I stammered. "I should never forgive myself."

"Yes, of course not. There was really no need for me to ask you. Then you promise you will do all I wish?" and once more she looked at me, adding, "Don't be ashamed, for you remember that I have been in touch with hidden things and am not quite as other women are. You will recollect I told you that which I have never breathed to any other living soul, years ago on that night when first we met."

"I promise," I answered and was about to add something, I forget what, when she cut me short, saying,

"That's enough, for I know your word is rather better than your bond. Now dress as quickly as you can or the dinner will be spoiled."

IV

THROUGH THE GATES

S hort as was the time at my disposal before the dinner-gong sounded, it proved ample for reflection. With every article of attire that I discarded went some of that boudoir glamour till its last traces vanished with my walking-boots. I was fallen indeed. I who had come to this place so full of virtuous resolutions, could now only reflect upon the true and universal meaning of our daily prayer that we might be kept from temptation. And yet what had tempted me? For my life's sake I could not say. The desire to please a most charming woman and to keep her from making solitary experiments of a dangerous nature, I suppose, though whether they should be less dangerous carried out jointly remained to be seen. Certainly it was not any wish to eat of her proffered apple of Knowledge, for already I knew a great deal more than I cared for about things in general. Oh! the truth was that woman is the mightiest force in the world, at any rate where the majority of us poor men is concerned. She commanded and I must obey.

I grew desperate and wondered if I could escape. Perhaps I might slip out of the back door and run for it, without my great coat or hat although the night was so cold and I should probably be taken up as a lunatic. No, it was impossible for I had forged a chain that might not be broken. I had passed my word of honour. Well, I was in for it and after all what was there of which I need be afraid that I should tremble and shrink back as though I were about to run away with somebody's wife, or rather to be run away with quite contrary to my own inclination? Nothing at all. A mere nonsensical ordeal much less serious than a visit to the dentist.

Probably that stuff had lost its strength by now—that is, unless it had grown more powerful by keeping, as is the case with certain sorts of explosives. And if it had not, the worst to be expected was a silly dream, followed perhaps by headache. That is, unless I did not chance to wake up again at all in this world, which was a most unpleasant possibility. Another thing, suppose I woke and she didn't! What should I say then? Of a certainty I should find myself in the dock. Yes, and there were further dreadful eventualities, quite conceivable, every one of them, the very thought of which plunged me into a cold perspiration and made me feel so weak that I was obliged to sit down.

Then I heard the gong; to me it sounded like the execution bell to a prisoner under sentence of death. I crept downstairs feebly and found Lady Ragnall waiting for me in the drawing-room, clothed with gaiety as with a garment. I remember that it made me most indignant that she could be so happy in such circumstances, but I said nothing. She looked me up and down and remarked,

"Really from your appearance you might have seen the Ragnall ghost, or be going to be married against your will, or—I don't know what. Also you have forgotten to fasten your tie."

I looked in the glass. It was true, for there hung the ends down my shirt front. Then I struggled with the wretched thing until at last she had to help me, which she did laughing softly. Somehow her touch gave me confidence again and enabled me to say quite boldly that I only wanted my dinner.

"Yes," she replied, "but you are not to eat much and you must only drink water. The priestesses in Kendah Land told me that this was necessary before taking *Taduki* in its strongest form, as we are going to do to-night. You know the prophet Harût only gave us the merest whiff in this room years ago."

I groaned and she laughed again.

That dinner with nothing to drink, although to avoid suspicion I let Moxley fill my glass once or twice, and little to eat for my appetite had vanished, went by like a bad dream. I recall no more about it until I heard Lady Ragnall tell Moxley to see that there was a good fire in the museum where we were going to study that night and must not be disturbed.

Another minute and I was automatically opening the door for her. As she passed she paused to do something to her dress and whispered,

"Come in a quarter of an hour. Mind—no port which clouds the intellect."

"I have none left to cloud," I remarked after her.

Then I went back and sat by the fire feeling most miserable and staring at the decanters, for never in my life do I remember wanting a bottle of wine more. The big clock ticked and ticked and at last chimed the quarter, jarring on my nerves in that great lonely banqueting hall. Then I rose and crept upstairs like an evil-doer and it seemed to me that the servants in the hall looked on me with suspicion, as well they might.

I reached the museum and found it brilliantly lit, but empty except for the cheerful company of the two mummies who also appeared to regard me with gleaming but doubtful eyes. So I sat down there in front of the fire, not even daring to smoke lest tobacco should complicate *Taduki*.

Presently I heard a low sound of laughter, looked up and nearly fell backwards, that is, metaphorically, for the chair prevented such a physical collapse.

It was not wonderful since before me, like a bride of ancient days adorned for her husband, stood the goddess Isis—white robes, feathered headdress, ancient bracelets, gold-studded sandals on bare feet, scented hair, ruby necklace and all the rest. I stared, then there burst from me words which were the last I meant to say,

"Great Heavens! how beautiful you are."

"Am I?" she asked. "I am glad," and she glided across the room and locked the door.

"Now," she said, returning, "we had better get to business, that is unless you would like to worship the goddess Isis a little first, to bring yourself into a proper frame of mind, you know."

"No," I replied, my dignity returning to me. "I do not wish to worship any goddess, especially when she isn't a goddess. It was not a part of the bargain."

"Quite so," she said, nodding, "but who knows what you will be worshipping before an hour is over? Oh! forgive me for laughing at you, but I can't help it. You are so evidently frightened."

"Who wouldn't be frightened?" I answered, looking with gloomy apprehension at the sandal-wood box which had appeared upon a case full of scarabs. "Look here, Lady Ragnall," I added, "why can't you leave all this unholy business alone and let us spend a pleasant evening talking, now that those Smith people have gone? I have lots of stories about my African adventures which would interest you."

"Because I want to hear my own African adventures, and perhaps yours too, which I am sure will interest me a great deal more," she exclaimed earnestly. "You think it is all foolishness, but it is not. Those Kendah priestesses told me much when I seemed to be out of my mind. For a long time I did not remember what they said, but of late years, especially since George and I began to excavate that temple, plenty has come back to me bit by bit, fragments, you know, that make me desire to learn the rest as I never desired anything else on earth. And the worst of it has always been that from the beginning I have known—and know—that this can only happen with you and through you, why I cannot say, or have forgotten. That's what sent me nearly wild with joy when I heard that you were not only alive, but in this country. You won't disappoint me, will you? There is nothing I can offer you which would have any value for you, so I can only beg you not to disappoint me—well, because I am your friend."

I turned away my head, hesitating, and when I looked up again I saw that her beautiful eyes were full of tears. Naturally that settled the matter, so I only said,

"Let us get on with the affair. What am I to do? Stop a bit. I may as well provide against eventualities," and going to a table I took a sheet of notepaper and wrote:

"Lady Ragnall and I, Allan Quatermain, are about to make an experiment with an herb which we discovered some years ago in Africa. If by any chance this should result in accident to either or both of us, the Coroner is requested to understand that it is not a case of murder or of suicide, but merely of unfortunate scientific research."

This I dated, adding the hour, 9.47 P.M., and signed, requesting her to do the same.

She obeyed with a smile, saying it was strange that one who had lived a life of such constant danger as myself, should be so afraid to die.

"Look here, young lady," I replied with irritation, "doesn't it occur to you that *I* may be afraid lest *you* should die—and *I* be hanged for it," I added by an afterthought.

"Oh! I see," she answered, "that is really very nice of you. But, of course, you would think like that; it is your nature."

"Yes," I replied. "Nature, not merit."

She went to a cupboard which formed the bottom of one of the mahogany museum cases, and extracted from it first of all a bowl of ancient appearance made of some black stone with projecting knobs for handles that were carved with the heads of women wearing ceremonial wigs; and next a low tripod of ebony or some other black wood. I looked at these articles and recognized them. They had stood in front of the sanctuary in the temple in Kendah Land, and over them I had once seen this very woman dressed as she was to-night, bend her head in the magic smoke before she had uttered the prophecy of the passing of the Kendah god.

"So you brought these away too," I said.

"Yes," she replied with solemnity, "that they might be ready at the appointed hour when we needed them."

Then she spoke no more for a while, but busied herself with certain rather eerie preparations. First she set the tripod and its bowl in an open space which I was glad to note was at some distance from the fire, since if either of us fell into that who would there be to take us off before cremation ensued? Then she drew up a curved settee with a back and arms, a comfortable-looking article having a seat that sloped backwards like those in clubs, and motioned to me to sit down. This I did with much the same sensations that are evoked by taking one's place upon an operation-table.

Next she brought that accursed *Taduki* box, I mean the inner silver one, the contents of which I heartily wished I had thrown upon the fire, and set it down, open, near the tripod. Lastly she lifted some glowing embers of wood from the grate with tongs, and dropped them into the stone bowl.

"I think that's all. Now for the great adventure," she said in a voice that was at once rapt and dreamy.

"What am I to do?" I asked feebly.

"That is quite simple," she replied, as she sat herself down beside me well within reach of the *Taduki* box, the brazier being between us with its tripod stand pressed against the edge of the couch, and in its curve, so that we were really upon each side of it. "When the smoke begins to rise thickly you have only to bend your head a little forward, with your shoulders still resting against the settee, and inhale until you find your senses leaving you, though I don't know that this is necessary for the stuff is subtle. Then throw your head back, go to sleep and dream."

"What am I to dream about?" I inquired in a vacuous way, for my senses were leaving me already.

"You will dream, I think, of past events in which both of us played a part, at least I hope so. I dreamt of them before in Kendah Land, but then I was not myself, and for the most part they are forgotten. Moreover, I learned that we can only see them all when we are together. Now speak no more."

This command, by the way, at once produced in me an intense desire for prolonged conversation. It was not to be gratified, however, for at that moment she stood up again facing the tripod and me, and began to sing in a rich and thrilling voice. What she sang I do not know for I could not understand the language, but I presume it was some ancient chant that she learned in Kendah Land. At any rate, there she stood, a lovely and inspired priestess clad in her sacerdotal robes, and sang, waving her arms and fixing her eyes upon mine. Presently she bent down, took a little of the *Taduki* weed and with words of incantation, dropped it upon the embers in the bowl. Twice she did this, then sat herself upon the couch and waited.

A clear flame sprang up and burned for thirty seconds or so, I suppose while it consumed the volatile oils in the weed. Then it died down and smoke began to come, white, rich and billowy, with a very pleasant odour resembling that of hot-house flowers. It spread out between us like a fan, and though its veil I heard her say,

"The gates are wide. Enter!"

I knew what she meant well enough, and though for a moment I thought of cheating, there is no other word for it, knew also that she had detected the thought and was scorning me in her mind. At any rate I felt that I must obey and thrust my head forward into the smoke, as a green ham is thrust into a chimney. The warm vapour struck against my face like fog, or rather steam, but without causing me to choke or my eyes to smart. I drew it down my throat with a deep inhalation—once, twice, thrice, then as my brain began to swim, threw myself back as I had been instructed to do. A deep and happy drowsiness stole over me, and the last thing I remember was hearing the clock strike the first two strokes of the hour of ten. The third stroke I heard also, but it sounded like to that of the richest-throated bell that ever boomed in all the world. I remember becoming aware that it was the signal for the rolling up of some vast proscenium, revealing behind it a stage that was the world—nothing less.

WHAT DID I SEE? WHAT did I see? Let me try to recall and record.

First of all something chaotic. Great rushes of vapour driven by mighty winds; great seas, for the most part calm. Then upheavals and volcanoes spouting fire. Then tropic scenes of infinite luxuriance. Terrific reptiles feeding on the brinks of marshes, and huge elephant-like animals moving between palms beyond. Then, in a glade, rough huts and about them a jabbering crowd of creatures that were only half human, for sometimes they stood upright and sometimes ran on their hands and feet. Also they were almost covered with hair which was all they had in the way of clothes, and at the moment that I met them, were terribly frightened by the appearance of a huge mammoth, if that is the right name for it, which walked into the glade and looked at us. At any rate it was a beast of the elephant tribe which I judged to be nearly twenty feet high, with enormous curving tusks.

The point of the vision was that I recognized myself among those hairy jabberers, not by anything outward and visible, but by something inward and spiritual. Moreover, I was being urged by a female of the race, I can scarcely call her a woman, to justify my existence by tackling the mammoth in her particular interest, or to give her up to someone who would. In the end I tackled it, rushing forward with a weapon, I think it was a sharp stone tied to a stick, though how I could expect to hurt a beast twenty feet high with such a thing is more than I can understand, unless perhaps the stone was poisoned.

At any rate the end was sudden. I threw the stone, whereat a great trunk shot out from between the tusks and caught me. Round and round I went in the air, reflecting as I did so, for I suppose at the time my normal consciousness had not quite left me, that this was my first encounter with the elephant Jana, also that it was very foolish to try to oblige a female regardless of personal risk. . .

All became dark, as no doubt it would have done, but presently, that is after a lapse of a great many thousands of years, or so it appeared to me, light grew again. This time I was a black man living in something not unlike a Kaffir kraal on the top of a hill.

There was shouting below and enemies attacked us; a woman rushed out of a hut and gave me a spear and a shield, the latter made of wood with white spots on it, and pointed to the path of duty which ran down the hill. I followed in company with others, though without enthusiasm, and presently met a roaring giant of a man at the bottom. I stuck my spear into him and he stuck his into me, through the stomach, which hurt me most abominably. After this I retired up the hill where the woman pulled the spear out and gave it to another man. I remember no more.

Then followed a whole maze of visions, but really I cannot disentangle them. Nor is it worth while doing so since after all they were only of the nature of an overture, jumbled incidents of former lives, real or imaginary, or so I suppose, having to do, all of them, with elementary things, such as hunger and wounds and women and death.

H. RIDER HAGGARD

At length these broken fragments of the past were swept away out of my consciousness and I found myself face to face with something connected and tangible, not too remote or unfamiliar for understanding. It was the beginning of the real story.

I, PLEASE REMEMBER ALWAYS THAT I knew it was I, Allan, and no one else, that is, the same personality or whatever it may be which makes each man different from any other man, saw myself in a chariot drawn by two horses with arched necks and driven by a charioteer who sat on a little seat in front. It was a highly ornamented, springless vehicle of wood and gilded, something like a packing-case with a pole, or as we should call it in South Africa, a disselboom, to which the horses were harnessed. In this cart I stood arrayed in flowing robes fastened round my middle by a studded belt, with strips of coloured cloth wound round my legs and sandals on my feet. To my mind the general effect of the attire was distinctly feminine and I did not like it at all.

I was glad to observe, however, that the I of those days was anything but feminine. Indeed I could never have believed that once I was so good-looking, even over two thousand years ago. I was not very tall but extremely stalwart, burly almost, with an arm that as I could observe, since it projected from the sleeve of my lady's gown, would have done no discredit to a prize-fighter, and a chest like a bull.

The face also I admired very much. The brow was broad; the black eyes were full and proud-looking, the features somewhat massive but well-cut and highly intelligent; the mouth firm and shapely, with lips that were perhaps a trifle too thick; the hair—well, there was rather a failure in the hair, at least according to modern ideas, for it curled so beautifully as to suggest that one of my ancestors might have fallen in love with a person of negroid origin. However there was lots of it, hanging down almost to the shoulders and bound about the brow by a very neat fillet of blue cloth with silver studs. The colour of my skin, I was glad to note, was by no means black, only a light and pleasing brown such as might have been produced by sunburn. My age, I might add, was anywhere between five and twenty and five and thirty, perhaps nearer the latter than the former, at any rate, the very prime of life.

For the rest, I held in my left hand a very stout, long bow of black wood which seemed to have seen much service, with a string of what looked like catgut, on which was set a broad-feathered, barbed arrow. This I kept in place with the fingers of my right hand, on one of which

I observed a handsome gold ring with strange characters carved upon the bezel.

Now for the charioteer.

He was black as night, black as a Sunday hat, with yellow rolling eyes set in a countenance of extraordinary ugliness and I may add, extraordinary humour. His big, wide mouth with thick lips ran up the left side of his face towards an ear that was also big and projecting. His hair, that had a feather stuck in it, was real nigger wool covering a skull like a cannon ball and I should imagine as hard. This head, by the way, was set plumb upon the shoulders, as though it had been driven down between them by a pile hammer. They were very broad shoulders suggesting enormous strength, but the gaily-clad body beneath, which was supported by two bowed legs and large, flat feet, was that of a dwarf who by the proportions of his limbs Nature first intended for a giant; yes, an Ethiopian dwarf.

Looking through this remarkable exterior, as it were, I recognized that inside of it was the soul, or animating principle, of—whom do you think? None other than my beloved old servant and companion, the Hottentot Hans whose loss I had mourned for years! Hans himself who died for me, slaying the great elephant, Jana, in Kendah Land, the elephant I could not hit, and thereby saving my life. Oh! although I had been obliged to go back to the days of I knew not what ancient empire to do so in my trance, or whatever it was, I could have wept with joy at finding him again, especially as I knew by instinct that as he loved the Allan Quatermain of to-day, so he loved this Egyptian in a wheeled packing-case, for I may as well say at once that such was my nationality in the dream.

Now I looked about me and perceived that my chariot was the second of a cavalcade. Immediately in front of it was one infinitely more gorgeous in which stood a person who even if I had not known it, I should have guessed to be a king, and who, as a matter of fact, was none other than the King of kings, at that time the absolute master of most of the known world, though what his name may have been, I have no notion. He wore a long flowing robe of purple silk embroidered with gold and bound in at the waist by a jewelled girdle from which hung the private, sacred seal; the little "White Seal" that, as I learned afterwards, was famous throughout the earth.

On his head was a stiff cloth cap, also purple in colour, round which was fastened a fillet of light blue stuff spotted with white. The best idea that I can give of its general appearance is to liken it to a tall hat of fashionable shape, without a brim, slightly squashed in so that it bulged at the top, and surrounded by a rather sporting necktie. Really, however, it was the *kitaris* or headdress of these monarchs worn by them alone. If anyone else had put on that hat, even by mistake in the dark, well, his head would have come off with it, that is all.

This king held a bow in his hand with an arrow set upon its string, just as I did, for we were out hunting, and as I shall have to narrate presently, lions are no respecters of persons. By his side, leaning against the back of the chariot, was a tall, sharp-pointed wand of cedar wood with a knob of some green precious stone, probably an emerald, fashioned to the likeness of an apple. This was the royal sceptre. Immediately behind the chariot walked several great nobles. One of them carried a golden footstool, another a parasol, furled at the moment; another a spare bow and a quiver of arrows, and another a jewelled fly-whisk made of palm fibre.

The king, I should add, was young, handsome with a curled beard and clear-cut, high-bred looking features; his face, however, was bad, cruel and stamped with an air of weariness, or rather, satiety, which was emphasized by the black circles beneath his fine dark eyes. Moreover pride seemed to emanate from him and yet there was something in his bearing and glances which suggested fear. He was a god who knows that he is mortal and is therefore afraid lest at any moment he may be called upon to lose his godship in his mortality.

Not that he dreaded the perils of the chase; he was too much of a man for that. But how could he tell lest among all that crowd of crawling nobles, there was not one who had a dagger ready for his back, or a phial of poison to mix with his wine or water? He with all the world in the hollow of his hand, was filled with secret terrors which as I learned since first I seemed to see him thus, fulfilled themselves at the appointed time. For this man of blood was destined to die in blood, though not by murder.

THE CAVALCADE HALTED. PRESENTLY A fat eunuch glittering in his gold-wrought garments like some bronzed beetle in the sunlight, came waddling back towards me. He was odious and I knew that we hated each other.

"Greeting, Egyptian," he said, mopping his brow with his sleeve for the sun was hot. "An honour for you! A great honour! The King of kings commands your presence. Yes, he would speak with you with his own lips, and with that abortion of a servant of yours also. Come! Come swiftly!"

"Swift as an arrow, Houman," I answered laughing, "seeing that for three moons I, like an arrow, have rested upon the string and flown no nearer to his Majesty."

"Three moons!" screeched the eunuch. "Why, many wait three years and many go to the grave still waiting; bigger men than you, Egyptian, though I hear you do claim to be of royal blood yonder on the Nile. But talk not of arrows flying towards the most High, for surely it is ill-omened and might earn you another honour, that of the string," and he made a motion suggestive of a cord encircling his throat. "Man, leave your bow behind! Would you appear before the King armed? Yes, and your dagger also."

"Perchance a lion might appear before the King and he does not leave his claws and teeth behind," I answered drily as I divested myself of my weapons.

Then we started, the three of us, leaving the chariot in charge of a soldier.

"Draw your sleeves over your hands," said the eunuch. "None must appear before the King showing his hands, and, dwarf, since you have no sleeves, thrust yours into your robe."

"What am I to do with my feet?" he answered in a thick, guttural voice. "Will it offend the King of kings to see my feet, most noble eunuch?"

"Certainly, certainly," answered Houman, "since they are ugly enough to offend even me. Hide them as much as possible. Now we are near, down on your faces and crawl forward slowly on your knees and elbows, as I do. Down, I say!"

So down I went, though with anger in my heart, for be it remembered that I, the modern Allan Quatermain, knew every thought and feeling that passed through the mind of my prototype.

It was as though I were a spectator at a play, with this difference. I could read the motives and reflections of this former *ego* as well as observe his actions. Also I could rejoice when he rejoiced, weep when he wept and generally feel all that he felt, though at the same time I retained the power of studying him from my own modern standpoint and with my own existing intelligence. Being two we still were one, or being one we still were two, whichever way you like to put it. Lastly I lacked these powers with reference to the other actors in the piece. Of these I knew just as much, or as little as my former self knew, that is if he ever really existed. There was nothing unnatural in my faculties where they were concerned. I had no insight into their souls any more than I have into those of the people about me to-day. Now I hope that I have made clear my somewhat uncommon position with reference to these pages from the Book of the Past.

Well, preceded by the eunuch and followed by the dwarf, I crawled though the sand in which grew some thorny plants that pricked my knees and fingers, towards the person of the Monarch of the World. He had descended from his chariot by help of a footstool, and was engaged in drinking from a golden cup, while his attendants stood around in various attitudes of adoration, he who had handed him the cup being upon his knees. Presently he looked up and saw us.

"Who are these?" he asked in a high voice that yet was not unmusical, "and why do you bring them into my presence?"

"May it please the King," answered our guide, knocking his head upon the ground in a very agony of humiliation, "may it please the King—"

"It would please me better, dog, if you answered my question. Who are they?"

"May it please the King, this is the Egyptian hunter and noble, Shabaka."

"I hear," said his Majesty with a gleam of interest in his tired eyes, "and what does this Egyptian here?"

"May it please the King, the King bade me bring him to the presence, but now when the chariots halted."

"I forgot; you are forgiven. But who is that with him? Is it a man or an ape?"

Here I screwed my head round and saw that my slave in his efforts to obey the eunuch's instructions and hide his feet, had made himself into a kind of ball, much as a hedgehog does, except that his big head appeared in front of the ball.

"O King, that I understand is the Egyptian's servant and charioteer."

Again he looked interested, and exclaimed,

"Is it so? Then Egypt must be a stranger country than I thought if such ape-men live there. Stand up, Egyptian, and bid your ape stand up also, for I cannot hear men who speak with their mouths in the dust."

So I rose and saluted by lifting both my hands and bowing as I had observed others do, trying, however, to keep them covered by my sleeves. The King looked me up and down, then said briefly,

"Set out your name and the business that brought you to my city."

"May the King live for ever," I replied. "As this lord said," and I pointed to the eunuch—

"He is not a lord but a dog," interrupted the Monarch, "who wears the robe of women. But continue."

"As this dog who wears the robe of women said"—here the King laughed, but the eunuch, Houman, turned green with rage and glowered at me—"my name is Shabaka. I am a descendant of the Ethiopian king of Egypt of that same name."

"It seems from all I hear that there are too many descendants of kings in Egypt. When I visit that land which perhaps soon I must do with an army at my back," here he stared at me coldly, "it may be well to lessen their number. There is a certain Peroa for instance."

He paused, but I made no answer, since Peroa was my father's cousin and of the fallen Royal House; also the protector of my youth.

"Well, Shabaka," he went on, "in Persia royal blood is common also, though some of us think it looks best when it is shed. What else are you?"

"A slayer of royal beasts, O King of kings, a hunter of lions and of elephants," (this statement interested me, Allan Quatermain, intensely, showing me as it did that our tastes are very persistent); "also when I am at home, a breeder of cattle and a grower of grain."

"Good trades, all of them, Shabaka. But why came you here?"

"Idernes the satrap of Egypt, servant of the King of kings, sought for one who would travel to the East because the King of kings desired to hear of the hunting of lions in the lands that lie to the south of Egypt towards the beginnings of the great river. Then I, who desired to see new countries, said, 'Here am I. Send me.' So I came and for three moons have dwelt in the royal city, but till this hour have scarcely so much as seen the face of the great King, although by many messengers I have announced my presence, showing them the letters of Idernes giving me safe-conduct. Therefore I propose to-morrow or the next day to return to Egypt."

The King said a word and a scribe appeared whom he commanded to take note of my words and let the matter be inquired of, since some should suffer for this neglect, a saying at which I saw Houman and certain of the nobles turn pale and whisper to each other.

"Now I remember," he exclaimed, "that I did desire Idernes to send me an Egyptian hunter. Well, you are here and we are about to hunt the lion of which there are many in yonder reeds, hungry and fierce beasts, since for three days they have been herded in so that they can kill no food. How many lions have you slain, Shabaka?"

"Fifty and three in all, O King, not counting the cubs."

He stared at me, answering with a sneer,

"You Egyptians have large mouths. I have always heard it of you. Well, to-day we will see whether you can kill a fifty-fourth. In an hour when the sun begins to sink, the hounds will be loosed in yonder reeds and since the water is behind them, the lions will come out, and then we shall see."

Now I saw that the King thought me to be a liar and the blood rose to my head.

"Why wait till the sun begins to sink, O King of kings?" I said. "Why not enter the reeds, as is our fashion in the Land of Kush, and rouse the lions from sleep in their own lair?"

Now the King laughed outright and called in a loud voice to his courtiers,

"Do ye hear this boasting Egyptian, who talks of entering the reeds and facing the lions in their lair, a thing that no man dare do where none can see to shoot? What say ye now? Shall we ask him to prove his words?"

Some great lord stepped forward, one who was a hunter though he looked little like it, for the scent on his hair reached me from four paces away and there was paint upon his face.

"Yes, O King," he said in a mincing voice, "let him enter and kill a lion. But if he fail, then let a lion kill him. There are some hungry in the palace den and it is not fit that the King's ears should be filled with empty words by foreigners from Egypt."

"So be it," said the King. "Egyptian, you have brought it on your own head. Prove that you can do what you say and I will give you great honour. Fail, and to the lions with him who lies of lions. Still," he added, "it is not right that you should go alone. Choose therefore one of these lords to keep you company; he who would put you to the test, if you will."

Now I looked at the scented noble who turned pale beneath his paint. Then I looked at the fat eunuch, Houman, who opened his mouth and gasped like a fish, and when I had looked, I shook my head and said as though to myself,

"Not so, no woman and no eunuch shall be my companion on this quest," whereat the King and all the rest laughed out loud. "The dwarf and I will go alone."

"The dwarf!" said the King. "Can he hunt lions also?"

"No, O King, but perchance he can smell them, for otherwise how shall I find them in that thicket within an hour?"

"Perchance they can smell him. How is the ape-man named?" asked the King.

"Bes, O King, after the god of the Egyptians whom he resembles."

"Dare you accompany your master on this hunt, O Bes?" inquired the King.

Then Bes looked up, rolling his yellow eyes, and answered in his thick and guttural voice,

"I am my master's slave and dare I refuse to accompany him? If I did he might kill me, as the King of kings kills his slaves. It is better to die with honour by the teeth of a lion, than with dishonour beneath the whip of a master. So at least we think in Ethiopia."

"Well spoken, dwarf Bes!" exclaimed the King. "So would I have all men think throughout the East. Let the words of this Ethiop be written down and copies of them sent to the satraps of all the provinces that they may be read to the peoples of the earth. I the King have decreed it."

V

THE WAGER

While the scribes were at their work I bowed before the King and prayed his leave and I and the dwarf Bes might get to ours.

"Go," he said, "and return here within an hour. If you do not return tidings of your death shall be sent to the satrap of Egypt to be told to your wives."

"I thank the King, but it is needless, for I have no wives, which are ill company for a hunter."

"Strange," he said, "since many women would be glad to name such a man their husband, at least here among us Easterns."

Walking backwards and bowing as we went, Bes and I returned to our chariot. There we stripped off our outer garments till Bes was naked save for his waistcloth and I was clad only in a jerkin. Then I took my bow, my arrows and my knife, and Bes took two spears, one light for throwing and the other short, broad and heavy for stabbing. Thus armed we passed back before the Easterns who stared at us, and advanced to the edge of the thicket of tall reeds that was full of lions.

Here Bes took dust and threw it into the air that we might learn from which quarter the light wind blew.

"We will go against the breeze, Lord," he said, "that I may smell the lions before they smell us."

I nodded, and answered,

"Hearken, Bes. Well may it be that we kill no lions in this place where it is hard to shoot. Yet I would not return to be thrown to wild beasts by yonder evil king. Therefore if we fail in this or in any other way, do you kill me, if you still live."

He rolled his eyes and grinned.

"Not so, Master. Then we will win through the reeds and lie hid in their edge till darkness comes, for in them those half-men will never dare to seek for us. Afterwards we will swim the water and disguise ourselves as jugglers and try to reach the coast, and so back to Egypt, having learned much. Never stretch out your hand to Death till he stretches out his to you, which he will do soon enough, Master."

Again I nodded and said,

"And if a lion should kill me, Bes, what then?"

"Then, Master, I will kill that lion if I can and go report the matter to the King."

"And if he should wish to throw you to the beasts, Bes, what then?"

"Then, first I will drag him down to the greatest of all beasts, he who waits to devour evil-doers in the Under-world, be they kings or slaves," and he stretched out his long arms and made a motion as of clutching a man by the throat. "Oh! have no fear, Master, I can break him like a stick, and afterwards we will talk the matter over among the dead, for I shall swallow my tongue and die also. It is a good trick, Master, which I wish you would learn."

Then he took my hand and kissed it and we entered the reeds, I, who was a hunter, feeling more happy than I had done since we set foot in the East.

Yet the quest was desperate for the reeds were tall and often I could not see more than a bow's length in front of me. Presently, however, we found a path made perchance by game coming down to drink, or by crocodiles coming up to sleep, and followed it, I with an arrow on my string and Bes with the throwing spear in his right hand and the stabbing spear in his left, half a pace ahead of me. On we crept, Bes drawing in the air through his great nostrils as a hound might do, till suddenly he stopped and sniffed towards the north.

"I smell lion near," he whispered, searching among the reed stems with his eyes. "I see lion," he whispered again, and pointed, but I could see nothing save the stems of the reeds.

"Rouse him," I whispered back, "and I will shoot as he bounds."

Then Bes poised the spear, shook it till it quivered, and threw. There was a roar and a lioness appeared with the spear fast in her flank. I loosed the arrow but it cut into the thick reeds and stuck there.

"Forward!" whispered Bes, "for where woman is, there look for man. The lion will be near."

We crept on, Bes stopping to cut the arrow from a reed and set it back in the quiver, for it was a good arrow made by himself. But now he shifted the broad spear to his right hand and in his left held his knife. We heard the wounded lioness roar not far away.

"She calls her man to help her," whispered Bes, and as the words left his lips the reeds down wind began to sway, for we were smelt.

They swayed, they parted and, half seen, half hid between their stems, appeared the head of a great, black-maned lion. I drew the string and shot, this time not in vain, for I heard the arrow thud upon his hide. Then before I could set another he was on us, reared upon his hind legs and roaring. As I drew my dagger he struck at me, but I bent down and his paw went over my head. Then his weight came against me and I fell beneath him, stabbing him in the belly as I fell. I saw his mighty jaws open to crush my head. Then they shut again and through them burst a whine like that of a hurt dog.

Bes had driven his spear into the lion's breast, so deep that the point of it came out through the back. Still he was not dead, only now it was Bes he sought. The dwarf ran at him as he reared up again, and casting his great arms about the brute's body, wrestled with him as man with man.

Then it was, for the first time I think, that I learned all the Ethiopian's strength. For he, a dwarf, threw that lion on its back and thrusting his big head beneath the jaws, struggled with it madly. I was up, the knife still in my hand, and oh! I too was strong. Into the throat I drove it, dragging it this way and that, and lo! the lion moaned and died and his blood gushed out over both of us. Then Bes sat up and laughed, and I too laughed, since neither of us had more than scratches and we had done what men could scarcely do.

"Do you remember, Master," said Bes when he had finished laughing, as he wiped his brow with some damp moss, "how, once far away up the Nile you charged a mad elephant with a spear and saved me who had fallen, from being trampled to death?"

I, Shabaka, answered that I did. (And I, Allan Quatermain, observing all these things in my psychic trance in the museum of Ragnall Castle, reflected that I also remembered how a certain Hans had saved me from a certain mad elephant, to wit, Jana, not so long before, which just shows how things come round.)

"Yes," went on Bes, "you saved me from that elephant, though it seemed death to you. And, Master, I will tell you something now. That very morning I had tried to poison you, only you would not wait to eat because the elephants were near."

"Did you?" I asked idly. "Why?"

"Because two years before you captured me in battle with some of my people, and as I was misshapen, or for pity's sake, spared my life and made me your slave. Well, I who had been a chief, a very great chief, Master, did not wish to remain a slave and did wish to avenge my people's blood. Therefore I tried to poison you, and that very day you saved my life, offering for it your own."

"I think it was because I wanted the tusks of the elephant, Bes."

"Perhaps, Master, only you will remember that this elephant was a young cow and had no tusks worth anything. Still had it carried tusks, it might have been so, since one white tusk is worth many black dwarfs. Well, to-day I have paid you back. I say it lest you should forget that had it not been for me, that lion would have eaten you."

"Yes, Bes, you have paid me back and I thank you."

"Master, hitherto I always thought you one who worshipped Maat, goddess of Truth. Now I see that you worship the god of Lies, whoever he may be, that god who dwells in the breasts of women and most men, but has no name. For, Master, it was *you* who saved *me* from the lion and not I you, since you cut its throat at the last. So that debt of mine is still to pay and by the great Grasshopper which we worship in my country, who is much better than all the gods of the Egyptians put together, I swear that I will pay it soon, or mayhap ten thousand years hence. At the last it shall be paid."

"Why do you worship a grasshopper and why is he better than the gods of the Egyptians?" I asked carelessly, for I was tired and his talk amused me while we rested.

"We worship the Grasshopper, Master, because he jumps with men's spirits from one life to another, or from this world to the next, yes, right through the blue sky. And he is better than your Egyptian gods because they leave you to find your own way there, and then eat you alive, that is if you have tried to poison people, as of course we have all done. But, Master, we are fresh again now, so let us be going, for the hour will soon be finished. Also when she has eaten the spear handle, that lioness may return."

"Yes," I said; "let us go and report to the King of kings that we have killed a lion."

"Master, it is not enough. Even common kings believe little that they do not see, wherefore it is certain that a King of kings will believe nothing and still more certain that he will not come here to look. So as we cannot carry the lion, we must take a bit of it," and straightway he cut off the end of the brute's tail.

Following the crocodile path, presently we reached the edge of the reeds opposite to the camp where the King now sat in state beneath a purple pavilion that had been reared, eating a meal, with his courtiers standing at a distance and looking very hungry.

Out of the reeds bounded Bes, naked and bloody, waving the lion's tail and singing some wild Ethiopian chant, while I, also bloody and half naked, for the lion's claws had torn my jerkin off me, followed with bow unstrung.

The King looked up and saw us.

"What! Do you live, Egyptian?" he asked. "Of a surety I thought that by now you would be dead."

"It was the lion that died, O King," I answered, pointing to Bes who, having ceased from his song, was jumping about carrying the beast's tail in his mouth as a dog carries a bone.

"It seems that this Egyptian has killed a lion," said the King to one of his lords, him of the painted face and scented hair.

"May be please the King," he answered, bowing, "a tail is not the whole beast and may have been taken thither, or cut from a lion lying dead already. The King knows that the Egyptians are great liars."

So he spoke because he was jealous of the deed.

"These men look as though they had met a live one, not one that is dead," said the King, scanning our blood-stained shapes. "Still, as you doubt it, you will wish to put the matter to the proof. Therefore, Cousin, take six men with you, enter the reeds and search. In that soft ground it will be easy to follow their footmarks."

"It is dangerous, O King," began the prince, for such he was, no less.

"And therefore the task will be the more to your taste, Cousin. Go now, and be swift."

So six hunters were called and the prince went, cursing me beneath his breath as he passed us. For he was terribly afraid, and with reason. Suddenly Bes ceased from his antics and prostrating himself, cried,

"A boon, O King. This noble lord throws doubt upon my master's word. Suffer that I may lead him to where the lion lies dead, since otherwise wandering in those reeds the great King's cousin might come to harm and the great King be grieved."

"I have many cousins," said the King. "Still go if you wish, Dwarf."

So Bes ran after the prince and catching him up, tapped him on the shoulder with the lion's tail to point out the way. Then they vanished into the reeds and I went to the chariot to wash off the blood from my body and clothes. As I fastened my robe I heard a sound of roaring, then one scream, after which all grew still. Now I drew near to the reeds and stood between them and the King's camp.

Presently on their edge appeared Bes dancing and singing as before, but this time he held a lion's tail in either hand. After him came the six hunters dragging between them the body of the lion we had killed. They staggered with it towards the King, and I followed.

"I see the dwarf," he said. "I see the dead lion and I see the hunters. But where is my cousin? Make report, O Bes."

"O King of kings," replied Bes, "the mighty prince your cousin lies flat yonder beneath the body of that lion's wife. She sprang upon him and killed him, and I sprang upon her and killed her with my spear. Here is her tail, O King of kings."

"Is this true?" he asked of the hunters.

"It is true, O King," answered their captain. "The lioness, which was wounded, leapt upon the prince, choosing him although he was behind us all. Then this dwarf leapt upon the lioness, being behind the prince and nearest to him, and drove his spear through her shoulders to her heart. So we brought the first lion as the King commanded us, since we could carry no more."

The face of the King grew red with rage.

"Seven of my people and one black dwarf!" he exclaimed. "Yet the lioness kills my cousin and the dwarf kills the lioness. Such is the tale that will go to Egypt concerning the hunters of the King of the world. Seize those men, Guards, and let them be fed to the wild beasts in the palace dens."

At once the unfortunates were seized and led away. Then the King called Bes to him, and taking the gold chain he wore about his neck, threw it over his head, thereby, though I knew nothing of it at the time, conferring upon him some noble rank. Next he called to me and said,

"It would seem that you are skilled in the use of the bow and in the hunting of lions, Egyptian. Therefore I will honour you, for this afternoon your chariot shall drive with my chariot, and we will hunt side by side. Moreover, I will lay you a wager as to which of us will kill the most lions, for know, Shabaka, that I also am skilled in the use of the bow, more skilled than any among the millions of my subjects."

"Then, O King, it is of little use for me to match myself against you, seeing that I have met men who can shoot better than I do, or, since in the East all must speak nothing but the truth, not being liars as the dead prince said we Egyptians are, one man."

"Who was that man, Shabaka?"

"The Prince Peroa, O King."

The King frowned as though the name displeased him, then answered,

"Am I not greater than this Peroa and cannot I therefore shoot better?"

"Doubtless, O King of kings, and therefore how can I who shoot worse than Peroa, match myself against you?"

"For which reason I will give you odds, Shabaka. Behold this rope of rose-hued pearls I wear. They are unequalled in the whole world, for twenty years the merchants sought them in the days of my father; half of them would buy a satrapy. I wager them"—here the listening nobles gasped and the fat eunuch, Houman, held up his hands in horror.

"Against what, O King?"

"Your slave Bes, to whom I have taken a fancy."

Now I trembled and Bes rolled his yellow eyes.

"Your pardon, O King of kings," I said, "but it is not enough. I am a hunter and to such, priceless pearls are of little use. But to me that dwarf is of much use in my hunting."

"So be it, Shabaka, then I will add to the wager. If you win, together with the pearls I will give you the dwarf's weight in solid gold."

"The King is bountiful," I answered, "but it is not enough, for even if I win against one who can shoot better than Peroa, which is impossible, what should I do with so much gold? Surely for the sake of it I should be murdered or ever I saw the coasts of Egypt."

"What shall I add then?" asked the King. "The most beauteous maiden in the House of Women?"

I shook my head. "Not so, O King, for then I must marry who would remain single."

"There is no need, you might sell her to your friend, Peroa. A satrapy?"

"Not so, O King, for then I must govern it, which would keep me from my hunting, until it pleased the King to take my head."

"By the name of the holy ones I worship what then do you ask added to the pearls and the pure gold?"

Now I tried to bethink me of something that the King could not grant, since I had no wish for this match which my heart warned me would end in trouble. As no thought came to me I looked at Bes and saw that he was rolling his eyes towards the six doomed hunters who were being led away, also in pretence of driving off a fly, pointing to them with one of the lion tails. Then I remembered that a decree once uttered by the King of the East could not be altered, and saw a road of escape.

"O King," I said, "together with the pearls and the gold I ask that the lives of those six hunters be added to the wager, to be spared if by chance I should win."

"Why?" asked the King amazed.

"Because they are brave men, O King, and I would not see the bones of such cracked by tame beasts in a cage."

"Is my judgment registered?" asked the King.

"Not yet, O King," answered the head scribe.

"Then it has no weight and can be suspended without the breaking of the law. Shabaka, thus stands our wager. If I kill more lions than you do this day, or, should but two be slain, I kill the first, or should none be slain, I plant more arrows in their bodies, I take your slave, Bes the dwarf, to be my slave. But should you have the better of me in any of these ways, then I give to you this girdle of rose pearls and the weight of the dwarf Bes in gold and the six hunters free of harm, to do with what you will. Let it be recorded, and to the hunt."

Soon Bes and I were in our chariot which by command took place in line with that of the King, but at a distance of some thirty steps. Bending over the dwarf who drove, I spoke with him, saying,

"Our luck is ill to-day, Bes, seeing that before the end of it we may well be parted."

"Not so, Master, our luck is good to-day seeing that before the end of it you will be the richer by the finest pearls in the whole world, by my weight in pure gold (and Master, I am twice as heavy as the king thought and will stuff myself with twenty pounds of meat before the weighing, if I have the chance, or at least with water, though in this hot place that will not last for long), and by six picked huntsmen, brave men as you thought, who will serve to escort us and our treasure to the coast."

"First I must win the match, Bes."

"Which you could do with one eye blinded, Master, and a sore finger. Kings think that they can shoot because all the worms that crawl about them and are named men, dare not show themselves their betters. Oh! I have heard tales in yonder city. There have been days when this Lord of the world has missed six lions with as many arrows, and they seated smiling in his face, being but tamed brutes brought from far in cages of wood, yes, smiling like cats in the sun. Look you, Master, he drinks too much wine and sits up too late in his Women's house—there are three hundred of them there, Master—to shoot as you and I can. If you doubt it, look at his eyes and hands. Oh! the pearls and the gold and the men are yours, and that painted prince who mocked us is where he ought to be—dead in the mud.

"Did I tell you how I managed that, Master? As you know better than I do, lions hate those that have on them the smell of their own blood. Therefore, while I pointed out the way to him, I touched the painted prince with the bleeding tail of that which we killed, pretending that it was by chance, for which he cursed me, as well he might. So when we came to the dead lion and, as I had expected, met there the lioness you had wounded, she charged through the hunters at him who smelt of her husband, and bit his head off."

"But, Bes, you smelt of him also, and worse."

"Yes, Master, but that painted cousin of the King came first. I kept well behind him, pretending to be afraid," and he chuckled quietly, adding, "I expect that he is now telling an angry tale about me to Osiris, or to the Grasshopper that takes him there, as it may happen."

"These Easterns worship neither Osiris, nor your Grasshopper, Bes, but a flame of fire."

"Then he is telling the tale to the fire, and I hope that it will get tired and burn him."

So we talked merrily enough because we had done great deeds and thought that we had outwitted the Easterns and the King, not knowing all their craft. For none had told us that that man who hunted with the King and yet dared to draw arrow upon the quarry before the King should be put to death as one who had done insult to his Majesty. This that royal fox remembered and therefore was sure that he would win the wager.

Now the chariots turned and passing down a path came to an open space that was cleared of reeds. Here they halted, that of the King and my own side by side with ten paces between them, and those of the court behind. Meanwhile huntsmen with dogs entered the great brake far away to the right and left of us, also in front, so that the lions might be driven backwards and forwards across the open space.

Soon we heard the hounds baying on all sides. Then Bes made a sucking noise with his great lips and pointed to the edge of the reeds in front of us some sixty paces away. Looking, I saw a yellow shape creeping along between their dark stems, and although the shot was far, forgetting all things save I was a hunter and there was my game, I drew the arrow to my ear, aimed and loosed, making allowance for its fall and for the wind.

Oh! that shot was good. It struck the lion in the body and pierced him through. Out he came, roaring, rolling, and tearing at the ground.

But by now I had another arrow on the string, and although the King lifted his bow, I loosed first. Again it struck, this time in the throat, and that lion groaned and died.

The King looked at me angrily, and from the court behind rose a murmur of wonder mingled with wrath, wonder at my marksmanship, and wrath because I had dared to shoot before the King.

"The wager looks well for us," muttered Bes, but I bade him be silent, for more lions were stirring.

Now one leapt across the open space, passing in front of the King and within thirty paces of us. He shot and missed it, sending his shaft two spans above its back. Then I shot and drove the arrow through it just where the head joins the neck, cutting the spine, so that it died at once.

Again that murmur went up and the King struck the charioteer on the head with his clenched fist, crying out that he had suffered the horses to move and should be scourged for causing his hand to shake.

This charioteer, although he was a lord—since in the East men of high rank waited on the King like slaves and even clipped his nails and beard—craved pardon humbly, admitting his fault.

"It is a lie," whispered Bes. "The horses never stirred. How could they with those grooms holding their heads? Nevertheless, Master, the pearls are as good as round your neck."

"Silence," I answered. "As we have heard, in the East all men speak the truth; it is only Egyptians who lie. Also in the East men's necks are encircled with bowstrings as well as pearls, and ears are long."

The hounds continued to bay, drawing nearer to us. A lioness bounded out of the reeds, ran towards the King's chariot and as though amazed, sat down like a dog, so near that a man might have hit it with a stone. The King shot short, striking it in the fore-paw only, whereon it shook out the arrow and rushed back into the reeds, while the court behind cried,

"May the King live for ever! The beast is dead."

"We shall see if it is dead presently," said Bes, and I nodded.

Another lion appeared to the right of the King. Again he shot and missed it, whereon he began to curse and to swear in his own royal oaths, and the charioteer trembled. Then came the end.

One of the hounds drew quite close and roused the lioness that had been pricked in the foot. She turned and killed it with a blow of her paw, then, being mad, charged straight at the King's chariot. The horses reared, lifting the grooms off their feet. The King shot wildly and fell backwards out of the chariot, as even Kings of the world must do when they have nothing left to stand on. The lioness saw that he was down and leapt at him, straight over the chariot. As she leapt I shot at her in the air and pierced her through the loins, paralysing her, so that although she fell down near the King, she could not come at him to kill him.

I sprang from my chariot, but before I could reach the lioness hunters had run up with spears and stabbed her, which was easy as she could not move.

The King rose from the ground, for he was unharmed, and said in a loud voice,

"Had not that shaft of mine gone home, I think that the East would have bowed to another lord to-night."

Now, forgetting that I was speaking to the King of the earth, forgetting the wager and all besides, I exclaimed,

"Nay, your shaft missed; mine went home," whereon one of the courtiers cried,

"This Egyptian is a liar, and calls the King one!"

"A liar?" I said astonished. "Look at the arrow and see from whose quiver it came," and I drew one from my own of the Egyptian make and marked with my mark.

Then a tumult broke out, all the courtiers and eunuchs talking at once, yet all bowing to the mud-stained person of the King, like ears of wheat to a tree in a storm. Not wishing to urge my claims further, for my part I returned to the chariot and the hunting being done, as I supposed, unstrung my bow which I prized above all things, and set it in its case.

While I was thus employed the eunuch Houman approached me with a sickly smile, saying,

"The King commands your presence, Egyptian, that you may receive your reward."

I nodded, saying that I would come, and he returned.

"Bes," I said when he was out of hearing, "my heart sinks. I do not trust that King who I think means mischief."

"So do I, Master. Oh! we have been great fools. When a god and a man climb a tree together, the man should allow the god to come first to the top, and thence tell the world that he is a god."

"Yes," I answered, "but who ever sees Wisdom until she is flying away? Now perhaps, the god being the stronger, will cast down the man."

Then both together we advanced towards the King, leaving the chariot in charge of soldiers. He was seated on a gilded chair which served him as a throne, and behind him were his officers, eunuchs and attendants, though not all of them, since at a little distance some of them were engaged in beating the lord who had served as his charioteer upon the feet with rods. We prostrated ourselves before him and waited till he spoke. At length he said,

"Shabaka the Egyptian, we made a wager with you, of which you will remember the terms. It seems that you have won the wager, since you slew two lions, whereas we, the King, slew but one, that which leapt upon us in the chariot."

Here Bes groaned at my side and I looked up.

"Fear nothing," he went on, "it shall be paid." Here he snatched off the girdle of priceless, rose-hued pearls and threw it in my face.

"At the palace too," he went on, "the dwarf shall be set in the scales and his full weight in pure gold shall be given to you. Moreover, the lives of the six hunters are yours, and with them the men themselves."

"May the King live for ever!" I exclaimed, feeling that I must say something.

"I hope so," he answered cruelly, "but, Egyptian, you shall not, who have broken the laws of the land."

"In what way, O King?" I asked.

"By shooting at the lions before the King had time to draw his bow, and by telling the King that he lied to his face, for both of which things the punishment is death."

Now my heart swelled till I thought it would burst with rage. Then of a sudden, a certain spirit entered into me and I rose to my feet and said,

"O King, you have declared that I must die and as this is so, I will kneel to you no more who soon shall sup at the table of Osiris, and there be far greater than any king, going before him with clean hands. Is it not your law that he who is condemned to die has first the right to set out his case for the honour of his name?"

"It is," said the King, I think because he was curious to hear what I had to say. "Speak on."

"O King, although my blood is as high as your own, of that I say nothing, for at the wish of your satrap I came to the East from Egypt as a hunter, to show you how we of Egypt kill lions and other beasts. For three months I have waited in the royal city seeking admission to the presence of the King, and in vain. At length I was bidden to this hunt when I was about to depart to my own land, and being taunted by your servants, entered the reeds with my slave, and there slew a lion. Then it pleased you to thrust a wager upon me which I did not wish to take, as to which of us would shoot the most lions; a wager as I now understand you did not mean that I should win, whatever might be my skill, since you thought I knew that I must shoot at nothing till you had first shot and killed the beasts or scared them away.

"So I matched myself against you, as hunter against hunter, for in the field, as before the gods, all are equal, not as a slave against a king who is determined to avenge defeat by death. We were posted and the lions came. I shot at those which appeared opposite to me, or upon my side, leaving those that appeared opposite to you, or on your side unshot at, as is the custom of hunters. My skill, or my fortune, was better than yours and I killed, whereas you missed or only wounded. In the end a lioness sprang at you and I shot it lest it should kill you; as could easily be proved by the arrow in its body. Now you say that I must die because I have broken some laws of yours which men should be ashamed to make, and to save your honour, pay me what I have won, knowing that pearls and gold and slaves are of no value to a dying man and can be taken back again. That is all the story.

"Yet I would add one word. You Easterns have two sayings which you teach to your children; that they should learn to shoot with the bow, and to tell the truth. O King, they are my last lessons to you. Learn to shoot with the bow—which you cannot do, and to tell the truth which you have not done. Now I have spoken and am ready to die and I thank you for the patience with which you have heard my words, that, as the King does *not* live for ever, I hope one day to repeat to you more fully beyond the grave."

Now at this bold speech of mine all those nobles and attendants gasped, for never had they heard such words addressed to his Majesty. The King turned red as though with shame, but made no answer, only he asked of those about him.

"What fate for this man?"

"Death, O King!" they cried with one voice.

"What death?" he asked again.

Then his Councillors consulted together and one of them answered,

"The slowest known to our law, *death by the boat*."

Hearing this and not knowing what was meant, it came into my mind that I was to be turned adrift in a boat and there left to starve.

"Behold the reward of good hunting!" I mocked in my rage. "O King, because of this deed of shame I call upon you the curse of all the gods of all the peoples. Henceforth may your sleep be ever haunted by evil dreams of what shall follow the last sleep, and in the end may you also die in blood."

The King opened his mouth as though to answer, but from it came nothing but a low cry of fear. Then guards rushed up and seized me.

VI

The Doom of the Boat

The guards led me to my chariot and thrust me into it, and with me Bes. I asked them if they would murder him also, to which the eunuch, Houman, answered No, since he had committed no crime, but that he must go with me to be weighed. Then soldiers took the horses by the bridles and led them, while others, having first snatched away my bow and all our other weapons, surrounded the chariot lest we should escape. So Bes and I were able to talk together in a Libyan tongue that none of them understood, even if they heard our words.

"Your life is spared," I said to him, "that the King may take you as a slave."

"Then he will take an ill slave, Master, since I swear by the Grasshopper that within a moon I will find means to kill him, and afterwards come to join you in a land where men hunt fair."

I smiled and Bes went on,

"Now I wish I had time to teach you that trick of swallowing your own tongue, since perhaps you will need it in this boat of which they talk."

"Did you not say to me an hour or two ago, Bes, that we are fools to stretch out our hands to Death until he stretches out his to us? I will not die until I must—now."

"Why 'now,' Master, seeing that only this afternoon you bade me kill you rather than let you be thrown to the wild beasts?" he asked peering at me curiously.

"Do you remember the old hermit, the holy Tanofir, who dwells in a cell over the sepulchre of the Apis bulls in the burial ground of the desert near to Memphis, Bes?"

"The magician and prophet who is the brother of your grandfather, Master, and the son of a king; he who brought you up before he became a hermit? Yes, I know him well, though I have seldom been very near to him because his eyes frighten me, as they frightened Cambyses the Persian when Tanofir cursed him and foretold his doom after he had stabbed the holy Apis, saying that by a wound from that same sword in his own body he should die himself, which thing came to pass. As they have frightened many another man also."

"Well, Bes, when yonder king told me that I must die, fear filled me who did not wish to die thus, and after the fear came a blackness in my mind. Then of a sudden in that blackness I saw a picture of Tanofir, my great uncle, seated in a sepulchre looking towards the East. Moreover I heard him speak, and to me, saying, 'Shabaka, my foster-son, fear nothing. You are in great danger but it will pass. Speak to the great King all that rises in your heart, for the gods of Vengeance make use of your tongue and whatever you prophesy to him shall be fulfilled.' So I spoke the words you heard and I feared nothing."

"Is it so, Master? Then I think that the holy Tanofir must have entered my heart also. Know that I was minded to leap upon that king and break his neck, so that all three of us might end together. But of a sudden something seemed to tell me to leave him alone and let things go as they are fated. But how can the holy Tanofir who grows blind with age, see so far?"

"I do not know, Bes, save that he is not as are other men, for in him is gathered all the ancient wisdom of Egypt. Moreover he lives with the gods while still upon earth, and like the gods can send his *Ka*, as we Egyptians call the spirit, or invisible self which companions all from the cradle to the grave and afterwards, whither he will. So doubtless to-day he sent it hither to me whom he loves more than anything on earth. Also I remember that before I entered on this journey he told me that I should return safe and sound. Therefore, Bes, I say I fear nothing."

"Nor do I, Master. Yet if you see me do strange things, or hear me speak strange words, take no note of them, since I shall be but playing a part as I think wisest."

After this we talked of that day's adventure with the lions, and of others that we had shared together, laughing merrily all the while, till the soldiers stared at us as though we were mad. Also the fat eunuch, Houman, who was mounted on an ass, rode up and said,

"What, Egyptian who dared to twist the beard of the Great King, you laugh, do you? Well, you will sing a different song in the boat to that which you sing in the chariot. Think of my words on the eighth day from this."

"I will think of them, Eunuch," I answered, looking at him fiercely in the eyes, "but who knows what kind of a song you will be singing before the eighth day from this?"

"What I do is done under the authority of the ancient and holy Seal of Seals," he answered in a quavering voice, touching the little cylinder of white shell which I had noted upon the person of the King, but that now hung from a gold chain about the eunuch's neck.

Then he made the sign which Easterns use to avert evil and rode off again, looking very frightened.

So we came to the royal city and went up to a wonderful palace. Here we were taken from the chariot and led into a room where food and drink in plenty were given to me as though I were an honoured guest, which caused me to wonder. Bes also, seated on the ground at a distance, ate and drank, for his own reasons filling himself to the throat as though he were a wineskin, until the serving slaves mocked at him for a glutton.

When we had finished eating, slaves appeared bearing a wooden framework from which hung a great pair of scales. Also there appeared officers of the King's Treasury, carrying leather bags which they opened, breaking the seals to show that the contents were pure gold coin. They set a number of these bags on one of the scales, and then ordered Bes to seat himself in the other. So much heavier did he prove than they expected him to be, that they were obliged to send back to the Treasury to fetch more bags of gold, for although Bes was so short in height, his weight was that of a large man. One of the treasurers grumbled, saying he should have been weighed before he had eaten and drunk. But the officer to whom he spoke grinned and answered that it mattered little, since the King was heir to criminals and that these bags would soon return to the Treasury, only they would need washing first, a remark that made me wonder.

At length, when the scales were even, the six hunters whose lives I had won and who had been given to me as slaves, were brought in and ordered to shoulder the bags of gold. I too was seized and my hands were bound behind me. Then I was led out in charge of the eunuch Houman, who informed me with a leer that it would be his duty to attend to my comfort till the end. With him were four black men all dressed in the same way. These, he said, were the executioners. Lastly came Bes watched by three of the king's guards armed with spears, lest he should attempt to rescue me or to do anyone a mischief.

Now my heart began to sink and I asked Houman what was to happen to me.

"This, O Egyptian slayer of lions. You will be laid upon a bed in a little boat upon the river and another boat will be placed over you, for these boats are called the Twins, Egyptian, in such a fashion that your head and your hands will project at one end and your feet at the other. There you will be left, comfortable as a baby in its cradle, and twice every day the best of food and drink will be brought to you. Should your appetite fail, moreover, it will be my duty to revive it by pricking your eyes with the point of a knife until it returns. Also after each meal I shall wash your face, your hands and your feet with milk and honey, lest the flies that buzz about them should suffer hunger, and to preserve your skin from burning by the sun. Thus slowly you will grow weaker and at length fall asleep. The last one who went into the boat—he, unlucky man, had by accident wandered into the court of the House of Women and seen some of the ladies there unveiled—only lived for twelve days, but you, being so strong, may hope to last for eighteen. Is there anything more that I can tell you? If so, ask it quickly for we draw near to the river."

Now when I heard this and understood all the horror of my fate, I forgot the vision of my great uncle, the holy Tanofir, and his comfortable prophecies, and my heart failed me altogether, so that I stood stock still.

"What, Lion-hunter and Bearder of kings, do you think it is too early to go to bed?" mocked this devilish eunuch. "On with you!" and he began to beat me about the face with the handle of his fly-whisk.

Then my manhood came back to me.

"When did the King tell you to touch me, you fatted swine?" I roared, and turning, since I could not reach him with my bound hands, kicked him in the body with all my strength, so that he fell down, writhing and screaming with agony. Indeed, had not the executioners leapt upon me, I would have trampled the life out of him where he lay. But they held me fast and presently, after he had been sick, Houman recovered enough to come forward leaning on the shoulders of two guards. Only now he mocked me no more.

We reached a quay just as the sun was setting. There in charge of a one-eyed black slave, a little square-ended boat floated at the river's edge, while on the quay itself lay a similar but somewhat shorter boat, bottom uppermost. Now the hunters whom I had won in the wager, with many glances of compassion, for they were brave men and knew that it was I who had saved their lives, placed the bags of gold in the bottom of the floating boat, and on the top of these a mattress stuffed with straw. Then the girdle of rose-hued pearls was made fast about my middle, my hands were untied, I was seized by the executioners and laid on my back on the mattress, and my wrists and ankles were fixed by cords to iron rings that were screwed to the thwarts of the boat. After this the other, shorter boat was laid over me in such a manner that it did not touch me, leaving my head, my hands and my feet exposed as the eunuch had said.

While this wicked work was going forward Bes sat on the quay, watching, till presently, after I had been made fast and covered up, he burst into shouts of laughter, clapped his hands and began to dance about as though with joy, till the eunuch, who had now recovered somewhat from my kick, grew curious and asked him why he behaved thus.

"O noble Eunuch," he answered, "once I was free and that man made me a slave, so that for many years I have been obliged to toil for him whom I hate. Moreover, often he has beaten me and starved me, which was why you saw me eat so much not long ago, and threatened to kill me, and now at last I have my revenge upon him who is about to die miserably. That is why I laugh and sing and dance and clap my hands, O most noble Eunuch, I who shall become the follower and servant of the glorious King of all the earth, and perhaps your friend, too, O Eunuch of eunuchs, whose sacred person my brutal master dared to kick."

"I understand," said Houman smiling, though with a twisted face, "and will make report of all you say to the King, and ask him to grant that you shall sometimes prick this Egyptian in the eye. Now go spit in his face and tell him what you think of him."

So Bes waded into the water which was quite shallow here, and spat into my face, or pretended to, while amid a torrent of vile language, he interpolated certain words in the Libyan tongue, which meant,

"O my most beloved father, mother, and other relatives, have no fear. Though things look very black, remember the vision of the holy Tanofir, who doubtless allows these things to happen to you to try your faith by direct order of the gods. Be sure that I will not leave you to perish, or if there should be no escape, that I will find a way to put you out of your misery and to avenge you. Yes, yes, I will yet see that accursed swine, Houman, take your place in this boat. Now I go to the Court to which it seems that this gold chain gives me a right of entry, or so the eunuch says, but soon I will be back again."

Then followed another stream or most horrible abuse and more spitting, after which he waded back to land and embraced Houman, calling him his best friend.

They went, leaving me alone in the boat save for the guard upon the quay who, now that darkness had come, soon grew silent. It was lonely, very lonely, lying there staring at the empty sky with only the stinging gnats for company, and soon my limbs began to ache. I thought of the poor wretches who had suffered in this same boat and wondered if their lot would be my lot.

Bes was faithful and clever, but what could a single dwarf do among all these black-hearted fiends? And if he could do nothing, oh! if he could do nothing!

The seconds seemed minutes, the minutes seemed hours, and the hours seemed years. What then would the days be, passed in torture and agony while waiting for a filthy death? Where now were the gods I had worshipped and—was there any god? Or was man but a self-deceiver who created gods instead of the gods creating him, because he did not love to think of an eternal blackness in which he would soon be swallowed up and lost? Well, at least that would mean sleep, and sleep is better than torment of mind or body.

It came to me, I think, who was so weary. At any rate I opened my eyes to see that the low moon had vanished and that some of the stars which I knew as a hunter who had often steered his way by them, had moved a little. While I was wondering idly why they moved, I heard the tramp of soldiers on the quay and the voice of an officer giving a command. Then I felt the boat being drawn in by the cord with which it was attached to the quay. Next the other boat that lay over me was lifted off, the ropes that bound we were undone and I was set upon my feet, for already I was so stiff that I could scarcely stand. A voice which I recognised as that of the eunuch Houman, addressed me in respectful tones, which made me think I must be dreaming.

"Noble Shabaka," said the voice, "the Great King commands your presence at his feast."

"Is it so?" I answered in my dream. "Then my absence from their feast will vex the gnats of the river," a saying at which Houman and others with him laughed obsequiously.

Next I heard the bags of gold being removed from the boat, after which we walked away, guards supporting me by either elbow until I found my strength again, and Houman following just behind, perhaps because he feared my foot if he went in front.

"What has chanced, Eunuch," I asked presently, "that I am disturbed from the bed where I was sleeping so well?"

"I do not know, Lord," he answered. "I only know that the King of kings has suddenly commanded that you should be brought before him as a guest clothed in a robe of honour, even if to do so, you must be awakened from your rest, yes, to his own royal table, for he holds a feast this night. Lord," he went on in a whining voice, "if perchance fortune should have changed her face to you, I pray you bear no malice to those who, when she frowned, were forced, yes, under the private Seal of Seals, against their will to carry out the commands of the King. Be just, O Lord Shabaka."

"Say no more. I will try to be just," I answered. "But what is justice in the East? I only know of it in Egypt."

Now we reached one of the doors of the palace and I was taken to a chamber where slaves who were waiting, washed and anointed me with scents, after which they clad me in a beautiful robe of silk, setting the girdle of rose-hued pearls about me.

When they had finished, preceded by Houman I was led to a great pillared hall closed in with silk hangings, where many feasted. Through them I went to a dais at the head of the hall where between half-drawn curtains surrounded by cup-bearers and other officers, the King sat in all his glory upon a cushioned golden throne. He had a glittering wine-cup in his hand and at a glance I saw that he was drunk, as it is the fashion for these Easterns to be at their great feasts, for he looked happy and human which he did not do when he was sober. Or perchance, as sometimes I thought afterwards, he only pretended to be drunk. Also I saw something else, namely, Bes, wondrously attired with the gold chain about his neck and wearing a red headdress. He was seated on the carpet before the throne, and saying things that made the King laugh and even caused the grave officers behind to smile.

I came to the dais and at a little sign from Bes who yet did not seem to see me, such a sign as he often made when he caught sight of game before I did, I prostrated myself. The King looked at me, then asked,

"Who is this?" adding, "Oh, I remember, the Egyptian whose arrows do not miss, the wonderful hunter whom Idernes sent to me from Memphis, which I hope to visit ere long. We quarrelled, did we not, Egyptian, something about a lion?"

"Not so, King," I answered. "The King was angry and with justice, because I could not kill a lion before it frightened his horses."

This I said because my hours in the boat had made me humble, also because the words came to my lips.

"Yes, yes, something like that, or at least you lie well. Whatever it may have been, it is done with now, a mere hunters' difference," and taking from his side his long sceptre that was headed with the great emerald, he stretched it out for me to touch in token of pardon.

Then I knew that I was safe for he to whom the King has extended his sceptre is forgiven all crimes, yes, even if he had attempted the royal life. The Court knew it also, for every man who saw bowed towards me, yes, even the officers behind the King. One of the cup-bearers too brought me a goblet of the King's own wine, which I drank thankfully, calling down health on the King.

"That was a wonderful shot of yours, Egyptian," he said, "when you sent an arrow through the lioness that dared to attack my Majesty. Yes, the King owes his life to you and he is grateful as you shall learn. This slave of yours," and he pointed to Bes in his gaudy attire, "has brought the whole matter to my mind whence it had fallen, and, Shabaka," here he hiccupped, "you may have noted how differently things look to the naked eye and when seen through a wine goblet. He has told me a wonderful story—what was the story, Dwarf?"

"May it please the great King," answered Bes, rolling his big eyes, "only a little tale of another king of my own country whom I used to think great until I came to the East and learned what kings could be. That king had a servant with whom he used to hunt, indeed he was my own father. One day they were out together seeking a certain elephant whose tusks were bigger than those of any other. Then the elephant charged the king and my father, at the risk of his life, killed it and claimed the tusks, as is the custom among the Ethiopians. But the king who greatly desired those tusks, caused my father to be poisoned that he might take them as his heir. Only before he died, my father, who could talk the elephant language, told all the other elephants of this wickedness, at which they were very angry, because they knew well that from the beginning of time their tusks have belonged to him who killed them, and the elephants are a people who do not like ancient laws to be altered. So the elephants made a league together and when the king next went out hunting, taking heed of nothing else they rushed at the king and tore him into pieces no bigger than a finger, and then killed the prince his son, who was behind him. That is the tale of the elephants who love Law, O King."

"Yes, yes," said his Majesty, waking up from a little doze, "but what became of the great tusks? I should like to have them."

"I inherited them as my father's son, O King, and gave them to my master, who doubtless will send them to you when he gets back to Egypt."

"A strange tale," said the King. "A very strange tale which seems to remind me of something that happened not long ago. What was it? Well, it does not matter. Egyptian, do you seek any reward for that shot of yours at the lioness? If so, it shall be given to you. Have you a grudge against anyone, for instance?"

"O King," I answered, "I do seek justice against a certain man. This evening I was led to the bank of the river in charge of the eunuch Houman, who desired to take me for a row in a boat. On the road, for no offence he struck me on the head with the handle of his fly-whip. See, here are the marks of it, O King. Unless the King commanded him to strike me which I do not remember, I seek justice against this eunuch."

Now the King grew very angry and cried,

"What! Did the dog dare to strike a freeborn noble Egyptian?"

Here Houman threw himself upon his face in terror and began to babble out I know not what about the punishment of the boat, which was unlucky for him, for it put the matter into the King's mind.

"The boat!" he cried. "Ah! yes, the boat; being so fat you will fit it well, Eunuch. To the boat with him, and before he enters it a hundred blows upon the feet with the rods," and he pointed at him with his sceptre.

Then guards sprang upon Houman and dragged him away. As he went he clutched at Bes, but hissing something into his ear, the dwarf bit him through the hand till he let go. So Houman departed and the King's guests laughed at the sight, for he had worked mischief to many.

When he had gone the King stared at me and asked,

"But why did I disturb you from your sleep, Egyptian? Oh! I remember. This dwarf says that he has seen the fairest woman in the whole world, and the most learned, some lady of Egypt, but that he does not know her name, that you alone know her name. I disturbed you that you might tell it to me but if you have forgotten it, you can go back to your bed and rest there till it returns to you. There are plenty of boats in the river, Egyptian."

"The fairest and most learned woman in the world?" I said astonished. "Who can that be, unless he means the lady Amada?" and I paused, wishing I had bitten out my tongue before I spoke, for I smelt a trap.

"Yes, Master," said Bes in a clear voice. "That was the name, the lady Amada."

"Who is this lady Amada?" asked the King, seeming to grow suddenly sober. "And what is she like?"

"I can tell you that, O King," said Bes. "She is like a willow shaken in the wind for slenderness and grace. She has eyes like those of a buck at gaze; she has lips like rosebuds; she has hair black as the night and soft as silk, the odour of which floats round her like that of flowers. She has a voice that whispers like the evening wind, and yet is rich as honey. Oh! she is beautiful as a goddess and when men see her their hearts melt like wax in the sun and for a long while they can look upon no other woman, not till the next day indeed if they meet her in the evening," and Bes smacked his thick lips and gazed upwards.

"By the holy Fire," laughed the King, "I feel my heart melting already. Say, Shabaka, what do you know of this Amada? Is she married or a maiden?"

Now I answered because I must, for after all that boat was not far away, nor did I dare to lie.

"She is married, O King of kings, to the goddess Isis whom she loves alone."

"A woman married to a woman, or rather to the Queen of women," he answered laughing, "well, that matters little."

"Nay, O King, it matters much since she is under the protection of Isis and inviolate."

"That remains to be seen, Shabaka. I think that I would dare the wrath of every false goddess in heaven to win such a prize. Learned also, you say, Shabaka."

"Aye, O King, full of learning to the finger tips, a prophetess also, one in whom the divine fire burns like a lamp in a vase of alabaster, one to whom visions come and who can read the future and the past."

"Still better," said the King. "One, then, who would be a fitting consort for the King of kings, who wearies of fat, round-eyed, sweetmeat-sucking fools whereof there are hundreds yonder," and he pointed towards the House of Women. "Who is this maid's father?"

"He is dead but she is the niece of the Prince Peroa, and by birth the Royal Lady of Egypt, O King."

"Good, then she is well born also. Hearken, O Shabaka, to-morrow you start back to Egypt, bearing letters from me to my vassal Peroa, and to my Satrap Idernes, bidding Peroa to hand over this lady Amada to Idernes and bidding Idernes to send her to the East with all honour and without delay, that she may enter my household as one of my wives."

Now I was filled with rage and horror, and about to refuse this mission when Bes broke in swiftly,

"Will the King of kings be pleased to give command as to my master's safe and honourable escort to Egypt?"

"It is commanded with all things necessary for Shabaka the Egyptian and the dwarf his servant, with the gold and gems and slaves he won from me in a wager, and everything else that is his. Let it be recorded."

Scribes sprang forward and wrote the King's words down, while like one in a dream I thought to myself that they could not now be altered. The King watched them sleepily for a while, then seemed to wake up and grow clear-minded again. At least he said to me,

"Fortune has shown you smiles and frowns to-day, Egyptian, and the smiles last. Yet remember that she has teeth behind her lips wherewith to tear out the throat of the faithless. Man, if you play me false or fail in your mission, be sure that you shall die and in such a fashion that will make you think of yonder boat as a pleasant bed, and with you this woman Amada and her uncle Peroa, and all your kin and hers; yes," he added with a burst of shrewdness, "and even that abortion of a dwarf to whom I have listened because he amused me, but who perhaps is more cunning than he seems."

"O King of kings," I said, "I will not be false." But I did not add to whom I would be true.

"Good. Ere long I shall visit Egypt, as I have told you, and there I shall pass judgment on you and others. Till then, farewell. Fear nothing, for you have my safe-conduct. Begone, both of you, for you weary me. But first drink and keep the cup, and in exchange, give me that bow of yours which shoots so far and straight."

"It is the King's," I answered as I pledged him in the golden, jewelled cup which a butler had handed to me.

Then the curtain fell in front of the throne and chamberlains came forward to lead me and Bes back to our lodging, one of whom took the cup and bore it in front of us. Down the hall we went between the feasting nobles who all bowed to one to whom the Great King had shown favour, and so out of the palace through the quiet night back to the house where I had dwelt while waiting audience of the King. Here the chamberlains bade me farewell, giving the cup to Bes to carry, and saying that on the morrow early my gold should be brought to me together with all that was needed for my journey, also one who would receive the bow I had promised to the King, which had already been returned to my lodgings with everything that was ours. Then they bowed and went.

We entered the house, climbing a stair to an upper chamber. Here Bes barred the door and the shutters, making sure that none could see or hear us.

Then he turned, threw his arms about me, kissed my hand and burst into tears.

VII

Bes Steals the Signet

O h! my Master," gulped Bes, "I weep because I am tired, so take no notice. The day was long and during it twice at least there has been but the twinkling of an eyelid, but the thickness of a finger nail, but the weight of a hair between you and death."

"Yes," I said, "and you were the eyelid, the finger nail and the hair."

"No, Master, not I, but something beyond me. The tool carves the statue and the hand holds the tool but the spirit guides the hand. Not once only since the sun rose has my mind been empty as a drum. Then something struck on it, perhaps the holy Tanofir, perhaps another, and it knew what note to sound. So it was when I cursed you in the boat. So it was when I walked back with the eunuch, meaning to kill him on the road, and then remembered that the death of one vile eunuch would not help you at all, whereas alive he could bring me to the presence of the King, if I paid him, as I did out of the gold in your purse which I carried. Moreover he earned his hire, for when the King grew dull, wine not yet having taken a hold on him, it was he who brought me to his mind as one who might amuse him, being so ugly and different from others, if only for a few minutes, after the women dancers had failed to do so."

"And what happened then, Bes?"

"Then I was fetched and did my juggling tricks with that snake I caught and tamed, which is in my pouch now. You should not hate it any more, Master, for it played your game well. After this the King began to talk to me and I saw that his mind was ill at ease about you whom he knew that he had wronged. So I told him that story of an elephant that my father killed to save a king—it grew up in my mind like a toadstool in the night, Master, did this story of an ungrateful king and what befell him. Then the King became still more unquiet in his heart about you and asked the eunuch, Houman, where you were, to which he answered that by his order you were sleeping in a boat and might not be disturbed. So that arrow of mine missed its mark because the King did not like to eat his own words and cause you to be brought from out the boat, whither he had sent you. Now when everything seemed lost, some god, or perhaps the holy Tanofir who is ever present with me to see that I have not forgotten him, put it into the King's mouth to begin to talk about women and to ask me if I had ever seen any fairer than those dancers whom I met going out as I came in. I answered that I had not noticed them much because they were so ugly, as indeed all women had seemed to me since once upon the banks of Nile I had looked upon one who was as Hathor herself for beauty. The King asked me who this might be and I answered that I did not know since I had never dared to ask the name of one whom even my master held to be as a goddess, although as boy and girl they had been brought up together.

"Then the King saw his opportunity to ease his conscience and inquired of an old councillor if there were not a law which gave the king power to alter his decree if thereby he could satisfy his soul and acquire knowledge. The councillor answered that there was such a law and began to give examples of its working, till the King cut him short and said that by virtue of it he commanded that you should be brought out of your bed in the boat and led before him to answer a question.

"So you were sent for, Master, but I did not go with the messengers, fearing lest if I did the King would forget all about the matter before you came. Therefore I stayed and amused him with tales of hunting, till I could not think of any more, for you were long in coming. Indeed I began to fear lest he should declare the feast at an end. But at the last, just as he was yawning and spoke to one of his councillors, bidding him send to the House of Women that they might make ready to receive him there, you came, and the rest you know."

Now I looked at Bes and said,

"May the blessing of all the gods of all the lands be on your head, since had it not been for you I should now lie in torment in that boat. Hearken, friend: If ever we reach Egypt again, you will set foot on it, not as a slave but as a free man. You will be rich also, Bes, that is, if we can take the gold I won with us, since half of it is yours."

Bes squatted down upon the floor and looked up at me with a strange smile on his ugly face.

"You have given me three things, Master," he said. "Gold, which I do not want at present; freedom, which I do not want at present and mayhap, never shall while you live and love me; and the title of friend. This I do want, though why I should care to hear it from your lips I am not sure, seeing that for a long while I have known that it was spoken in your heart. Since you have said it, however, I will tell you something which hitherto I have hid even from you. I have a right to that name, for if your blood is high, O Shabaka, so is mine. Know that this poor dwarf whom you took captive and saved long years ago was more than the petty chief which he declared himself to be. He was and is by right the King of the Ethiopians and that throne with all its wealth and power he could claim to-morrow if he would."

"The King of the Ethiopians!" I said. "Oh! friend Bes, I pray you to remember that we no longer stand in yonder court lying for our lives."

"I speak no lie, O Shabaka, I before you am King of the Ethiopians. Moreover, I laid that kingship down of my own will and should I so desire, can take it up again when I will, since the Ethiopians are faithful to their kings."

"Why?" I asked, astonished.

"Master, for so I will still call you who am not yet upon the land of Egypt where you have promised me freedom, do you remember anything strange about the people of that tribe from among whom you and the Egyptian soldiers captured me by surprise, because they wished to drive you and your following from their country?"

Now I thought and answered,

"Yes, one thing. I saw no women in their camp, nor any sign of children. This I know because I gave orders that such were to be spared and it was reported to me that there were none, so I supposed that they had fled away."

"There were none to fly, Master. That tribe was a brotherhood which had abjured women. Look on me now. I am misshapen, hideous, am I not? Born thus, it is said, because before my birth my mother was frightened by a dwarf. Yet the law of the Ethiopians is that their kings must marry within a year of their crowning. Therefore I chose a woman to be the queen whom I had long desired in secret. She scorned me, vowing that not for all the thrones of all the world would she be mated to a monster, and that if it were done by force she would kill herself, a saying that went abroad throughout the land. I said that she had spoken well and sent her in safety from the country, after which I too laid down my crown and departed with some who loved me, to form a brotherhood of women-haters further down the Nile, beyond the borders of Ethiopia. There the Egyptian force of which you were in command, attacked us unprepared, and you made me your slave. That is all."

"But why did you do this, Bes, seeing that maidens are many and all would not have thought thus?"

"Because I wished for that one only, Master; also I feared lest I should become the father of a breed of twisted dwarfs. So I who was a king am now a slave, and yet, who knows which way the Grasshopper will jump? One day from a slave I may again grow into a king. And now let us seek that wherein kings are as slaves and slaves as kings—sleep."

So we lay down and slept, I thanking the gods that my bed was not yonder in the boat upon the great river.

When I woke refreshed, though after all I had gone through on the yesterday my brain still swam a little, the light was pouring through the carved work of the shuttered windows. By it I saw Bes seated on the floor engaged in doing something to his bow, which, as I have said, had been restored to us with our other weapons, and asked him sleepily what it was.

"Master," he said, "yonder King demanded your bow and therefore a bow must be sent to him. But there is no need for it to be that with which you shot the lions, which, too, you value above anything you have, seeing that it came down to you from your forefather who was a Pharaoh of Egypt, and has been your companion from boyhood ever since you were strong enough to draw it. As you may remember I copied that bow out of a somewhat lighter wood, which I could bend with ease, and it is the copy that we will give to the King. Only first I must set your string upon it, for that may have been noted; also make one or two marks that are on your bow which I am finishing now, having begun the task with the dawn."

"You are clever," I said laughing, "and I am glad. The holy Tanofir, looking on my bow, once had a vision. It was that an arrow loosed from it would drink the blood of a great king and save Egypt. But what king and when, he did not see."

The dwarf nodded and answered,

"I have heard that tale and so have others. Therefore I play this trick since it is better that yonder palace dweller should get the arrow than the bow. There, it is finished to the last scratch, and none, save you and I, would know them apart. Till we are clear of this cursed land your bow is mine, Master, and you must find you another of the Eastern make."

"Master," I repeated after him. "Say, Bes, did I dream or did you in truth tell me last night that you are by birth and right the king of a great country?"

"I told you that, Master and it is true, no dream, since joy and suffering mixed unseal the lips and from them comes that at times which the heart would hide. Now I ask a favour of you, that you will speak no more of this matter either to me or to any other, man or woman, unless I should speak of it first. Let it be as though it were indeed a dream."

"It is granted," I said as I rose and clothed myself, not in my own garments which had been taken from me in the palace, but in the splendid silken robes that had been set upon me after I was loosed from the boat. When this was done and I had washed and combed my long, curling hair, we descended to a lower chamber and called for the woman of the house to bring us food, of which I ate heartily. As we finished our meal we heard shouts in the street outside of, "Make way for the servants of the King!" and looking through the window-place, saw a great cavalcade approaching, headed by two princes on horseback.

"Now I pray that yonder Tyrant has not changed his mind and that these do not come to take me back to the boat," I said in a low voice.

"Have no fear, Master," answered Bes, "seeing that you have touched his sceptre and drunk from his cup which he gave to you. After these things no harm can happen to you in any land he rules. Therefore be at ease and deal with these fellows proudly."

A minute later two princes entered followed by slaves who bore many things, among them those hide bags filled with gold that had been set beneath me in the boat. The elder of them bowed, greeting me with the title of "Lord," and I bowed back to him. Then he handed me certain rolls tied up with silk and sealed, which he said I was to deliver as the King had commanded to the King's Satrap in Egypt, and to the Prince Peroa. Also he gave me other letters addressed to the King's servants on the road and written on tablets of clay in a writing I could not read, with all of which I touched my forehead in the Eastern fashion.

After this he told me that by noon all would be ready for my journey which I should make with the rank of the King's Envoy, duly provisioned and escorted by his servants, with liberty to use the royal horses from post to post. Then he ordered the slaves to bring in the gifts which the King sent to me, and these were many, including even suits of flexible armour that would turn any sword-thrust or arrow.

I thanked him, saying that I would be ready to start by noon, and asked whether the King wished to see me before I rode. He replied that he had so wished, but that as he was suffering in his head from the effects of the sun, he could not. He bade me, however, remember all that he had said to me and to be sure that the beauteous lady Amada, of whom I had spoken, was sent to him without delay. In that case my reward should be great; but if I failed to fulfil his commands, then his wrath would be greater and I should perish miserably as he had promised.

I bowed and made no answer, after which he and his companions opened the bags of gold to show me that it was there, offering to weigh it again against my servant, the dwarf, so that I could see that nothing had been taken away.

I replied that the King's word was truer than any scale, whereon the bags were tied up again and sealed. Then I produced the bow, or rather its counterfeit, and having shown it to the princes, wrapped it and six of my own arrows in a linen cloth, to be taken to the King, with a message that though hard to draw it was the deadliest weapon in the world. The elder of them took it, bowed and bade me farewell, saying that perhaps we should meet again ere long in Egypt, if my gods gave me a safe journey. So we parted and I was glad to see the last of them.

Scarcely had they gone when the six hunters whom I had won in the wager and thereby saved from death, entered the chamber and fell upon their knees before me, asking for orders as to making ready my gear for the journey. I inquired of them if they were coming also, to which their spokesman replied that they were my slaves to do what I commanded.

"Do you desire to come?" I inquired.

"O Lord Shabaka," answered their spokesman, "we do, though some of us must leave wives and children behind us."

"Why?" I asked.

"For two reasons, Lord. Here we are men disgraced, though through no fault of our own and if you were to leave us in this land, soon the anger of the King would find us out and we should lose not only our wives and children, but with them our lives. Whereas in another land we may get other wives and more children, but never shall we get another life. Therefore we would leave those dear ones to our friends, knowing that soon the women will forget and find other husbands, and that the children will grow up to whatever fate is appointed them, thinking of us, their fathers, as dead. Secondly we are hunters by trade, and we have seen that you are a great hunter, one whom we shall always be proud to serve in the chase or in war, one, too, who went out of his path to save our lives, because he saw that we had been unjustly doomed to a cruel death. Therefore we desire nothing better than to be your slaves, hoping that perchance we may earn our liberty from you in days to come by our good service."

"Is that the wish of all of you?" I asked.

Speaking one by one, they said that it was, though tears rose in the eyes of some of them who were married at the thought of parting from their women and their little ones, who, it seemed might not be brought with them because they were the people of the King and had not been named in the bet. Moreover, horses could not be found for so many, nor could they travel fast.

"Come then," I said, "and know that while you are faithful to me, I will be good to you, men of my own trade, and perhaps in the end set you free in a land where brave fellows are not given to be torn to pieces by wild beasts at the word of any kind. But if you fail me or betray me, then either I will kill you, or sell you to those who deal in slaves, to work at the oar, or in the mines till you die."

"Henceforth we have no lord but you, O Shabaka," they said, and one after another took my hand and pressed it to their foreheads, vowing to be true to me in all things while we lived.

So I bade them begone to bid farewell to those they loved and return again within half an hour of noon, never expecting, to tell the truth, that they would come. Indeed I did this to give them the opportunity of escaping if they saw fit, and hiding themselves where they would. But as I have often noted, the trade of hunting breeds honesty in the blood and at the hour appointed all of these men appeared, one of them with a woman who carried a child in her arms, clinging to him and weeping bitterly. When her veil slipped aside I saw that she was young and very fair to look on.

So AT NOON WE LEFT the city of the Great King in the charge of two of his officers who brought me his thanks for the bow I had sent him, which he said he should treasure above everything he possessed, a saying at which Bes rolled his yellow eyes and grinned. We were mounted on splendid stallions from the royal stables and clad in the shirts of mail that had been presented to us, though when we were clear of the city we took these off because of the heat, also because that which Bes wore chafed him, being too long for his squat shape. Our goods together with the bags of gold were laden on sumpter horses which were led by my six hunter slaves. Four picked soldiers brought up the rear, mighty men from the King's own bodyguard, and two of the royal postmen who served us as guides. Also there were cooks and grooms with spare horses.

Thus we started in state and a great crowd watched us go. Our road ran by the river which we must cross in barges lower down, so that in a few minutes we came to that quay whither I had been led on the previous night to die. Yes, there were the watching guards, and there floated the hateful double boat, at the prow of which appeared the tortured face of the eunuch Houman, who rolled his head from side to side to rid himself of the torment of the flies. He caught sight of us and began to scream for pity and forgiveness, whereat Bes smiled. The officers halted our cavalcade and one of them approaching me said,

"It is the King's command, O Lord Shabaka, that you should look upon this villain who traduced you to the King and afterwards dared to strike you. If you will, enter the water and blind him, that your face may be the last thing he sees before he passes into darkness."

I shook my head, but Bes into whose mind some thought had come, whispered to me,

"I wish to speak with yonder eunuch, so give me leave and fear nothing. I will do him no hurt, only good, if I find the chance."

Then I said to the officer,

"It is not for great lords to avenge themselves upon the fallen. Yet my slave here was also wronged and would say a word to yonder Houman."

"So be it," said the officer, "only let him be careful not to hurt him too sorely, lest he should die before the time and escape his punishment."

Then Bes tucked up his robes and waded into the river, flourishing a great knife, while seeing him come, Houman began to scream with fear. He reached the boat and bent over the eunuch, talking to him in a low voice. What he did there I could not see because his cloak was spread out on either side of the man's head. Presently, however, I caught sight of the flash of a knife and heard yells of agony followed by groans, whereat I called to him to return and let the fellow be. For when I remembered that his fate was near to being my own, those sounds made me sick at heart and I grew angry with Bes, though the cruel Easterns only laughed.

At length he came back grinning and washing the blade of his knife in the water. I spoke fiercely to him in my own language, and still he grinned on, making no answer. When we were mounted again and riding away from that horrible boat with its groaning prisoner, watching Bes whose behaviour and silence I could not understand, I saw him sweep his hand across his great mouth and thrust it swiftly into

H. RIDER HAGGARD

his bosom. After this he spoke readily enough, though in a low voice lest someone who understood Egyptian should overhear him.

"You are a fool, Master," he said, "to think that I should wish to waste time in torturing that fat knave."

"Then why did you torture him?" I asked.

"Because my god, the Grasshopper, when he fashioned me a dwarf, gave me a big mouth and good teeth," he answered, whereon I stared at him, thinking that he had gone mad.

"Listen, Master. I did not hurt Houman. All I did was to cut his cords nearly through from the under side, so that when night comes he can break them and escape, if he has the wit. Now, Master, you may not have noticed, but I did, that before the King doomed you to death by the boat yesterday, he took a certain round, white seal, a cylinder with gods and signs cut on it, which hung by a gold chain from his girdle, and gave it to Houman to be his warrant for all he did. This seal Houman showed to the Treasurer whereon they produced the gold that was weighed in the scales against me, and to others when he ordered the boat to be prepared for you to lie in. Moreover he forgot to return it, for when he himself was dragged off to the boat by direct command of the King, I caught sight of the chain beneath his robe. Can you guess the rest?"

"Not quite," I answered, for I wished to hear the tale in his own words.

"Well, Master, when I was walking with Houman after he had put you in the boat, I asked him about this seal. He showed it to me and said that he who bore it was for the time the king of all the Empire of the East. It seems that there is but one such seal which has descended from ancient days from king to king, and that of it every officer, great or small, has an impress in all lands. If the seal is produced to him, he compares it with the impress and should the two agree, he obeys the order that is brought as though the King had given it in person. When we reached the Court doubtless Houman would have returned the seal, but seeing that the King was, or feigned to be drunk, waited for fear lest it should be lost, and with it his life. Then he was seized as you saw, and in his terror forgot all about the seal, as did the King and his officers."

"But, surely, Bes, those who took Houman to the boat would have removed it."

"Master, even the most clear-sighted do not see well at night. At any rate my hope was that they had not done so, and that is why I waded out to prick the eyes of Houman. Moreover, as I had hoped, so it was; there beneath his robe I saw the chain. Then I spoke to him, saying,

"'I am come to put out your eyes, as you deserve, seeing how you have treated my master. Still I will spare you at a price. Give me the King's ancient white seal that opens all doors, and I will only make a pretence of blinding you. Moreover I will cut your cords nearly through, so that when the night comes you can break them, roll into the river and escape.'

"'Take it if you can,' he said, 'and use it to injure or destroy that accursed one.'"

"So you took it, Bes."

"Yes, Master, but not easily. Remember, it was on a chain about the man's neck, and I could not draw it over his head, for, like his hands, his throat was tied by a cord, as you remember yours was."

"I remember very well," I said, "for my throat is still sore from the rope that ran to the same staples to which my hands were fastened."

"Yes, Master, and therefore if I drew the chain off his neck, it would still have been on the ropes. I thought of trying to cut it with the knife, but this was not easy because it is thick, and if I had dragged it up on the blade of the knife it would have been seen, for many eyes were watching me, Master. Then I took another counsel. While I pretended to be putting out the eyes of Houman, I bent down and getting the chain between my teeth I bit it through. One tooth broke—see, but the next finished the business. I ate through the soft gold, Master, and then sucked up the chain and the round white seal into my mouth, and that is why I could not answer you just now, because my cheeks were full of chain. So we have the King's seal that all the subject countries know and obey. It may be useful, yonder in Egypt, and at least the gold is of value."

"Clever!" I exclaimed, "very clever. But you have forgotten something, Bes. When that knave escapes, he will tell the whole story and the King will send after us and kill us who have stolen his royal seal."

"I don't think so, Master. First, it is not likely that Houman will escape. He is very fat and soft and already suffers much. After a day in the sun also he will be weak. Moreover I do not think that he can swim, for eunuchs hate the water. So if he gets out of the boat it is probable that he will drown in the river, since he dare not wade to the quay where the guards will be waiting. But if he does escape by swimming across the river, he will hide for his life's sake and never be seen again, and if by chance he is caught, he will say that the seal fell into the water when he was taken to the boat, or that one of the guards had stolen it. What he will not say is that he had bargained it away with someone who in return, cut his cords, since for that crime he must die by worse tortures than those of the boat. Lastly we shall ride so fast that with six hours' start none will catch us. Or if they do I can throw away the chain and swallow the seal."

As Bes said, so it happened. The fate of Houman I never learned, and of the theft of the seal I heard no more until a proclamation was issued to all the kingdoms that a new one was in use. But this was not until long afterwards when it had served my turn and that of Egypt.

VIII

THE LADY AMADA

N ow day by day, hour by hour and minute by minute every detail of that journey appeared before me, but to set it all down is needless. As I, Allan Quatermain, write the record of my vision, still I seem to hear the thunder of our horses' hoofs while we rushed forward at full gallop over the plains, over the mountain passes and by the banks of rivers. The speed at which we travelled was wonderful, for at intervals of about forty miles were post-houses and at these, whatever might be the hour of day or night, we found fresh horses from the King's stud awaiting us. Moreover, the postmasters knew that we were coming, which astonished me until we discovered that they had been warned of our arrival by two King's messengers who travelled ahead of us.

These men, it would seem, although our officers and guides professed ignorance of the matter, must have left the King's palace at dawn on the day of our departure, whereas we did not mount in the city till a little after noon. Therefore they had six hours good start of us, and what is more, travelled lighter than we did, having no sumpter beasts with them, and no cooks or servants. Moreover, always they had the pick of the horses and chose the three swiftest beasts, leading the third in case one of their own should founder or meet with accident. Thus it came about that we never caught them up although we covered quite a hundred miles a day. Only once did I see them, far off upon the skyline of a mountain range which we had to climb, but by the time we had reached its crest they were gone.

At length we came to the desert without accident and crossed it, though more slowly. But even here the King had his posts which were in charge of Arabs who lived in tents by wells of water, or sometimes where there was none save what was brought to them. So still we galloped on, parched by the burning sand beneath and the burning sand above, and reached the borders of Egypt.

Here, upon the very boundary line, the two officers halted the cavalcade saying that their orders were to return thence and make report to the King. There then we parted, Bes and I with the six hunters who still chose to cling to me, going forward and the officers of the

King with the guides and servants going back. The good horses that we rode from the last post they gave to us by the King's command, together with the sumpter beasts, since horses broken to the saddle were hard to come by in Egypt where they were trained to draw chariots. These we took, sending back my thanks to the King, and started on once more, Bes leading that beast which bore the gold and the hunters serving as a guard.

Indeed I was glad to see the last of those Easterns although they had brought us safely and treated us well, for all the while I was never sure but that they had some orders to lead us into a trap, or perhaps to make away with us in our sleep and take back the gold and the priceless, rose-hued pearls, any two of which were worth it all. But such was not their command nor did they dare to steal them on their own account, since then, even if they escaped the vengeance of the King, their wives and all their families would have paid the price.

Now we entered Egypt near the Salt Lakes that are not far from the head of the Gulf, crossing the canal that the old Pharaohs had dug, which proved easy for it was silted up. Before we reached it we found some peasant folk labouring in their gardens and I heard one of them call to another,

"Here come more of the Easterns. What is toward, think you, neighbour?"

"I do not know," answered the other, "but when I passed down the canal this morning, I saw a body of the Great King's guards gathering from the fort. Doubtless it is to meet these men of whose coming the other two who went by fifty hours ago, have warned the officers."

"Now what does that mean?" I asked of Bes.

"Neither more nor less than we have heard, Master. The two King's messengers who have gone ahead of us all the way from the city, have told the officer of the frontier fort that we are coming, so he has advanced to the ford to meet us, for what purpose I do not know."

"Nor do I," I said, "but I wish we could take another road, if there were one."

"There is none, Master, for above and below the canal is full of water and the banks are too steep for horses to climb. Also we must show no doubt or fear."

He thought a while, then added,

"Take the royal seal, Master. It may be useful."

He gave it to me, and I examined it more closely than I had done before. It was a cylinder of plain white shell hung on a gold chain, that which Bes had bitten through, but now mended again by taking out the broken link. On this cylinder were cut figures; as I think of a priest presenting a noble to a god, over whom was the crescent of the moon, while behind the god stood a man or demon with a tall spear. Also between the figures were mystic signs, meaning I know not what. The workmanship of the carving was grown shallow with time and use for the cylinder seemed to be very ancient, a sacred thing that had descended from generation to generation and was threaded through with a bar of silver on which it turned.

I put the seal which was like no other that I had seen, being the work of an early and simpler age, round my neck beneath my mail and we went on.

Descending the steep bank of the canal we came to the ford where the sand that had silted in was covered by not more than a foot of water. As we entered it, on the top of the further bank appeared a body of about thirty armed and mounted men, one of whom carried the Great King's banner, on which I noted was blazoned the very figures that were cut upon the cylinder. Now it was too late to retreat, so we rode through the water and met the soldiers. Their officer advanced, crying,

"In the name of the Great King, greeting, my lord Shabaka!

"In the name of the Great King, greeting!" I answered. "What would you with Shabaka, Officer of the King?"

"Only to do him honour. The word of the King has reached us and we come to escort you to the Court of Idernes, the Satrap of the King and Governor of Egypt who sits at Sais."

"That is not my road, Officer. I travel to Memphis to deliver the commands of the King to my cousin, Peroa, the ruler of Egypt under the King. Afterwards, perchance, I shall visit the high Idernes."

"To whom our commands are to take you now, my lord Shabaka, not afterwards," said the officer sternly, glancing round at his armed escort.

"I come to give commands, not to receive them, Captain of the King."

"Seize Shabaka and his servants," said the officer briefly, whereon the soldiers rode forward to surround us.

I waited till they were near at hand. Then suddenly I plunged my hand beneath my robe and drew out the small, white seal which I held before the eyes of the officer, saying,

"Who is it that dares to lay a finger upon the holder of the King's White Seal? Surely that man is ready for death."

The officer stared at it, then leapt from his horse and flung himself face downwards on the ground, crying,

"It is the ancient signet of the Kings of the East, given to their first forefather by Samas the Sungod, on which hangs the fortunes of the Great House! Pardon, my lord Shabaka."

"It is granted," I answered, "because what you did you did in ignorance. Now go to the Satrap Idernes and say to him that if he would have speech with the bearer of the King's seal which all must obey, he will find him at Memphis. Farewell," and with Bes and the six hunters I rode through the guards, none striving to hinder me.

"That was well done, Master," said Bes.

"Yes," I said. "Those two messengers who went ahead of us brought orders to the frontier guard of Idernes that I should be taken to him as a prisoner. I do not know why, but I think because things are passing in Egypt of which we know nothing and the King did not desire that I should see the Prince Peroa and give him news that I might have gathered. Mayhap we have been outwitted, Bes, and the business of the lady Amada is but a pretext to pick a quarrel suddenly before Peroa can strike the first blow."

"Perhaps, Master, for these Easterns are very crafty. But, Master, what happens to those who make a false use of the King's ancient, sacred signet? I think they have cut the ropes which tie them to earth," and he looked upwards to the sky rolling his yellow eyes.

"They must find new ropes, Bes, and quickly, before they are caught. Hearken. You have sat upon a throne and I can speak out to you. Think you that my cousin, the Prince Peroa, loves to be the servant of this distant, Eastern king, he who by right is Pharaoh of Egypt? Peroa must strike or lose his niece and perchance his life. Forward, that we may warn him."

"And if he will not strike, Master, knowing the King's might and being somewhat slow to move?"

"Then, Bes, I think that you and I had best go hunting far away in those lands you know, where even the Great King cannot follow us."

"And where, if only I can find a woman who does not make me ill to look on, and whom I do not make ill, I too can once more be a king, Master, and the lord of many thousand brave armed men. I must speak of that matter to the holy Tanofir."

"Who doubtless will know what to advise you, Bes; or, if he dies not, I shall."

For a while we rode on in silence, each thinking his own thoughts. Then Bes said,

"Master, before so very long we shall reach the Nile, and having with us gold in plenty can buy boats and hire crews. It comes into my mind that we should do well for our own safety and comfort to start at once on a hunting journey far from Egypt; in the land of the Ethiopians, Master. There perchance I could gather together some of the wise men in whose hands I left the rule of my kingdom, and submit to them this question of a woman to marry me. The Ethiopians are a faithful people, Master, and will not reject me because I have spent some years seeing the world afar, that I might learn how to rule them better."

"I have remembered that it cannot be, Bes," I said.

"Why not, Master?"

"For this reason. You left your country because of a woman? I cannot leave mine again because of a woman."

Bes rolled his eyes around as though he thought to see that woman in the desert. Not discovering her, he stared upwards and there found light.

"Is she perchance named the lady Amada, Master?"

I nodded.

"So. The lady Amada who you told the Great King is the most beautiful one in the whole world, causing the fire of Love to burn up in his royal heart, and with it many other things of which we do not know at present."

"*You* told him, Bes," I said angrily.

"I told him of a beautiful one; I did not tell him her name, Master, and although I never thought of it at the time, perhaps she will be angry with him who told her name."

Now fear took hold of me, and Bes saw it in my face.

"Do not be afraid, Master. If there is trouble I will swear that I told the Great King that lady's name."

"Yes, Bes, but how would that fit in with the story, seeing that I was brought out of the boat for this very purpose?"

"Quite easily, Master, since I will say that you were led from the boat to confirm my tale. Oh! she will be angry with me, no doubt, but in Egypt even a dwarf cannot be killed because he has declared a certain lady to be the most beautiful in the world. But, Master, tell me, when did you learn to love her?"

"When we were boy and girl, Bes. We used to play together, being cousins, and I used to hold her hand. Then suddenly she refused to let me hold her hand any more, and I being quite grown up then, though she was younger, understood that I had better go away."

"I should have stopped where I was, Master."

"No, Bes. She was studying to be a priestess and my great uncle, the holy Tanofir, told me that I had better go away. So I went down south hunting and fighting in command of the troops, and met you, Bes."

"Which perhaps was better for you, Master, than to stop to watch the lady Amada acquire learning. Still, I wonder whether the holy Tanofir is *always* right. You see, Master, he thinks a great deal of priests and priestesses, and is so very old that he has forgotten all about love and that without it there never would have been a holy Tanofir."

"The holy Tanofir thinks of souls, not of bodies, Bes."

"Yes, Master. Still, oil is of no use without a lamp, or a soul without a body, at least here underneath the sun, or so we were taught who worship the Grasshopper. But, Master, when you came back from all your hunting, what happened then?"

"Then I found, Bes, that the lady Amada, having acquired all the learning possible, had taken her first vows to Isis, which she said she would not break for any man on earth although she might have done so without crime. Therefore, although I was dear to her, as a brother would have been had she had one, and she swore that she had never even thought of another man, she refused so much as to think of marrying who dreamed only of the heavenly perfections of the lady Isis."

"Ump!" said Bes. "We Ethiopians have Priestesses of the Grasshopper, or the Grasshopper's wife, but they do not think of her like that. I hope that one day something stronger than herself will not cause the lady Amada to break her vows to the heavenly Isis. Only then, perhaps, it may be for the sake of another man who did not go off to the East on account of such fool's talk. But here is a village and the horses are spent. Let us stop and eat, as I suppose even the lady Amada does sometimes."

ON THE FOLLOWING AFTERNOON WE crossed the Nile, and towards sunset entered the vast and ancient city of Memphis. On its white walls floated the banners of the Great King which Bes pointed out to me, saying that wherever we went in the whole world, it seemed that we could never be free from those accursed symbols.

"May I live to spit upon them and cast them into the moat," I answered savagely, for as I drew near to Amada they grew ten times more hateful to me than they had been before.

In truth I was nearer to Amada than I thought, for after we had passed the enclosure of the temple of Ptah, the most wonderful and the mightiest in the whole world, we came to the temple of Isis. There near to the pylon gate we met a procession of her priests and priestesses advancing to offer the evening sacrifice of song and flowers, clad, all of them, in robes of purest white. It was a day of festival, so singers went with them. After the singers came a band of priestesses bearing flowers, in front of whom walked another priestess shaking a *sistrum* that made a little tinkling music.

Even at a distance there was something about the tall and slender shape of this priestess that stirred me. When we came nearer I saw why, for it was Amada herself. Through the thin veil she wore I could see her dark and tender eyes set beneath the broad brow that was so full of thought, and the sweet, curved mouth that was like no other woman's. Moreover there could be no doubt since the veil parting above her breast showed the birth-mark for which she was famous, the mark of the young moon, the sign of Isis.

I sprang from my horse and ran towards her. She looked up and saw me. At first she frowned, then her face grew wondering, then tender, and I thought that her red lips shaped my name. Moreover in her confusion she let the *sistrum* fall.

I muttered "Amada!" and stepped forward, but priests ran between us and thrust me away. Next moment she had recovered the *sistrum* and passed on with her head bowed. Nor did she lift her eyes to look back.

"Begone, man!" cried a priest, "Begone, whoever you may be. Because you wear Eastern armour do you think that you can dare the curse of Isis?"

Then I fell back, the holy image of the goddess passed and the procession vanished through the pylon gate. I, Shabaka the Egyptian, stood by my horse and watched it depart. I was happy because the lady Amada was alive, well, and more beautiful than ever; also because she had shown signs of joy and confusion at seeing me again. Yet I was unhappy because I met her still filling a holy office which built a wall between us, also because it seemed to me an evil omen that I should have been repelled from her by a priest of Isis who talked of the curse of the goddess. Moreover the sacred statue, I suppose by accident, turned towards me as it passed and perhaps by the chance of light, seemed to frown upon me.

Thus I thought as Shabaka hundreds of years before the Christian era, but as Allan Quatermain the modern man, to whom it was given so marvellously to behold all these things and who in beholding them, yet never quite lost the sense of his own identity of to-day, I was amazed. For I knew that this lady Amada was the same being though clad in different flesh, as that other lady with whom I had breathed the magical *Taduki* fumes which had power to rend the curtain of the past, or, perhaps, only to breed dreams of what it might have been.

To the outward eye, indeed she was different, as I was different, taller, more slender, larger-eyed, with longer and slimmer hands than those of any Western woman, and on the whole even more beautiful and alluring. Moreover that mysterious look which from time to time I had seen on Lady Ragnall's face, was more constant on that of the lady Amada. It brooded in the deep eyes and settled in a curious smile about the curves of the lips, a smile that was not altogether human, such a smile as one might wear who had looked on hidden things and heard voices that spoke beyond the limits of the world.

Somehow neither then nor at any other time during all my dream, could I imagine this Amada, this daughter of a hundred kings, whose blood might be traced back through dynasty on dynasty, as nothing but a woman who nurses children upon her breast. It was as though something of our common nature had been bred out of her and something of another nature whereof we have no ken, had entered to fill its place. And yet these two women were the same, that I *knew*, or at any rate, much of them was the same, for who can say what part of us we leave behind as we flit from life to life, to find it again elsewhere in the abysms of Time and Change? One thing too was quite identical—the birthmark of the new moon above the breast which the priests of the Kendah had declared was always the seal that marked their prophetess, the guardian of the Holy Child.

WHEN THE PROCESSION HAD QUITE departed and I could no longer hear the sound of singing, I remounted and rode on to my house, or rather to that of my mother, the great lady Tiu, which was situated beneath the wall of the old palace facing towards the Nile. Indeed my heart was full of this mother of mine whom I loved and who loved me, for I was her only child, and my father had been long dead; so long that I could not remember him. Eight months had gone by since I saw her face and in eight months who knew what might have happened? The thought made me cold for she, who was aged and not too strong, perhaps had been gathered to Osiris. Oh! if that were so!

I shook my tired horse to a canter, Bes riding ahead of me to clear a road through the crowded street in which, at this hour of sundown, all the idlers of Memphis seemed to have gathered. They stared at me because it was not common to see men riding in Memphis, and with little love, since from my dress and escort they took me to be some envoy from their hated master, the Great King of the East. Some even threatened to bar the way; but we thrust through and presently turned into a thoroughfare of private houses standing in their own gardens. Ours was the third of these. At its gate I leapt from my horse, pushed open the closed door and hastened in to seek and learn.

I had not far to go for, there in the courtyard, standing at the head of our modest household and dressed in her festal robes, was my mother, the stately and white-haired lady Tiu, as one stands who awaits the coming of an honoured guest. I ran to her and kneeling, kissed her hand, saying,

"My mother! My mother, I have come safe home and greet you."

"I greet you also, my son," she answered, bending down and kissing me on the brow, "who have been in far lands and passed so many dangers. I greet you and thank the guardian gods who have brought you safe home again. Rise, my son."

I rose and kissed her on the face, then looked at the servants who were bowing their welcome to me, and said,

"How comes it, Lady of the House, that all are gathered here? Did you await some guest?"

"We awaited you, my son. For an hour have we stood here listening for the sound of your feet."

"Me!" I exclaimed. "That is strange, seeing that I have ridden fast and hard from the East, tarrying only a few minutes, and those since I entered Memphis, when I met—" and I stopped.

"Met whom, Shabaka?"

"The lady Amada walking in the procession of Isis."

"Ah! the lady Amada. The mother waits that the son may stop to greet the lady Amada!"

"But *why* did you wait, my mother? Who but a spirit or a bird of the air could have told you that I was coming, seeing that I sent no messenger before me?"

"You must have done so, Shabaka, since yesterday one came from the holy Tanofir, our relative who dwells in the desert in the burial-ground of Sekera. He bore a message from Tanofir to me, telling me to make ready since before sundown to-night you, my son, would be with me, having escaped great dangers, accompanied by the dwarf Bes, your servant, and six strange Eastern men. So I made ready and waited; also I prepared lodging for the six strange men in the outbuildings behind the house and sent a thank offering to the temple. For know, my son, I have suffered much fear for you."

"And not without cause, as you will say when I tell you all," I answered laughing. "But how Tanofir knew that I was coming is more than I can guess. Come, my mother, greet Bes here, for had it not been for him, never should I have lived to hold your hand again."

So she greeted him and thanked him, whereon Bes rolled his eyes and muttered something about the holy Tanofir, after which we entered the house. Thence I despatched a messenger to the Prince Peroa saying that if it were his pleasure I would wait on him at once, seeing that I had much to tell him. This done I bathed and caused my hair and beard to be trimmed and, discarding the Eastern garments, clothed myself in those of Egypt, and so felt that I was my own man again. Then I came out refreshed and drank a cup of Syrian wine and the night having fallen, sat down by my mother in the chamber with a lamp between us, and, holding her hand, told her something of my story, showing her the sacks of gold that had come with me safely from the East, and the chain of priceless, rose-hued pearls that I had won in a wager from the Great King.

Now when she learned how Bes by his wit had saved me from a death of torment in the boat, my mother clapped her hands to summon a servant and sent for Bes, and said to him,

"Bes, hitherto I have looked on you as a slave taken by my son, the noble Shabaka, in one of his far journeys that it pleases him to make to fight and to hunt. But henceforth I look upon you as a friend and give you a seat at my table. Moreover it comes into my mind that although so strangely shaped by some evil god, perhaps you are more than you seem to be."

Now Bes looked at me to see if I had told my mother anything, and when I shook my head answered,

"I thank you, O Lady of the House, who have but done my duty to my master. Still it is true that as a goatskin often holds good wine, so a dwarf should not always be judged by what can be seen of him."

Then he went away.

"It seems that we are rich again, Son, who have been somewhat poor of late years," said my mother, looking at the bags of gold. "Also, there are the pearls which doubtless are worth more than the gold. What are you going to do with them, Shabaka?"

"I thought of offering them as a gift to the lady Amada," I replied hesitatingly, "that is unless you—"

"I? No, I am too old for such gems. Yet, Son, it might be well to keep them for a time, seeing that while they are your own they may give you more weight in the eyes of the Prince Peroa and others. Whereas if you gave them the lady Amada and she took them, perchance it might only be to see them return to the East, whither you tell me she is summoned by one whose orders may not be disobeyed."

Now I turned white with rage and answered,

"While I live, Mother, Amada shall never go to the East to be the woman of yonder King."

"While you live, Son. But those who cross the will of a great king, are apt to die. Also this is a matter which her uncle, the Prince Peroa, must decide as policy dictates. Now as ever the woman is but a pawn in the game. Oh! my son," she went on, "do not pin all your heart to the robe of this Amada. She is very fair and very learned, but is she one who will love? Moreover, if so she is a priestess and it would be difficult for her to wed who is sworn to Isis. Lastly, remember this: If Egypt were free, she would be its heiress, not her uncle, Peroa. For hers is the true blood, not his. Would he, therefore, be willing to give her to any man who, according to the ancient custom, through her would acquire the right to rule?"

"I do not seek to rule, Mother; I only seek to wed Amada whom I love."

"Amada whom you love and whose name you, or rather your servant Bes, which is the same thing since it will be held that he did it by your order, gave to the King of the East, or so I understand. Here is a pretty tangle, Shabaka, and rather would I be without all that gold and those priceless pearls than have the task of its unravelling."

Before I could answer and explain all the truth to her, the curtain was swung aside and through it came a messenger from the Prince

Peroa, who bade me come to eat with him at once at the palace, since he must see me this night.

So my mother having set the rope of rose-hued pearls in a double chain about my neck, I kissed her and went, with Bes who was also bidden. Outside a chariot was waiting into which we entered.

"Now, Master," said Bes to me as we drove to the palace, "I almost wish that we were back in another chariot hunting lions in the East."

"Why?" I asked.

"Because then, although we had much to fear, there was no woman in the story. Now the woman has entered it and I think that our real troubles are about to begin. Oh! to-morrow I go to seek counsel of the holy Tanofir."

"And I come with you," I answered, "for I think it will be needed."

IX

The Messengers

We descended at the great gate of the palace and were led through empty halls that were no longer used now when there was no king in Egypt, to the wing of the building in which dwelt the Prince Peroa. Here we were received by a chamberlain, for the Prince of Egypt still kept some state although it was but small, and had about him men who bore the old, high-sounding titles of the "Officers of Pharaoh."

The chamberlain led me and Bes to an ante-chamber of the banqueting hall and left us, saying that he would summon the Prince who wished to see me before he ate. This, however, was not necessary since while he spoke Peroa, who as I guessed had been waiting for me, entered by another door. He was a majestic-looking man of middle age, for grey showed in his hair and beard, clad in white garments with a purple hem and wearing on his brow a golden circlet, from the front of which rose the *uræus* in the shape of a hooded snake that might be worn by those of royal blood alone. His face was full of thought and his black and piercing eyes looked heavy as though with sleeplessness. Indeed I could see that he was troubled. His gaze fell upon us and his features changed to a pleasant smile.

"Greeting, Cousin Shabaka," he said. "I am glad that you have returned safe from the East, and burn to hear your tidings. I pray that they may be good, for never was good news more needed in Egypt."

"Greeting, Prince," I answered, bowing my knee. "I and my servant here are returned safe, but as for our tidings, well, judge of them for yourself," and drawing the letter of the Great King from my robe, I touched my forehead with the roll and handed it to him.

"I see that you have acquired the Eastern customs, Shabaka," he said as he took it. "But here in my own house which once was the palace of our forefathers, the Pharaohs of Egypt, by your leave I will omit them. Amen be my witness," he added bitterly, "I cannot bear to lay the letter of a foreign king against my brow in token of my country's vassalage."

Then he broke the silk of the seals and read, and as he read his face grew black with rage.

"What!" he cried, casting down the roll and stamping on it. "What!

Does this dog of an Eastern king bid me send my niece, by birth the Royal Princess of Egypt, to be his toy until he wearies of her? First I will choke her with my own hands. How comes it, Shabaka, that you care to bring me such a message? Were I Pharaoh now I think your life would pay the price."

"As it would certainly have paid the price, had I not done so. Prince, I brought the letter because I must. Also a copy of it has gone, I believe, to Idernes the Satrap at Sais. It is better to face the truth, Prince, and I think that I may be of more service to you alive than dead. If you do not wish to send the lady Amada to the King, marry her to someone else, after which he will seek her no more."

He looked at me shrewdly and said,

"To whom then? I cannot marry her, being her uncle and already married. Do you mean to yourself, Shabaka?"

"I have loved the lady Amada from a child, Prince," I answered boldly. "Also I have high blood in me and having brought much gold from the East, am rich again and one accustomed to war."

"So you have brought gold from the East! How? Well, you can tell me afterwards. But you fly high. You, a Count of Egypt, wish to marry the Royal Lady of Egypt, for such she is by birth and rank, which, if ever Egypt were free again, would give you a title to the throne."

"I ask no throne, Prince. If there were one to fill I should be content to leave that to you and your heirs."

"So you say, no doubt honestly. But would the children of Amada say the same? Would you even say it if you were her husband, and would she say it? Moreover she is a priestess, sworn not to wed, though perhaps that trouble might be overcome, if she wishes to wed, which I doubt. Mayhap you might discover. Well, you are hungry and worn with long travelling. Come, let us eat, and afterwards you can tell your story. Amada and the others will be glad to hear it, as I shall. Follow me, Count Shabaka."

So we went to the lesser banqueting-hall, I filled with joy because I should see Amada, and yet, much afraid because of that story which I must tell. Gathered there, waiting for the Prince, we found the Princess his wife, a large and kindly woman, also his two eldest daughters and his young son, a lad of about sixteen. Moreover, there were certain officers, while at the tables of the lower hall sat others of the household, men of smaller rank, and their wives, since Peroa still maintained some kind of a shadow of the Court of old Egypt.

The Princess and the others greeted me, and Bes also who had always been a favourite with them, before he went to take his seat at the lowest table, and I greeted them, looking all the while for Amada whom I did not see. Presently, however, as we took our places on the couches, she entered dressed, not as a priestess, but in the beautiful robes of a great lady of Egypt and wearing on her head the *uræus* circlet that signified her royal blood. As it chanced the only seat left vacant was that next to myself, which she took before she recognized me, for she was engaged in asking pardon for her lateness of the Prince and Princess, saying that she had been detained by the ceremonies at the temple. Seeing suddenly that I was her neighbour, she made as though she would change her place, then altered her mind and stayed where she was.

"Greeting, Cousin Shabaka," she said, "though not for the first time to-day. Oh! my heart was glad when looking up, outside the temple, I caught sight of you clad in that strange Eastern armour, and knew that you had returned safe from your long wanderings. Yet afterwards I must do penance for it by saying two added prayers, since at such a time my thoughts should have been with the goddess only."

"Greeting, Cousin Amada," I answered, "but she must be a jealous goddess who grudges a thought to a relative—and friend—at such a time."

"She is jealous, Shabaka, as being the Queen of women she must be who demands to reign alone in the hearts of her votaries. But tell me of your travels in the East and how you came by that rope of wondrous pearls, if indeed there can be pearls so large and beautiful."

This at the time I had little chance of doing, however, since the young Princess on the other side of her began to talk to Amada about some forthcoming festival, and the Prince's son next to me who was fond of hunting, to question me about sport in the East and when, unhappily, I said that I had shot lions there, gave me no peace for the rest of that feast. Also the Princess opposite was anxious to learn what food noble people ate in the East, and how it was cooked and how they sat at table, and what was the furniture of their rooms and did women attend feasts as in Egypt, and so forth. So it came about that what between these things and eating and drinking, which, being well-nigh starved, I was obliged to do, for, save a cup of wine, I had taken nothing in my mother's house, I found little chance of talking with the lovely Amada, although I knew that all the while she was studying me out of the corners of her large eyes. Or perhaps it was the rose-hued pearls she studied, I was not sure.

Only one thing did she say to me when there was a little pause while the cup went round, and she pledged me according to custom and passed it on. It was,

"You look well, Shabaka, though somewhat tired, but sadder than you used, I think."

"Perhaps because I have seen things to sadden me, Amada. But you too look well but somewhat lovelier than you used, I think, if that be possible."

She smiled and blushed as she replied,

"The Eastern ladies have taught you how to say pretty things. But you should not waste them upon me who have done with women's vanities and have given myself to learning and—religion."

"Have learning and religion no vanities of their own?" I began, when suddenly the Prince gave a signal to end the feast.

Thereon all the lower part of the hall went away and the little tables at which we ate were removed by servants, leaving us only wine-cups in our hands which a butler filled from time to time, mixing the wine with water. This reminded me of something, and having asked leave, I beckoned to Bes, who still lingered near the door, and took from him that splendid, golden goblet which the Great King had given me, that by my command he had brought wrapped up in linen and hidden beneath his robe. Having undone the wrappings I bowed and offered it to the Prince Peroa.

"What is this wondrous thing?" asked the Prince, when all had finished admiring its workmanship. "Is it a gift that you bring me from the King of the East, Shabaka?"

"It is a gift from myself, O Prince, if you will be pleased to accept it," I answered, adding, "Yet it is true that it comes from the King of the East, since it was his own drinking-cup that he gave me in exchange for a certain bow, though not the one he sought, after he had pledged me."

"You seem to have found much favour in the eyes of this king, Shabaka, which is more than most of us Egyptians do," he exclaimed, then went on hastily, "Still, I thank you for your splendid gift, and however you came by it, shall value it much."

"Perhaps my cousin Shabaka will tell us his story," broke in Amada, her eyes still fixed upon the rose-hued pearls, "and of how he came to win all the beauteous things that dazzle our eyes to-night."

Now I thought of offering her the pearls, but remembering my mother's words, also that the Princess might not like to see another woman bear off such a prize, did not do so. So I began to tell my story instead, Bes seated on the ground near to me by the Prince's wish, that he might tell his.

The tale was long for in it was much that went before the day when I saw myself in the chariot hunting lions with the King of kings, which I, the modern man who set down all this vision, now learned for the first time. It told of the details of my journey to the East, of my coming to the royal city and the rest, all of which it is needless to repeat. Then I came to the lion hunt, to my winning of the wager, and all that happened to me; of my being condemned to death, of the weighing of Bes against the gold, and of how I was laid in the boat of torment, a story at which I noticed Amada turn pale and tremble.

Here I ceased, saying that Bes knew better than I what had chanced at the Court while I was pinned in the boat, whereon all present cried out to Bes to take up the tale. This he did, and much better than I could have done, bringing out many little things which made the scene appear before them, as Ethiopians have the art of doing. At last he came to the place in his story where the king asked him if he had ever seen a woman fairer than the dancers, and went on thus:

"O Prince, I told the Great King that I had; that there dwelt in Egypt a lady of royal blood with eyes like stars, with hair like silk and long as an unbridled horse's tail, with a shape like to that of a goddess, with breath like flowers, with skin like milk, with a voice like honey, with learning like to that of the god Thoth, with wit like a razor's edge, with teeth like pearls, with majesty of bearing like to that of the king himself, with fingers like rosebuds set in pink seashells, with motion like that of an antelope, with grace like that of a swan floating upon water, and—I don't remember the rest, O Prince."

"Perhaps it is as well," exclaimed Peroa. "But what did the King say then?"

"He asked her name, O Prince."

"And what name did you give to this wondrous lady who surpasses all the goddesses in loveliness and charm, O dwarf Bes?" inquired Amada much amused.

"What name, O High-born One? Is it needful to ask? Why, what name could I give but your own, for is there any other in the world of whom a man whose heart is filled with truth could speak such things?"

Now hearing this I gasped, but before I could speak Amada leapt up, crying,

"Wretch! You dared to speak my name to this king! Surely you should be scourged till your bones are bare."

"And why not, Lady? Would you have had me sit still and hear those fat trollops of the East exalted above you? Would you have had me so disloyal to your royal loveliness?"

"You should be scourged," repeated Amada stamping her foot. "My Uncle, I pray you cause this knave to be scourged."

"Nay, nay," said Peroa moodily. "Poor simple man, he knew no better and thought only to sing your praises in a far land. Be not angry with the dwarf, Niece. Had it been Shabaka who gave your name, the thing would be different. What happened next, Bes?"

"Only this, Prince," said Bes, looking upwards and rolling his eyes, as was his fashion when unloading some great lie from his heart. "The King sent his servants to bring my master from the boat, that he might inquire of him whether he had always found me truthful. For, Prince, those Easterns set much store by truth which here in Egypt is worshipped as a goddess. There they do not worship her because she lives in the heart of every man, and some women."

Now all stared at Bes who continued to stare at the ceiling, and I rose to say something, I know not what, when suddenly the doors opened and through them appeared heralds, crying,

"Hearken, Peroa, Prince of Egypt by grace of the Great King. A message from the Great King. Read and obey, O Peroa, Prince of Egypt by grace of the Great King!"

As they cried thus from between them emerged a man whose long Eastern robes were stained with the dust of travel. Advancing without salute he drew out a roll, touched his forehead with it, bowing deeply, and handed it to the prince, saying,

"Kiss the Word. Read the Word. Obey the Word, O servant of our Master, the King of kings, beneath whose feet we are all but dust."

Peroa took the roll, made a semblance of lifting it to his forehead, opened and read it. As he did so I saw the veins swell upon his neck and his eyes flash, but he only said,

"O Messenger, to-night I feast, to-morrow an answer shall be given to you to convey to the Satrap Idernes. My servants will find you food and lodging. You are dismissed."

"Let the answer be given early lest you also should be dismissed, O Peroa," said the man with insolence.

Then he turned his back upon the prince, as one does on an inferior, and walked away, accompanied by the herald.

When they were gone and the doors had been shut, Peroa spoke in a voice that was thick with fury, saying,

"Hearken, all of you, to the words of the writing."

Then he read it.

"From the King of kings, the Ruler of all the earth, to Peroa, one of his servants in the Satrapy of Egypt,

"Deliver over to my servant Idernes without delay, the person of Amada, a lady of the blood of the old Pharaohs of Egypt, who is your relative and in your guardianship, that she may be numbered among the women of my house."

Now all present looked at each other, while Amada stood as though she had been frozen into stone. Before she could speak, Peroa went on,

"See how the King seeks a quarrel against me that he may destroy me and bray Egypt in his mortar, and tan it like a hide to wrap about his feet. Nay, hold your peace, Amada. Have no fear. You shall not be sent to the East; first will I kill you with my own hands. But what answer shall we give, for the matter is urgent and on it hang all our lives? Bethink you, Idernes has a great force yonder at Sais, and if I refuse outright, he will attack us, which indeed is what the King means him to do before we can make preparation. Say then, shall we fight, or shall we fly to Upper Egypt, abandoning Memphis, and there make our stand?"

Now the Councillors present seemed to find no answer, for they did not know what to say. But Bes whispered in my ear,

"Remember, Master, that you hold the King's seal. Let an answer be sent to Idernes under the White Seal, bidding him wait on you."

Then I rose and spoke.

"O Peroa," I said, "as it chances I am the bearer of the private signet of the Great King, which all men must obey in the north and in the south, in the east and in the west, wherever the sun shines over the dominions of the King. Look on it," and taking the ancient White Seal from about my neck, I handed it to him.

He looked and the Councillors looked. Then they said almost with one voice,

"It is the White Seal, the very signet of the Great Kings of the East," and they bowed before the dreadful thing.

"How you came by this we do not know, Shabaka," said Peroa. "That can be inquired of afterwards. Yet in truth it seems to be the old Signet of signets, that which has come down from father to son for countless generations, that which the King of kings carries on his person and affixes to his private orders and to the greatest documents of State, which afterwards can never be recalled, that of which a copy is emblazoned on his banner."

"It is," I answered, "and from the King's person it came to me for a while. If any doubt, let the impress be brought, that is furnished to all the officers throughout the Empire, and let the seal be set in the impress."

Now one of the officers rose and went to bring the impress which was in his keeping, but Peroa continued,

"If this be the true seal, how would you use it, Shabaka, to help us in our present trouble?"

"Thus, Prince," I answered. "I would send a command under the seal to Idernes to wait upon the holder of the seal here in Memphis. He will suspect a trap and will not come until he has gathered a great army. Then he will come, but meanwhile, you, Prince, can also collect an army."

"That needs gold, Shabaka, and I have little. The King of kings takes all in tribute."

"I have some, Prince, to the weight of a heavy man, and it is at the service of Egypt."

"I thank you, Shabaka. Believe me, such generosity shall not go unrewarded," and he glanced at Amada who dropped her eyes. "But if we can collect the army, what then?"

"Then you can put Memphis into a state of defence. Then too when Idernes comes I will meet him and, as the bearer of the seal, command him under the seal to retreat and disperse his army."

"But if he does, Shabaka, it will only be until he has received fresh orders from the Great King, whereon he will advance again."

"No, Prince, *he* will not advance, or that army either. For when they are in retreat we will fall on them and destroy them, and declare you, O Prince, Pharaoh of Egypt, though what will happen afterwards I do not know."

When they heard this all gasped. Only Amada whispered,

"Well said!" and Bes clapped his big hands softly in the Ethiopian fashion.

"A bold counsel," said Peroa, "and one on which I must have the night to think. Return here, Shabaka, an hour after sunrise to-morrow, by which time I can gather all the wisest men in Memphis, and we will discuss this matter. Ah! here is the impress. Now let the seal be tried."

A box was brought and opened. In it was a slab of wood on which was an impress of the King's seal in wax, surrounded by those of other seals certifying that it was genuine. Also there was a writing describing the appearance of the seal. I handed the signet to Peroa who, having compared it with the description in the writing, fitted it to the impress on the wax.

"It is the same," he said. "See, all of you."

They looked and nodded. Then he would have given it back to me but I refused to take it, saying,

"It is not well that this mighty symbol should hang about the neck of a private man whence it might be stolen or lost."

"Or who might be murdered for its sake," interrupted Peroa.

"Yes, Prince. Therefore take it and hide it in the safest and most secret place in the palace, and with it these pearls that are too priceless to be flaunted about the streets of Memphis at night, unless indeed——" and I turned to look for Amada, but she was gone.

So the seal and the pearls were taken and locked in the box with the impress and borne away. Nor was I sorry to see the last of them, wisely as it happened. Then I bade the Prince and his company good night, and presently was driving homeward with Bes in the chariot.

Our way led us past some large houses once occupied by officers of the Court of Pharaoh, but now that there was no Court, fallen into ruins. Suddenly from out of these houses sprang a band of men disguised as common robbers, whose faces were hidden by cloths with eye-holes cut in them. They seized the horses by the bridles, and before we could do anything, leapt upon us and held us fast. Then a tall man speaking with a foreign accent, said,

"Search that officer and the dwarf. Take from them the seal upon a gold chain and a rope of rose-hued pearls which they have stolen. But do them no harm."

So they searched us, the tall man himself helping and, aided by others, holding Bes who struggled with them, and searched the chariot also, by the light of the moon, but found nothing. The tall man muttered that I must be the wrong officer, and at a sign they left us and ran away.

"That was a wise thought of mine, Bes, which caused me to leave certain ornaments in the palace," I said. "As it is they have taken nothing."

"Yes, Master," he answered, "though I have taken something from them," a saying that I did not understand at the time. "Those Easterns whom we met by the canal told Idernes about the seal, and he ordered this to be done. That tall man was one of the messengers who came to-night to the palace."

"Then why did they not kill us, Bes?"

"Because murder, especially of one who holds the seal, is an ugly business, that is easily tracked down, whereas thieves are many in Memphis and who troubles about them when they have failed? Oh! the Grasshopper, or Amen, or both, have been with us to-night."

So I thought although I said nothing, for since we had come off scatheless, what did it matter? Well, this. It showed me that the signet of the Great King was indeed to be dreaded and coveted, even here in Egypt. If Idernes could get it into his possession, what might he not do with it? Cause himself to be proclaimed Pharaoh perhaps and become the forefather of an independent dynasty. Why not, when the Empire of the East was taxed with a great war elsewhere? And if this was so why should not Peroa do the same, he who had behind him all Old Egypt, maddened with its wrongs and foreign rule?

That same night before I slept, but after Bes and I had hidden away the bags of gold by burying them beneath the clay floor, I laid the whole matter before my mother who was a very wise woman. She heard me out, answering little, then said,

"The business is very dangerous, and of its end I will not speak until I have heard the counsel of your great-uncle, the holy Tanofir. Still, things having gone so far, it seems to me that boldness may be the best course, since the great King has his Grecian wars to deal with, and whatever he may say, cannot attack Egypt yet awhile. Therefore if Peroa is able to overcome Idernes and his army he may cause himself to be proclaimed Pharaoh and make Egypt free if only for a time."

"Such is my mind, Mother."

"Not all your mind, Son, I think," she answered smiling, "for you think more of the lovely Amada than of these high policies, at any rate to-night. Well, marry your Amada if you can, though I misdoubt me somewhat of a woman who is so lost in learning and thinks so much about her soul. At least if you marry her and Egypt should become free, as it was for thousands of years, you will be the next heir to the throne as husband of the Great Royal Lady."

"How can that be, Mother, seeing that Peroa has a son?"

"A vain youth with no more in him than a child's rattle. If once Amada ceases to think about her soul she will begin to think about her throne, especially if she has children. But all this is far away and for the present I am glad that neither she nor the thieves have got those pearls, though perhaps they might be safer here than where they are. And now, my son, go rest for you need it, and dream of nothing, not even Amada, who for her part will dream of Isis, if at all. I will wake you before the dawn."

So I went, being too tired to talk more, and slept like a crocodile in the sun, till, as it seemed to me, but a few minutes later I saw my mother standing over me with a lamp, saying that it was time to rise. I rose, unwillingly enough, but refreshed, washed and dressed myself, by which time the sun had begun to appear. Then I ate some food and, calling Bes, made ready to start for the palace.

"My son," said my mother, the lady Tiu, before we parted, "while you have been sleeping I have been thinking, as is the way of the old. Peroa, your cousin, will be glad enough to make use of you, but he does not love you over much because he is jealous of you and fears lest you should become his rival in the future. Still he is an honest man and will keep a bargain which he once has made. Now it seems that above everything on earth you desire Amada on whom you have set your heart since boyhood, but who has always played with you and spoken to you with her arm stretched out. Also life is short and may come to an end any day, as you should know better than most men who have lived among dangers, and therefore it is well that a man should take what he desires, even if he finds afterwards that the rose he crushes to his breast has thorns. For then at least he will have smelt the rose, not only have looked on and longed to smell it. Therefore, before you hand over your gold, and place your wit and strength at the service of Peroa, make your bargain with him; namely, that if thereby you save Amada from the King's House of Women and help to set Peroa on the throne, he shall promise her to you free of any priestly curse, you giving her as dowry the priceless rose-hued pearls that are worth a kingdom. So you will get your rose till it withers, and if the thorns prick, do not blame me, and one day you may become a king—or a slave, Amen knows which."

Now I laughed and said that I would take her counsel who desired Amada and nothing else. As for all her talk about thorns, I paid no heed to it, knowing that she loved me very much and was jealous of Amada who she thought would take her place with me.

X

SHABAKA PLIGHTS HIS TROTH

B es and I went armed to the palace, walking in the middle of the road, but now that the sun was up we met no more robbers. At the gate a messenger summoned me alone to the presence of Peroa, who, he said, wished to talk with me before the sitting of the Council. I went and found him by himself.

"I hear that you were attacked last night," he said after greeting me.

I answered that I was and told him the story, adding that it was fortunate I had left the White Seal and the pearls in safe keeping, since without doubt the would-be thieves were Easterns who desired to recover them.

"Ah! the pearls," he said. "One of those who handled them, who was once a dealer in gems, says that they are without price, unmatched in the whole world, and that never in all his life has he seen any to equal the smallest of them."

I replied that I believed this was so. Then he asked me of the value of the gold of which I had spoken. I told him and it was a great sum, for gold was scarce in Egypt. His eyes gleamed for he needed wealth to pay soldiers.

"And all this you are ready to hand over to me, Shabaka?"

Now I bethought me of my mother's words, and answered,

"Yes, Prince, at a price."

"What price, Shabaka?"

"The price of the hand of the Royal Lady, Amada, freed from her vows. Moreover, I will give her the pearls as a marriage dowry and place at your service my sword and all the knowledge I have gained in the East, swearing to stand or fall with you."

"I thought it, Shabaka. Well, in this world nothing is given for nothing and the offer is a fair one. You are well born, too, as well as myself, and a brave and clever man. Further, Amada has not taken her final vows and therefore the high priests can absolve her from her marriage to the goddess, or to her son Horus, whichever it may be, for I do not understand these mysteries. But, Shabaka, if Fortune should chance to go with us and I should became the first Pharaoh of a new dynasty in Egypt, he who was married to the Royal Princess of the true blood might become a danger to my throne and family."

"I shall not be that man, Prince, who am content with my own station, and to be your servant."

"And my son's, Shabaka? You know that I have but one lawful son."

"And your son's, Prince."

"You are honest, Shabaka, and I believe you. But how about your sons, if you have any, and how about Amada herself? Well, in great businesses something must be risked, and I need the gold and the rest which I cannot take for nothing, for you won them by your skill and courage and they are yours. But how you won the seal you have not told us, nor is there time for you to do so now."

He thought a little, walking up and down the chamber, then went on,

"I accept your offer, Shabaka, so far as I can."

"So far as you can, Prince?"

"Yes; I can give you Amada in marriage and make that marriage easy, but only if Amada herself consents. The will of a Royal Princess of Egypt of full age cannot be forced, save by her father if he reigns as Pharaoh, and I am not her father, but only her guardian. Therefore it stands thus. Are you willing to fulfil your part of the bargain, save only as regards the pearls, if she does not marry you, and to take your chance of winning Amada as a man wins a woman, I on my part promising to do all in my power to help your suit?"

Now it was my turn to think for a moment. What did I risk? The gold and perhaps the pearls, no more, for in any case I should fight for Peroa against the Eastern king whom I hated, and through him for Egypt. Well, these came to me by chance, and if they went by chance what of it? Also I was not one who desired to wed a woman, however much I worshipped her, if she desired to turn her back on me. If I could win her in fair love—well. If not, it was my misfortune, and I wanted her in no other way. Lastly, I had reason to think that she looked on me more favourably than she had ever done on any other man, and that if it had not been for what my mother called her soul and its longings, she would have given herself to me before I journeyed to the East. Indeed, once she had said as much, and there was something in her eyes last night which told me that in her heart she loved me, though with what passion at the time I did not know. So very swiftly I made up my mind and answered,

"I understand and I accept. The gold shall be delivered to you to-day, Prince. The pearls are already in your keeping to await the end."

"Good!" he exclaimed. "Then let the matter be reduced to writing and at once, that afterwards neither of us may have cause to complain of the other."

So he sent for his secret scribe and dictated to him, briefly but clearly, the substance of our bargain, nothing being added, and nothing taken away. This roll written on papyrus was afterwards copied twice, Peroa taking one copy, I another, and a third being deposited according to custom, in the library of the temple of Ptah.

When all was done and Peroa and I had touched each other's breasts and given our word in the name of Amen, we went to the hall in which we had dined, where those whom the Prince had summoned were assembled. Altogether there were about thirty of them, great citizens of Memphis, or landowners from without who had been called together in the night. Some of these men were very old and could remember when Egypt had a Pharaoh of its own before the East set its heel upon her neck, of noble blood also.

Others were merchants who dealt with all the cities of Egypt; others hereditary generals, or captains of fleets of ships; others Grecians, officers of mercenaries who were supposed to be in the pay of the King of kings, but hated him, as did all the Greeks. Then there were the high priests of Ptah, of Amen, of Osiris and others who were still the most powerful men in the land, since there was no village between Thebes and the mouths of the Nile in which they had not those who were sworn to the service of their gods.

Such was the company representing all that remained or could be gathered there of the greatness of Egypt the ancient and the fallen.

To these when the doors had been closed and barred and trusty watchmen set to guard them, Peroa expounded the case in a low and earnest voice. He showed them that the King of the East sought a new quarrel against Egypt that he might grind her to powder beneath his heel, and that he did this by demanding the person of Amada, his own niece and the Royal Lady of Egypt, to be included in his household like any common woman. If she were refused then he would send a great army under pretext of taking her, and lay the land waste as far as Thebes. And if she were granted some new quarrel would be picked and in the person of the royal Amada all of them be for ever shamed.

Next he showed the seal, telling them that I—who was known to many of them, at least by repute—had brought it from the East, and repeating to them the plan that I had proposed upon the previous night. After this he asked their counsel, saying that before noon he must send an answer to Idernes, the King's Satrap at Sais.

Then I was called upon to speak and, in answer to questions, answered frankly that I had stolen the ancient White Seal from the King's servant who carried it as a warrant for the King's private vengeance on one who had bested him. How I did not mention. I told them also of the state of the Great King's empire and that I had heard that he was about to enter upon a war with the Greeks which would need all its strength, and that therefore if they wished to strike for liberty the time was at hand.

Then the talk began and lasted for two hours, each man giving his judgment according to precedence, some one way and some another. When all had done and it became clear that there were differences of opinion, some being content to live on in slavery with what remained to them and others desiring to strike for freedom, among whom were the high priests who feared lest the Eastern heretics should utterly destroy their worship, Peroa spoke once more.

"Elders of Egypt," he said briefly, "certain of you think one way, and certain another, but of this be sure, such talk as we have held together cannot be hid. It will come to the ears of spies and through them to those of the Great King, and then all of us alike are doomed. If you refuse to stir, this very day I with my family and household and the Royal Lady Amada, and all who cling to me, fly to Upper Egypt and perhaps beyond it to Ethiopia, leaving you to deal with the Great King, as you will, or to follow me into exile. That he will attack us there is no doubt, either over the pretext of Amada or some other, since Shabaka has heard as much from his own lips. Now choose."

Then, after a little whispering together, every man of them voted for rebellion, though some of them I could see with heavy hearts, and bound themselves by a great oath to cling together to the last.

The matter being thus settled such a letter was written to Idernes as I had suggested on the night before, and sealed with the Signet of signets. Of the yielding up of Amada it said nothing, but commanded Idernes, under the private White Seal that none dared disobey, to wait upon the Prince Peroa at Memphis forthwith, and there learn from him, the Holder of the Seal, what was the will of the Great King. Then the Council was adjourned till one hour after noon, and most of them departed to send messengers bearing secret word to the various cities and nomes of Egypt.

Before they went, however, I was directed to wait upon my relative, the holy Tanofir, whom all acknowledged to be the greatest magician in Egypt, and to ask of him to seek wisdom and an oracle from his Spirit as to the future and whether in it we should fare well or ill. This I promised to do.

When most of the Council were gone the messengers of Idernes were summoned, and came proudly, and with them, or rather before them, Bes for whom I had sent as he was not present at the Council.

"Master," he whispered to me, "the tallest of those messengers is the man who captained the robbers last night. Wait and I will prove it."

Peroa gave the roll to the head messenger, bidding him bear it to the Satrap in answer to the letter which he had delivered to him. The man took it insolently and thrust it into his robe, as he did so revealing a silver chain that had been broken and knotted together, and asked whether there were words to bear besides those written in the roll. Before Peroa could answer Bes sprang up saying,

"O Prince, a boon, the boon of justice on this man. Last night he and others with him attacked my master and myself, seeking to rob us, but finding nothing let us go."

"You lie, Abortion!" said the Eastern.

"Oh! I lie, do I?" mocked Bes. "Well, let us see," and shooting out his long arm, he grasped the chain about the messenger's neck and broke it with a jerk. "Look, O Prince," he said, "you may have noted last night, when that man entered the hall, that there hung about his neck this chain to which was tied a silver key."

"I noted it," said Peroa.

"Then ask him, O Prince, where is the key now."

"What is that to you, Dwarf?" broke in the man. "The key is my mark of office as chief butler to the High Satrap. Must I always bear it for your pleasure?"

"Not when it has been taken from you, Butler," answered Bes. "See, here it is," and from his sleeve he produced the key hanging to a piece of the chain. "Listen, O Prince," he said. "I struggled with this man and the key was in my left hand though he did not know it at the time, and with it some of the chain. Compare them and judge. Also his mask slipped and I saw his face and knew him again."

Peroa laid the pieces of the chain together and observed the workmanship which was Eastern and rare. Then he clapped his hands, at which sign armed men of his household entered from behind him.

"It is the same," he said. "Butler of Idernes, you are a common thief."

The man strove to answer, but could not for the deed was proved against him.

"Then, O Prince," asked Bes, "what is the punishment of those thieves who attack passers-by with violence in the streets of Memphis, for such I demand on him?"

"The cutting off of the right hand and scourging," answered Peroa, at which words the butler turned to fly. But Bes leapt on him like an ape upon a bird, and held him fast.

"Seize that thief," said Peroa to his servants, "and let him receive fifty blows with the rods. His hand I spare because he must travel."

They laid the man down and the rods having been fetched, gave him the blows until at the thirtieth he howled for mercy, crying out that it was true and that it was he who had captained the robbers, words which Peroa caused to be written down. Then he asked him why he, a messenger from the Satrap, had robbed in the streets of Memphis, and as he refused to answer, commanded the officer of justice to lay on. After three more blows the man said,

"O Prince, this was no common robbery for gain. I did what I was commanded to do, because yonder noble had about him the ancient White Seal of the Great King which he showed to certain of the Satrap's servants by the banks of the canal. That seal is a holy token, O Prince, which, it is said, has descended for twice a thousand years in the family of the Great King, and as the Satrap did not know how it had come into the hands of the noble Shabaka, he ordered me to obtain it if I could."

"And the pearls too, Butler?"

"Yes, O Prince, since those gems are a great possession with which any Satrap could buy a larger satrapy."

"Let him go," said Peroa, and the man rose, rubbing himself and weeping in his pain.

"Now, Butler," he went on, "return to your master with a grateful heart, since you have been spared much that you deserve. Say to him that he cannot steal the Signet, but that if he is wise he will obey it, since otherwise his fate may be worse than yours, and to all his servants say the same. Foolish man, how can you, or your master, guess what is in the mind of the Great King, or for what purpose the Signet of signets is here in Egypt? Beware lest you fall into a pit, all of you together, and let Idernes beware lest he find himself at the very bottom of that pit."

"O Prince, I will beware," said the humbled butler, "and whatever is written over the seal, that I will obey, like many others."

"You are wise," answered Peroa; "I pray for his own sake that the Satrap Idernes may be as wise. Now begone, thanking whatever god you worship that your life is whole in you and that your right hand remains upon your wrist."

So the butler and those with him prostrated themselves before Peroa and bowed humbly to me and even to Bes because in their hearts now they believed that we were clothed by the Great King with terrible powers that might destroy them all, if so we chose. Then they went, the butler limping a little and with no pride left in him.

"That was good work," said Peroa to me afterwards when we were alone, "for now yonder knave is frightened and will frighten his master."

"Yes," I answered, "you played that pipe well, Prince. Still, there is no time to lose, since before another moon this will all be reported in the East, whence a new light may arise and perchance a new signet."

"You say you stole the White Seal?" he asked.

"Nay, Prince, the truth is that Bes bought it—in a certain fashion—and I used it. Perhaps it is well that you should know no more at present."

"Perhaps," he answered, and we parted, for he had much to do.

That afternoon the Council met again. At it I gave over the gold and by help of it all was arranged. Within a week ten thousand armed men would be in Memphis and a hundred ships with their crews upon the Nile; also a great army would be gathering in Upper Egypt, officered for the most part by Greeks skilled in war. The Greek cities too at the mouths of the Nile would be ready to revolt, or so some of their citizens declared, for they hated the Great King bitterly and longed to cast off his yoke.

For my part, I received the command of the bodyguard of Peroa in which were many Greeks, and a generalship in the army; while to Bes, at my prayer, was given the freedom of the land which he accepted with a smile, he who was a king in his own country.

At length all was finished and I went out into the palace garden to rest myself before I rode into the desert to see my great uncle, the holy Tanofir. I was alone, for Bes had gone to bring our horses on which we were to ride, and sat myself down beneath a palm-tree, thinking of the great adventure on which we had entered with a merry heart, for I loved adventures.

Next I thought of Amada and was less merry. Then I looked up and lo! she stood before me, unaccompanied and wearing the dress, not of a priestess, but of an Egyptian lady with the little circlet of her rank upon her hair. I rose and bowed to her and we began to walk together beneath the palms, my heart beating hard within me, for I knew that my hour had come to speak.

Yet it was she who spoke the first, saying,

"I hear that you have been playing a high part, Shabaka, and doing great things for Egypt."

"For Egypt and for you who are Egypt," I answered.

"So I should have been called in the old days, Cousin, because of my blood and the rank it gives, though now I am but as any other lady of the land."

"And so you shall be called in days to come, Amada, if my sword and wit can win their way."

"How so, Cousin, seeing that you have promised certain things to my uncle Peroa and his son?"

"I have promised those things, Amada, and I will abide by my promise; but the gods are above all, and who knows what they may decree?"

"Yes, Cousin, the gods are above all, and in their hands we will let these matters rest, provoking them in no manner and least of all by treachery to our oaths."

We walked for a little way in silence. Then I spoke.

"Amada, there are more things than thrones in the world."

"Yes, Cousin, there is that in which all thrones end—death, which it seems we court."

"And, Amada, there is that in which all thrones begin—love, which I court from you."

"I have known it long," she said, considering me gravely, "and been grateful to you who are more to me than any man has been or ever will be. But, Shabaka, I am a priestess bound to set the holy One I serve above a mortal."

"That holy One was wed and bore a child, Amada, who avenged his father, as I trust that we shall avenge Egypt. Therefore she looks with a kind eye upon wives and mothers. Also you have not taken your final vows and can be absolved."

"Yes," she said softly.

"Then, Amada, will you give yourself into my keeping?"

"I think so, Shabaka, though it has been in my mind for long, as you know well, to give myself only to learning and the service of the heavenly Lady. My heart calls me to you, it is true, day and night it calls, how loudly I will not tell; yet I would not yield myself to that alone. But Egypt calls me also, since I have been shown in a dream while I watched in the sanctuary, that you are the only man who can free her, and I think that this dream came from on high. Therefore I will give myself, but not yet."

"Not yet," I said dismayed. "When?"

"When I have been absolved from my vows, which must be done on the night of the next new moon, which is twenty-seven days from this. Then, if nothing comes between us during those twenty-seven days, it shall be announced that the Royal Lady of Egypt is to wed the noble Shabaka."

"Twenty-seven days! In such times much may happen in them, Amada. Still, except death, what can come between us?"

"I know of nothing, Shabaka, whose past is shadowless as the noon."

"Or I either," I replied.

Now we were standing in the clear sunlight, but as I said the words a wind stirred the palm-trees and the shadow from one of them fell full upon me, and she who was very quick, noted it.

"Some might take that for an omen," she said with a little laugh, pointing to the line of the shadow. "Oh! Shabaka, if you have aught to confess, say it now and I will forgive it. But do not leave me to discover it afterwards when I may not forgive. Perchance during your journeyings in the East——"

"Nothing, nothing," I exclaimed joyfully, who during all that time had scarcely spoken to a youthful woman.

"I am glad that nothing happened in the East that could separate us, Shabaka, though in truth my thought was not your own, for there are more things than women in the world. Only it seems strange to me that you should return to Egypt laden with such priceless gifts from him who is Egypt's greatest enemy."

"Have I not told you that I put my country before myself? Those gifts were won fairly in a wager, Amada, whereof you heard the story but last night. Moreover you know the purpose to which they are to be put," I replied indignantly.

"Yes, I know and now I am sure. Be not angry, Shabaka, with her who loves you truly and hopes ere long to call you husband. But till that day take it not amiss if I keep somewhat aloof from you, who must break with the past and learn to face a future of which I did not dream."

For the rest she stretched out her hand and I kissed it, for while she was still a priestess her lips she would not suffer me to touch. Another moment and smiling happily, she had glided away, leaving me alone in the garden.

Then it was for the first time that I bethought me of the warnings of Bes and remembered that it was I, not he, who had told the Great King the name of the most beautiful woman in Egypt, although in all innocence. Yes, I remembered, and felt as if all the shadows on the earth had wrapped me round. I thought of finding her, but she had gone whither I knew not in that great palace. So I determined that the next time we were alone I would tell her of the matter, explaining all, and with this thought I comforted myself who did not know that until many days were past we should be alone no more.

After this I went home and told my mother all my joy, for in truth there was no happier man in Egypt. She listened, then answered, smiling a little.

"When your father wished to take me to wife, Shabaka, it was not my hand that I gave him to kiss, and as you know, I too have the blood of kings in me. But then I was not a priestess of Isis, so doubtless all is well. Only in twenty-seven days much may happen, as you said to Amada. Now I wonder why did she——? Well, no matter, since priestesses are not like other women who only think of the man they have won and of naught before or after. The blessing of the gods and mine be on you both, my son," and she went away to attend to her household matters.

As we rode to Sekera to find the holy Tanofir I told Bes also, adding that I had forgotten to reveal that it was I who had spoken Amada's name to the king, but that I intended to do so ere long.

Bes rolled his eyes and answered,

"If I were you, Master, as I had forgotten, I should continue to forget, for what is welcome in one hour is not always welcome in another. Why speak of the matter at all, which is one hard to explain to a woman, however wise and royal? I have already said that *I* spoke the name to the King and that you were brought from the boat to say whether I was noted for my truthfulness. Is not that enough?"

While I considered, Bes went on,

"You may remember, Master, that when I told, well—the truth about this story, the lady Amada asked earnestly that I should be scourged, even to the bones. Now if you should tell another truth which will make mine dull as tarnished silver, she will not leave me even my bones, for I shall be proved a liar, and what will happen to you I am sure I do not know. And, Master, as I am no longer a slave here in Egypt, to say nothing of what I may be elsewhere, I have no fancy for scourgings, who may not kiss the hand that smites me as you can."

"But, Bes," I said, "what is, is and may always be learned in this way or in that."

"Master, if what is were always learned, I think the world would fall to pieces, or at least there would be no men left on it. Why should this matter be learned? It is known to you and me alone, leaving out the Great King who probably has forgotten as he was drunk at the time. Oh! Master, when you have neither bow nor spear at hand, it is not wise to kick a sleeping lion in the stomach, for then he will remember its emptiness and sup off you. Beside, when first I told you that tale I made a mistake. I did tell the Great King, as I now remember quite clearly, that the beautiful lady was named Amada, and he only sent for you to ask if I spoke the truth."

"Bes," I exclaimed, "you worshippers of the Grasshopper wear virtue easily."

"Easily as an old sandal, Master, or rather not at all, since the Grasshopper has need of none. For ages they have studied the ways of those who worship the gods of Egypt, and from them have learned——"

"What?"

"Amongst other things, Master, that woman, being modest, is shocked at the sight of the naked Truth."

XI

THE HOLY TANOFIR

We entered the City of Graves that is called Sekera. In the centre towered pyramids that hid the bones of ancient and forgotten kings, and everywhere around upon the desert sands was street upon street of monuments, but save for a priest or two hurrying to patter his paid office in the funeral chapels of the departed, never a living man. Bes looked about him and sniffed with his wide nostrils.

"Is there not death enough in the world, Master," he asked, "that the living should wish to proclaim it in this fashion, rolling it on their tongues like a morsel they are loth to swallow, because it tastes so good? Oh! what a waste is here. All these have had their day and yet they need houses and pyramids and painted chambers in which to sleep, whereas if they believed the faith they practised, they would have been content to give their bones to feed the earth they fed on, and fill heaven with their souls."

"Do your people thus, Bes?"

"For the most part, Master. Our dead kings and great ones we enclose in pillars of crystal, but we do this that they may serve a double purpose. One is that the pillars may support the roof of their successors, and the other, that those who inherit their goods may please themselves by reflecting how much handsomer they are than those who went before them. For no mummy looks really nice, Master, at least with its wrappings off, and our kings are put naked into the crystal."

"And what becomes of the rest, Bes?"

"Their bodies go to the earth or the water and the Grasshopper carries off their souls to—where, Master?"

"I do not know, Bes."

"No, Master, no one knows, except the lady Amada and perhaps the holy Tanofir. Here I think is the entrance to his hole," and he pulled up his beast with a jerk at what looked like the doorway of a tomb.

Apparently we were expected, for a tall and proud-looking girl clad in white and with extraordinarily dark eyes, appeared in the doorway and asked in a soft voice if we were the noble Shabaka and Bes, his slave.

"I am Shabaka," I answered, "and this is Bes, who is not my slave but a free citizen of Egypt."

The girl contemplated the dwarf with her big eyes, then said, "And other things, I think."

"What things?" inquired Bes with interest, as he stared at this beautiful lady.

"A very brave and clever man and one perhaps who is more than he seems to be?"

"Who has been telling you about me?" exclaimed Bes anxiously.

"No one, O Bes, at least not that I can remember."

"Not that you can remember! Then who and what are you who learn things you know not how?"

"I am named Karema and desert-bred, and my office is that of Cup to the holy Tanofir."

"If hermits drink from such a cup I shall turn hermit," said Bes, laughing. "But how can a woman be a man's cup and what kind of a wine does he drink from her?"

"The wine of wisdom, O Bes," she replied colouring a little, for like many Arabs of high blood she was very fair in hue.

"Wine of wisdom," said Bes. "From such cups most drink the wine of folly, or sometimes of madness."

"The holy Tanofir awaits you," she interrupted, and turning, entered the doorway.

A little way down the passage was a niche in which stood three lamps ready lighted. One of these she took and gave the others to us. Then we followed her down a steep incline of many steps, till at length we found ourselves in a hot and enormous hall hewn from the living rock and filled with blackness.

"What is this place?" said Bes, who looked frightened, and although he spoke in a low whisper, our guide overheard him and turning, answered,

"This is the burial place of the Apis bulls. See, here lies the last, not yet closed in," and holding up her lamp she revealed a mighty sarcophagus of black granite set in a niche of the mausoleum.

"So they make mummies of bulls as well as of men," groaned Bes. "Oh! what a land. But when I have seen the holy Tanofir it was in a brick cell beneath the sky."

"Doubtless that was at night, O Bes," answered Karema, "for in such a house he sleeps, spending his days in the Apis tomb, because of all the evil that is worked beneath the sun."

"Hump," said Bes, "I should have thought that more was worked beneath the moon, but doubtless the holy Tanofir knows better, or being asleep does not mind."

Now in front of each of the walled-up niches was a little chapel, and at the fourth of these whence a light came, the maiden stopped, saying,

"Enter. Here dwells the holy Tanofir. He tended this god during its life-days in his youth, and now that the god is dead he prays above its bones."

"Prays to the bones of a dead bull in the dark! Well, give me a live grasshopper in the light; he is more cheerful," muttered Bes.

"O Dwarf," cried a deep and resounding voice from within the chapel, "talk no more of things you do not understand. I do not pray to the bones of a dead bull, as you in your ignorance suppose. I pray to the spirit whereof this sacred beast was but one of the fleshly symbols, which in this haunted place you will do well not to offend."

Then for once I saw Bes grow afraid, for his great jaw dropped and he trembled.

"Master," he said to me, "when next you visit tombs where maidens look into your heart and hermits hear your very thoughts, I pray you leave me behind. The holy Tanofir I love, if from afar, but I like not his house, or his——" Here he looked at Karema who was regarding him with a sweet smile over the lamp flame, and added, "There is something the matter with me, Master; I cannot even lie."

"Cease from talking follies, O Shabaka and Bes, and enter," said the tremendous voice from within.

So we entered and saw a strange sight. Against the back wall of the chapel which was lit with lamps, stood a life-sized statue of Maat, goddess of Law and Truth, fashioned of alabaster. On her head was a tall feather, her hair was covered with a wig, on her neck lay a collar of blue stones; on her arms and wrists were bracelets of gold. A tight robe draped her body. In her right hand that hung down by her side, she held the looped Cross of Life, and in her left which was advanced, a long, lotus-headed sceptre, while her painted eyes stared fixedly at the darkness. Crouched upon the ground, at the feet of the statue, scribe fashion, sat my great-uncle Tanofir, a very aged man with sightless eyes and long hands, so thin that one might see through them against the lamp-flame. His head was shaven, his beard was long and white; white too was his robe. In front of him was a low altar, on which stood a shallow silver vessel filled with pure water, and on either side of it a burning lamp.

We knelt down before him, or rather I knelt, for Bes threw himself flat upon his face.

"Am I the King of kings whom you have so lately visited, that you should prostrate yourselves before me?" said Tanofir in his great voice, which, coming from so frail and aged a man seemed most unnatural. "Or is it to the goddess of Truth beyond that you bow yourselves? If so, that is well, since one, if not both of you, greatly needs her pardon and her help. Or is it to the sleeping god beyond who holds the whole world on his horns? Or is it to the darkness of this hallowed place which causes you to remember the nearness of the awaiting tomb?"

"Nay, my Uncle," I said, "we would greet you, no more, who are so worthy of our veneration, seeing we believe, both of us, that you saved us yonder in the East, from that tomb of which you speak, or rather from the jaws of lions or a cruel death by torments."

"Perchance I did, I or the gods of which I am the instrument. At least I remember that I sent you certain messages in answer to a prayer for help that reached me, here in my darkness. For know that since we parted I have gone quite blind so that I must use this maiden's eyes to read what is written in yonder divining-cup. Well, it makes the darkness of this sepulchre easier to bear and prepares me for my own. 'Tis full a hundred and twenty years since first I looked upon the light, and now the time of sleep draws near. Come hither, my nephew, and kiss me on the brow, remembering in your strength that a day will dawn when as I am, so shall you be, if the gods spare you so long."

So I kissed him, not without fear, for the old man was unearthly. Then he sent Karema from the place and bade me tell him my story, which I did. Why he did this I cannot say, since he seemed to know it already and once or twice corrected me in certain matters that I had forgotten, for instance as to the exact words that I had used to the Great King in my rage and as to the fashion in which I was tied in the boat. When I had done, he said,

"So you gave the name of Amada to the Great King, did you? Well, you could have done nothing else if you wished to go on living, and therefore cannot be blamed. Yet before all is finished I think it will bring you into trouble, Shabaka, since among many gifts, the gods did not give that of reason to women. If so, bear it, since it is better to have trouble and be alive than to have none and be dead, that is, for those whose work is still to do in the world. And you, or rather Bes, stole the White Signet of signets of which, although it is so simple and ancient, there is not the like for power in the whole world. That was well done since it will be useful for a while. And now Peroa has determined to rebel against the King, which also is well done. Oh! trouble not to tell me of that business for I know all. But what would you learn of me, Shabaka?"

"I am instructed to learn from you the end of these great matters, my Uncle."

"Are you mad, Shabaka, that you should think me a god who can read the future?"

"Not at all, my Uncle, who know that you can if you will."

"Call the maiden," he said.

So Bes went out and brought her in.

"Be seated, Karema, there in front of the altar, and look into my eyes."

She obeyed and presently seemed to go to sleep for her head nodded. Then he said,

"Wake, woman, look into the water in the bowl upon the altar and tell me what you see."

She appeared to wake, though I perceived that this was not really so, for she seemed a different woman with a fixed face that frightened me, and wide and frozen eyes. She stared into the silver bowl, then spoke in a new voice, as though some spirit used her tongue.

"I see myself crowned a queen in a land I hate," she said coldly, a saying at which I gasped. "I am seated on a throne beside yonder dwarf," a saying at which Bes gasped. "Although so hideous, this dwarf is a great man with a good heart, a cunning mind and the courage of a lion. Also his blood is royal."

Here Bes rolled his eyes and smiled, but Tanofir did not seem in the least astonished, and said,

"Much of this is known to me and the rest can be guessed. Pass on to what will happen in Egypt, before the spirit leaves you."

"There will be war in Egypt," she answered. "I see fightings; Shabaka and others lead the Egyptians. The Easterns are driven away or slain. Peroa rules as Pharaoh, I see him on his throne. Shabaka is driven away in his turn, I see him travelling south with the dwarf and with myself, looking very sad. Time passes. I see the moons float by; I see messengers reach Shabaka, sent by Peroa and you O holy Tanofir; they tell of trouble in Egypt. I see Shabaka and the dwarf coming north at the head of a great army of black men armed with bows. With them I come rejoicing, for my heart seems to shine. He reaches a temple on the Nile about which is camped another great army, a countless army of Easterns under the command of the King of kings. Shabaka and the dwarf give battle to that army and the fray is desperate. They destroy it, they drive it into the Nile; the Nile runs red with blood. The Great King falls, an arrow from the bow of Shabaka is in his heart. He enters the temple, a conqueror, and there lies Peroa, dying or dead. A veiled priestess is there before an image, I cannot see her face. Shabaka looks on her. She stretches out her arms to him, her eyes burn with woman's love, her breast heaves, and above the image frowns and threatens. All is done, for Tanofir, Master of spirits, you die, yonder in the temple on the Nile, and therefore I can see no more. The power that comes through you, has left me."

Then once more she became as a woman asleep.

"You have heard, Shabaka and Bes," said Tanofir quietly and stroking his long white beard, "and what that maiden seemed to read in the water you may believe or disbelieve as you will."

"What do you believe, O holy Tanofir?" I asked.

"The only part of the story whereof I am sure," he replied, evading a direct answer, "is that which said that I shall die, and that when I am dead I shall no longer be able to cause the maiden Karema to see visions. For the rest I do not know. These things may happen or they may not. But," he added with a note of warning in his voice, "whether they happen or not, my counsel to you both is that you say nothing of them beforehand."

"What then shall we report to those who bid me seek the oracle of your wisdom, O Tanofir?"

"You can tell them that my wisdom declared that the omens were mixed with good and evil, but that time would show the truth. Hush now, the maiden is about to awake and must not be frightened. Also it is time for me to be led from this sepulchre to where I sleep, for I think that Ra has set and I am weary. Oh! Shabaka, why do you seek to peer into the future, which from day to day will unroll itself as does a scroll? Be content with the present, man, and take what Fate gives you of good or ill, not seeking to learn what offerings he hides beneath his robe in the days and the years and the centuries to come."

"Yet you have sought to learn those things, O Tanofir, and not in vain."

"Aye and what have they made of me? A blind old hermit weighed down with the weight of years and holding in my fingers but some few threads that with pain and grief I have plucked from the fringe of Wisdom's robe. Be warned by me, Nephew. While you are a man, live the life of a man, and when you become a spirit, live the life of a spirit. But do not seek to mix the two together like oil and wine, and thus spoil both. I am glad to learn, O Bes, that you are going to make a king's, or a slave's wife, whichever it may be, of this maiden, seeing that I love her well and hold this trade unwholesome for her. She will be better bearing babes than reading visions in a diviner's cup, and I will pray the gods that they may not be dwarfs as you are, but take on the likeness of their mother, who tells me that she is fair. Hush! she stirs.

"Karema, are you awake? Good. Then lead me from the sepulchre, that I may make my evening prayer beneath the stars. Go, Shabaka and Bes, you are brave men, both of you, and I am glad to have the one for nephew and the other for pupil. My greetings to your mother, Tiu. She is a good woman and a true, one to whom you will do well to hearken. To the lady Amada also, and bid her study her beauteous face in a mirror and not be holy overmuch, since too great holiness often thwarts itself and ends in trouble for the unholy flesh. Still she loves pearls like other women, does she not, and even the statue of Isis likes to be adorned. As for you, Bes, though I think that is not your name, do not lie except when you are obliged, for jugglers who play with too many knives are apt to cut their fingers. Also give no more evil counsel to your Master on matters that have to do with woman. Now farewell. Let me hear how fortune favours you from time to time, Shabaka, for you take part in a great game, such as I loved in my youth before I became a holy hermit. Oh! if they had listened to me, things would have been different in Egypt to-day. But it was written otherwise, and as ever, women were the scribes. Good night, good night, good night! I am glad that my thought reached you yonder in the East, and taught you what to say and do. It is well to be wise sometimes, for others' sake, but not for our own, oh! not for our own."

"MASTER," SAID BES AS WE ambled homewards beneath the stars, "the holy Tanofir is a man for thought to feed on, since having climbed to the topmost peak of holiness, he does not seem to like its cold air and warns off those who would follow in his footsteps."

"Then he might have spared himself the pains in your case, Bes, or in my own for that matter, since we shall never come so high."

"No, Master, and I am glad to have his leave to stay lower down, since that hot place of dead bulls is not one which I wish to inhabit in my age, making use of a maiden to stare into a pot of water, and there read marvels, which I could invent better for myself after a jug or two of wine. Oh! the holy Tanofir is quite right. If these things are going to happen let them happen, for we cannot change them by knowing of them beforehand. Who wishes to know, Master, if his throat will be cut?"

"Or that he will be married," I suggested.

"Just so, Master, seeing that such prophecies end in becoming truths because we make them true, feeling that we must. Thus, now I must marry yonder Karema if she will marry me for fear lest I should prove the holy Tanofir to be what he called me—a liar."

I laughed and then asked Bes if he had taken note of what the seeress said of our flight south and our return thence with a great army of black men armed with bows.

"Yes, Master," he answered gravely, "and I think this army can be none other than that of the Ethiopians of whom by right I am the King. This very night I send messengers to tell those who rule in my place that I still live and am changing my mind on the matter of marriage. Also that if I do change it I may return to them, the wisest man who ever wore the crown of Ethiopia, having journeyed all about the world and collected much knowledge."

"Perhaps, Bes, those who rule in your place may not wish to give it up to you. Perhaps they will kill you."

"Have no fear, Master; as I have told you, the Ethiopians are a faithful people. Moreover they know that such a deed would bring the curse of the Grasshopper on them, since then the locusts would appear and eat up all their land, and when they were starving their enemies would attack them. Lastly they are a very tall folk and simple-minded and would not wish to miss the chance of being ruled over by the wisest dwarf in all the world, if only because it would be something new to them, Master."

Again I laughed thinking that Bes was jesting according to his fashion. But when that night, chancing to go round the corner of the house, I came upon him with a circlet of feathers round his head and his big bow in his hand, addressing three great black men who knelt before him as though he were a god, I changed my mind. As I withdrew he caught sight of me and said,

"I pray you, my lord Shabaka, stay one moment." Then he spoke to the three men in his own language, translating sentence by sentence to me what he said to them. Briefly it was this:—

"Say to the Lords and Councillors of the Ancient Kingdom that I, the Karoon" (for such it seemed was his title) "have a friend named the lord Shabaka, he whom you see before you, who again and again has saved my life, nursing me in his arms as a mother nurses her babe, and who is, after me, the bravest and the wisest man in all the world. Say to them that if indeed I double myself by marriage and return having fulfilled the law, I will beg this mighty prince to accompany me, and that if he consents that will be the most joyful day which the Ethiopians have seen for a thousand years, since he will teach them wisdom and lead their armies in great and glorious battles. Let the priests of the Grasshopper pray therefore that he may consent to do so. Now salute the mighty lord Shabaka who can send one arrow through all three of you and two more behind, and depart, tarrying not day or night till you reach the land of Ethiopia. Then when you have delivered the message of Karoon to the Captains and the Councillors, return, or let others return and seek me out wherever I may be, bringing of the gold of Ethiopia and other gifts, together with their answer, seeing that I and the lord Shabaka who have the world beneath our feet, will not come to a land where we are not welcome."

So these great men saluted me as though I were the King of kings himself, after which they rubbed their foreheads in the dust before Bes, said something which I did not understand, leapt to their feet, crying "Karoon" and sprang away into the night.

"It is good to have been a slave, Master," said Bes when they had gone, "since it teaches one that it is even better to be a king, at least sometimes."

Here I may add that during the days which followed Bes was often absent. When I asked him where he had gone, he would answer, to drink in the wisdom of the holy Tanofir by help of a certain silver vessel that the maiden Karema held to his lips. From all of which I gathered that he was wooing the lady who had called herself the Cup of Tanofir, and wondered how the business went, though as he said no more I did not ask him.

Indeed I had little time to talk with Bes about such light matters, since things moved apace in Memphis. Within six days all the great lords left in Upper Egypt were sworn to the revolt under the leadership of Peroa, and hour by hour their vassals or hired mercenaries flowed into the city. These it was my duty to weld into an army, and at this task I toiled without cease, separating them into regiments and drilling them, also arranging for the arming and victualling of the boats of war. Then news came that Idernes was advancing from Sais with a great force of Easterns, all the garrison of Lower Egypt indeed, as his messengers said, to answer the summons conveyed to him under the private Seal of seals.

Of Amada during this time I saw little, only meeting her now and again at the table of Peroa, or elsewhere in public. For the rest it pleased her to keep away from me. Once or twice I tried to find her alone, only to discover that she was engaged in the service of the goddess. Once, too, as she left Peroa's table, I whispered into her ear that I wished to speak with her. But she shook her head, saying,

"After the new moon, Shabaka. Then you shall speak with me as much as you wish."

Thus it came about that never could I find opportunity to tell her of that matter of what had happened at the court of the Great King. Still every morning she sent me some token, flowers or trifling gifts, and once a ring that must have belonged to her forefathers, since on its bezel was engraved the royal *uræus*, together with the signs of long life and health, which ring I wore hung about my neck but not upon my finger, fearing lest that emblem of royalty might offend Peroa or some of his House, if they chanced to see it. So in answer I also sent her flowers and other gifts, and for the rest was content to wait.

All of which things my mother noted with a smile, saying that the lady Amada showed a wonderful discretion, such as any man would value in a wife of so much beauty, which also must be most pleasing to her mistress, the goddess Isis. To this I answered that I valued it less as a lover than I might do as a husband. My mother smiled again and spoke of something else.

Thus things went on while the storm-clouds gathered over Egypt.

One night I could not sleep. It was that of the new moon and I knew that during those hours of darkness, before the solemn conclave of the high priests, with pomp and ceremony in the sanctuary of the temple, Amada had undergone absolution of her vows to Isis and been given liberty to wed as other women do. Indeed my mother, in virtue of her rank as a Singer of Amen, had been present at the rite, and returning, told me all that happened.

H. RIDER HAGGARD

She described how Amada had appeared, clad as a priestess, how she had put up her prayer to the four high priests seated in state, demanding to be loosed from her vow "for the sake of her heart and of Egypt."

Then one of the high priests, he of Amen, I think, as the chief of them all, had advanced to the statue of the goddess Isis and whispered the prayer to it, whereon after a pause the goddess nodded thrice in the sight of all present, thereby signifying her assent. This done the high priest returned and proclaimed the absolution in the ancient words "for the sake of the suppliant's heart and of Egypt" and with it the blessing of the goddess on her union, adding, however, the formula, "at thy prayer, daughter and spouse, I, the goddess Isis, cut the rope that binds thee to me on earth. Yet if thou should'st tie it again, know that it may never more be severed, for if thou strivest so to do, it shall strangle thee in whatever shape thou livest on the earth throughout the generations, and with thee the man thou choosest and those who give thee to him. Thus saith Isis the Queen of Heaven."

"What does that mean?" I asked my mother.

"It means, my son, that if, having broken her vows to Isis, a woman should repeat them and once more enter the service of the goddess, and then for the second time seek to break them, she and the man for whom she did this thing would be like flies in a spider's web, and that not only in this life, but in any other that may be given to them in the world."

"It seems that Isis has a long arm," I said.

"Without doubt a very long arm, my son, since Isis, by whatever name she is called, is a power that does not die or forget."

"Well, Mother, in this case she can have no reason to remember, since never again will Amada be her priestess."

"I think not, Shabaka. Yet who can be sure of what a woman will or will not do, now or hereafter? For my part I am glad that I have served Amen and not Isis, and that after I was wed."

XII

THE SLAYING OF IDERNES

Whilst I was still talking to my mother I received an urgent summons to the palace. I went and in a little ante-chamber met Amada alone, who, I could see, was waiting there for me. She was arrayed in her secular dress and wore the insignia of royalty, looking exceedingly beautiful. Moreover, her whole aspect had changed, for now she was no longer a priestess sworn to mysteries, but just a lovely and a loving woman.

"It is done, Shabaka," she whispered, "and thou art mine and I am thine."

Then I opened my arms and she sank upon my breast and for the first time I kissed her on the lips, kissed her many times and oh! my heart almost burst with joy. But all too fleeting was that sweet moment of love's first fruits, whereon I had sown the seed so many years ago, for while we yet clung together, whispering sweet things into each other's ears, I heard a voice calling me and was forced to go away before I had even time to ask when we might be wed.

Within the Council was gathered. The news before it was that the Satrap Idernes lay camped upon the Nile with some ten thousand men, not far from the great pyramids, that is, within striking distance of Memphis. Moreover his messengers announced that he purposed to visit the Prince Peroa that day with a small guard only, to inquire into this matter of the Signet, for which visit he demanded a safe-conduct sworn in the name of the Great King and in those of the gods of Egypt and the East. Failing this he would at once attack Memphis notwithstanding any commands that might be given him under the Signet, which, until he beheld it with his own eyes, he believed to be a forgery.

The question was—what answer should be sent to him? The debate that followed proved long and earnest. Some were in favour of attacking Idernes at once although his camp was reported to be strongly entrenched and flanked on one side by the Nile and on the other by the rising ground whereon stood the great sphinx and the pyramids. Others, among whom I was numbered, thought otherwise, for I hold that some evil god led me to give counsel that day which, if it were good for Egypt was most ill for my own fortunes. Perchance this god was Isis, angry at the loss of her votary.

I pointed out that by receiving Idernes Peroa would gain time which would enable a body of three thousand men, if not more, who were advancing down the Nile, to join us before they were perhaps cut off from the city, and thus give us a force as large as his, or larger. Also I showed that having summoned Idernes under the Signet, we should put ourselves in the wrong if we refused to receive him and instead attacked him at once.

A third party was in favour of allowing him to enter Memphis with his guard and then making him prisoner or killing him. As to this I pointed out again that not only would it involve the breaking of a solemn oath, which might bring the curse of the gods upon our cause and proclaim us traitors to the world, but it would also be foolish since Idernes was not the only general of the Easterns and if we cut off him and his escort, it would avail us little for then the rest of the Easterns would fight in a just cause.

So in the end it was agreed that the safe-conduct should be sent and that Peroa should receive Idernes that very day at a great feast given in his honour. Accordingly it was sent in the ancient form, the oaths being taken before the messengers that neither he nor those with him who must not number more than twenty men, would be harmed in Memphis and that he would be guarded on the road back until he reached the outposts of his own camp.

This done, I was despatched up the Nile bank in a chariot accompanied only by Bes, to hurry on the march of those troops of which I have spoken, so that they might reach Memphis by sundown. Before I went, however, I had some words alone with Peroa. He told me that my immediate marriage with the lady Amada would be announced at the feast that night. Thereon I prayed him to deliver to Amada the rope of priceless rose-hued pearls which was in his keeping, as my betrothal gift, with the prayer that she would wear them at the feast for my sake. There was no time for more.

The journey up Nile proved long for the road was bad being covered with drifted sand in some places and deep in mud from the inundation waters in others. At length I found the troops just starting forward after their rest, and rejoiced to see that there were more of them than I had thought. I told the case to their captains, who promised to make a forced march and to be in Memphis two hours before midnight.

As we drove back Bes said to me suddenly,

"Do you know why you could not find me this morning?"

I answered that I did not.

"Because a good slave should always run a pace ahead of his master, to clear the road and tell him of its pitfalls. I was being married. The Cup of the holy Tanofir is now by law and right Queen of the Ethiopians. So when you meet her again you must treat her with great respect, as I do already."

"Indeed, Bes," I said laughing, "and how did you manage that business? You must have wooed her well during these days which have been so full for both of us."

"I did not woo her over much, Master; indeed, the time was lacking. I wooed the holy Tanofir, which was more important."

"The holy Tanofir, Bes?" I exclaimed.

"Yes, Master. You see this beautiful Cup of his is after all—his beautiful Cup. Her mind is the shadow of his mind and from her he pours out his wisdom. So I told him all the case. At first he was angry, for, notwithstanding the words he spoke to you and me, when it came to a point the holy Tanofir, being after all much like other men, did not wish to lose his Cup. Indeed had he been a few score of years younger I am not sure but that he would have forgotten some of his holiness because of her. Still he came to see matters in the true light at last—for your sake, Master, not for mine, since his wisdom told him it was needful that I should become King of the Ethiopians again, to do which I must be married. At any rate he worked upon the mind of that Cup of his—having first settled that she should procure a younger sister of her own to fill her place—in such fashion that when at length I spoke to her on the matter, she did not say no."

"No doubt because she was fond of you for yourself, Bes. A woman would not marry even to please the holy Tanofir."

"Oh! Master," he replied in a new voice, a very sad voice, "I would that I could think so. But look at me, a misshapen dwarf, accursed from birth. Could a fair lady like this Karema wed such a one for his own sake?"

"Well, Bes, there might be other reasons besides the holy Tanofir," I said hurriedly.

"Master, there were no other reasons, unless the Cup, when it is awake, remembers what it has held in trance, which I do not believe. I wooed her as I was, not telling her that I am also King of the Ethiopians, or any more than I seem to be. Moreover the holy Tanofir told her nothing, for he swore as much to me and he does not lie."

"And what did she say to you, Bes?" I asked, for I was curious.

"She lied fast enough, Master. She said—well, what she said when first we met her, that there was more in me than the eye saw and that she who had lived so much with spirits looked to the spirit rather than to the flesh, and that dwarf or no she loved me and desired nothing better than to marry me and be my true and faithful wife and helpmeet. She lied so well that once or twice almost I believed her. At any rate I took her at her word, not altogether for myself, believe me, Master, but because without doubt what the holy Tanofir has shown us will come to pass, and it is necessary to you that I should be married."

"You married her to help me, Bes?"

"That is so, Master—after all, but a little thing, seeing that she is beautiful, well born and very pleasant, and I am fond of her. Also I do her no wrong for she has bought more than she bargained for, and if she has any that are not dwarfs, her children may be kings. I do not think," he added reflectively, "that even the faithful Ethiopians could accept a second dwarf as their king. One is very well for a change, but not two or three. The stomach of a tall people would turn against them."

I took Bes's hand and pressed it, understanding the depth of his love and sacrifice. Also some spirit—doubtless it came from the holy Tanofir—moved me to say,

"Be comforted, Bes, for I am sure of this. Your children will be strong and straight and tall, more so than any of their forefathers that went before them."

This indeed proved to be the case, for their father's deformity was but an accident, not born in his blood.

"Those are good-omened words, Master, for which I thank you, though the holy Tanofir said the like when he wed us with the sacred words this morning and gave us his blessing, endowing my wife with certain gifts of secret wisdom which he said would be of use to her and me."

"Where is she now, Bes?"

"With the holy Tanofir, Master, until I fetch her, training her younger sister to be a diviner's worthy Cup. Only perhaps I shall never send, seeing that I think there will be fighting soon."

"Yes, Bes, but being newly married you will do well to leave it to others."

"No, no, Master. Battle is better than wives. Moreover, could you think that I would leave you to stand alone in the fray? Why if I did and harm came to you I should die of shame or hang myself and then Karema would never be a queen. So both her trades would be gone, since after marriage she cannot be a Cup, and her heart would break. But here are the gates of Memphis, so we will forget love and think of war."

An hour later I and my mother, the lady Tiu, stood in the banqueting hall of the palace with many others, and learned that the Satrap Idernes and his escort had reached Memphis and would be present at the feast. A while later trumpets blew and a glittering procession entered the hall. At the head of it was Peroa who led Idernes by the hand. This Eastern was a big, strong man with tired and anxious eyes, such as I had noted were common among the servants of the Great King who from day to day never knew whether they would fill a Satrapy or a grave. He was clad in gorgeous silks and wore a cap upon his head in which shone a jewel, but beneath his robes I caught the glint of mail.

As he came into the hall and noted the number and quality of the guests and the stir and the expectant look upon their faces, he started as though he were afraid, but recovering himself, murmured some courteous words to his host and advanced towards the seat of honour which was pointed out to him upon the Prince's right. After these two followed the wife of Peroa with her son and daughters. Then, walking alone in token of her high rank, appeared Amada, the Royal Lady of Egypt, wonderfully arrayed. Now, however, she wore no emblems of royalty, either because it was not thought wise that these should be shown in the presence of the Satrap, or because she was about to be given in marriage to one who was not royal. Indeed, as I noted with joy, her only ornament was the rope of rose-hued pearls which were arranged in a double row upon her breast.

She searched me out with her eyes, smiled, touching the pearls with her finger, and passed on to her place next to the daughters of Peroa, at one end of the head table which was shaped like a horse's hoof.

After her came the nobles who had accompanied Idernes, grave Eastern men. One of these, a tall captain with eyes like a hawk, seemed familiar to me. Nor was I mistaken, for Bes, who stood behind me and whose business it would be to wait on me at the feast, whispered in my ear,

"Note that man. He was present when you were brought before the Great King from the boat and saw and heard all that passed."

"Then I wish he were absent now," I whispered back, for at the words a sudden fear shot through me, of what I could not say.

By degrees all were seated in their appointed places. Mine was by that of my mother at a long table that stood as it were across the ends of the high table but at a little distance from them, so that I was almost opposite to Peroa and Idernes and could see Amada, although she was too far away for me to be able to speak to her.

The feast began and at first was somewhat heavy and silent, since, save for the talk of courtesy, none spoke much. At length wine, whereof I noted that Idernes drank a good deal, as did his escort, but Peroa and the Egyptians little, loosened men's tongues and they grew merrier. For it was the custom of the people of the Great King to discuss both private and public business when full of strong drink, but of the Egyptians when they were quite sober. This was well known to Peroa and many of us, especially to myself who had been among them, which was one of the reasons why Idernes had been asked to meet us at a feast, where we might have the advantage of him in debate.

Presently the Satrap noted the splendid cup from which he drank and asked some question concerning it of the hawk-eyed noble of whom I have spoken. When it had been answered he said in a voice loud enough for me to overhear,

"Tell me, O Prince Peroa, was this cup ever that of the Great King which it so much resembles?"

"So I understand, O Idernes," answered Peroa. "That is, until it became mine by gift from the lord Shabaka, who received it from the Great King."

An expression of horror appeared upon the face of the Satrap and upon those of his nobles.

"Surely," he answered, "this Shabaka must hold the King's favours lightly if he passes them on thus to the first-comer. At the least, let not the vessel which has been hallowed by the lips of the King of kings be dishonoured by the humblest of his servants. I pray you, O Prince, that I may be given another cup."

So a new goblet was brought to him, Peroa trying to pass the matter off as a jest by appealing to me to tell the story of the cup. Then I said while all listened,

"O Prince, the most high Satrap is mistaken. The King of kings did not give me the cup, I bought it from him in exchange for a certain famous bow, and therefore held it not wrong to pass it on to you, my lord."

Idernes made no answer and seemed to forget the matter.

A while later, however, his eye fell upon Amada and the rose-hued pearls she wore, and again he asked a question of the hawk-eyed captain, then said,

"Think me not discourteous, O Prince, if I seem to look upon yonder lovely lady which in our country, where women do not appear in public, we should think it an insult to do. But on her fair breast I see certain pearls like to some that are known throughout the world, which for many years have been worn by those who sit upon the throne of the East. I would ask if they are the same, or others?"

"I do not know, O Idernes," answered Peroa; "I only know that the lord Shabaka brought them from the East. Inquire of him, if it be your pleasure."

"Shabaka again——" began Idernes, but I cut him short, saying,

"Yes, O Satrap, Shabaka again. I won those pearls in a bet from the Great King, and with them a certain weight of gold. This I think you knew before, since your messenger of a while ago was whipped for trying to steal them, which under the rods he said he did by command, O Satrap."

To this bold speech Idernes made no answer. Only his captains frowned and many of the Egyptians murmured approval.

After this the feast went on without further incident for a while, the Easterns always drinking more wine, till at length the tables were cleared and all of the meaner sort departed from the hall, save the butlers and the personal servants such as Bes, who stood behind the seats of their masters. There came a silence such as precedes the bursting of a storm, and in the midst of it Idernes spoke, somewhat thickly.

"I did not come here, O Peroa," he said, "from the seat of government at Sais to eat your meats and drink your wine. I came to speak of high matters with you."

"It is so, O Satrap," answered Peroa. "And now what may be your will? Would you retire to discuss them with me and my Councillors?"

"Where is the need, O Peroa, seeing that I have naught to say which may not be heard by all?"

"As it pleases you. Speak on, O Satrap."

"I have been summoned here, Prince Peroa, by a writing under what seems to be the Signet of signets—the ancient White Seal that for generations unknown has been worn by the forefathers of the King of kings. Where is this Signet?"

"Here," said the Prince, opening his robe. "Look on it, Satrap, and let your lords look, but let none of you dare to touch it."

Idernes looked long and earnestly, and so did some of his people, especially the lord with the hawk eyes. Then they stared at each other bewildered and whispered together.

"It seems to be the very Seal—the White Seal itself!" exclaimed Idernes at length. "Tell me now, Peroa. How came this sacred thing that dwells in the East hither into Egypt?"

"The lord Shabaka brought it to me with certain letters from the Great King, O Satrap."

"Shabaka for the third time, by the holy Fire!" cried Idernes. "He brought the cup; he brought the famous pearls; he brought the gold, and he brought the Signet of signets. What is there then that he did not bring? Perchance he has the person of the King of kings himself in his keeping!"

"Not that, O Satrap, only the commands of the King of kings which are prepared ready to deliver to you under the White Seal that you acknowledge."

"And what may they be, Egyptian?"

"This, O Satrap: That you and all the army which you have brought with you retire to Sais and thence out of Egypt as quickly as you may, or pay for disobedience with your lives."

Now Idernes and his captains gasped.

"Why this is rebellion!" he said.

"No, O Satrap, only the command of the Great King given under the White Seal," and drawing a roll from his breast, Peroa laid it on his brow and cast it down before Idernes, adding,

"Obey the writing and the Signet, or by virtue of my commission, as soon as you are returned to your army and your safe-conduct is expired, I fall upon you and destroy you."

Idernes looked about him like a wolf in a trap, then asked,

"Do you mean to murder me here?"

"Not so," answered Peroa, "for you have our safe-conduct and Egyptians are honourable men. But you are dismissed your office and ordered to leave Egypt."

Idernes thought a little while, then said,

"If I leave Egypt, there is at least one whom I am commanded to take with me under orders and writings that you will not dispute, a maiden named Amada whom the Great King would number among his women. I am told it is she who sits yonder—a jewel indeed, fair as the pearls upon her breast which thus will return into the King's keeping. Let her be handed over, for she rides with me at once."

Now in the midst of an intense silence Peroa answered,

"Amada, the Royal Lady of Egypt, cannot be sent to dwell in the House of Women of the Great King without the consent of the lord Shabaka, whose she is."

"Shabaka for the fourth time!" said Idernes, glaring at me. "Then let Shabaka come too. Or his head in a basket will suffice, since that will save trouble afterwards, also some pain to Shabaka. Why, now I remember. It was this very Shabaka whom the Great King condemned to death by the boat for a crime against his Majesty, and who bought his life by promising to deliver to him the fairest and most learned woman in the world—the lady Amada of Egypt. And thus does the knave keep his oath!"

Now I leapt to my feet, as did most of those present. Only Amada kept her seat and looked at me.

"You lie!" I cried, "and were it not for your safe-conduct I would kill you for the lie."

"I lie, do I?" sneered Idernes. "Speak then, you who were present, and tell this noble company whether I lie," and he pointed to the hawk-eyed lord.

"He does not lie," said the Captain. "I was in the Court of the Great King and heard yonder Shabaka purchase pardon by promising to hand over his cousin, the lady Amada, to the King. The pearls were entrusted to him as a gift to her and I see she wears them. The gold also of which mention has been made was to provide for her journey in state to the East, or so I heard. The cup was his guerdon, also a sum for his own purse."

"It is false," I shouted. "The name of Amada slipped my lips by chance—no more."

"So it slipped your lips by chance, did it?" sneered Idernes. "Now, if you are wise, you will suffer the lady Amada to slip your hand, and not by chance. But let us have done with this cunning knave. Prince, will you hand over yonder fair woman, or will you not?"

"Satrap, I will not," answered Peroa. "The demand is an insult put forward to force us to rebellion, since there is no man in Egypt who will not be ready to die in defence of the Royal Lady of Egypt."

This statement was received with a shout of applause by every Egyptian in the hall. Idernes waited until it had died away, then said,

"Prince Peroa and Egyptians, you have conveyed to me certain commands sealed with the Signet of signets, which I think was stolen by yonder Shabaka. Now hearken; until this matter is made clear I will obey those commands thus far. I will return with my army to Sais and there wait until I have received the orders of the Great King, after report made to him. If so much as an arrow is shot at us on our march, it will be open rebellion, as the price of which Egypt shall be crushed as she was never crushed before, and every one of you here present shall lose his head, save only the lady Amada who is the property of the Great King. Now I thank you for your hospitality and demand that you escort me and those with me back to my camp, since it seems that here we are in the midst of enemies."

"Before you go, Idernes," I shouted, "know that you and your lying captain shall pay with your lives for your slander on me."

"Many will pay with their lives for this night's work, O thief of pearls and seals," answered the Satrap, and turning, left the hall with his company.

Now I searched for Amada, but she also had gone with the ladies of Peroa's household who feared lest the feast should end in blows and bloodshed, also lest she should be snatched away. Indeed of all the women in the hall, only my mother remained.

"Search out the lady Amada," I said to her, "and tell her the truth."

"Yes, my son," she answered thoughtfully; "but what is the truth? I understood it was Bes who first gave the name of the lady Amada to the Great King. Now we learn from your own lips that it was you. Wise would you have been, my son, if you had bitten out your tongue before you said it, since this is a matter that any woman may well misunderstand."

"Her name was surprised out of me, Mother. It was Bes who spoke to the King of the beauty of a certain lady of Egypt."

"And I think, my son, it was Bes who told Peroa and his guests that he and not you had given the King her name, which you do not seem to have denied. Well, doubtless both of you are to blame for foolishness, no more, since well I know that you would have died ten times over rather than buy your life at the price of the honour of the Lady of Egypt. This I will say to her as soon as I may, praying that it may not be too late, and afterwards you shall tell me everything, which you would have done well to do at first, if Bes, as I think, had not been over cunning after the fashion of black people, and counselled you otherwise. See, Peroa calls you and I must go, for there are greater matters afoot than that of who let slip the name of the lady Amada to the King of kings."

So she went and there followed a swift council of war, the question being whether we were to strike at the Satrap's army or to allow it to retreat to Sais. In my turn I was asked for my judgment of the issue, and answered,

"Strike and at once, since we cannot hope to storm Sais, which is far away. Moreover such strength as we have is now gathered and if it is idle and perhaps unpaid, will disperse again. But if we can destroy Idernes and his army, it will be long before the King of kings, who is sending all his multitudes against the Greeks, can gather another, and during this time Egypt may again become a nation and able to protect herself under Peroa her own Pharaoh."

In the end I, and those who thought like me, prevailed, so that before the dawn I was sailing down the Nile with the fleet, having two thousand men under my command. Also I took with me the six hunters whom I had won from the Great King, since I knew them to be faithful, and thought that their knowledge of the Easterns and their ways might be of service. Our orders were to hold a certain neck of land between the river and the hills where the army of Idernes must pass, until Peroa and all his strength could attack him from behind.

Four hours later, the wind being very favourable to us, we reached that place and there took up our station and having made all as ready as we could, rested.

In the early afternoon Bes awakened me from the heavy sleep into which I had fallen, and pointed to the south. I looked and through the desert haze saw the chariots of Idernes advancing in ordered ranks, and after them the masses of his footmen.

Now we had no chariots, only archers, and two regiments armed with long spears and swords. Also the sailors on the boats had their slings and throwing javelins. Lastly the ground was in our favour since it sloped upwards and the space between the river and the hills was narrow, somewhat boggy too after the inundation of the Nile, which meant that the chariots must advance in a column and could not gather sufficient speed to sweep over us.

Idernes and his captains noted all this also, and halted. Then they sent a herald forward to ask who we were and to command us in the name of the Great King to make way for the army of the Great King.

I answered that we were Egyptians, ordered by Peroa to hold the road against the Satrap who had done affront to Egypt by demanding that its Royal Lady should be given over to him to be sent to the East as a woman-slave, and that if the Satrap wished to clear a road, he could come and do so. Or if it pleased him he could go back towards Memphis, or stay where he was, since we did not wish to strike the first blow. I added this,

"I who speak on behalf of the Prince Peroa, am the lord Shabaka, that same man whom but last night the Satrap and a certain captain of his named a liar. Now the Easterns are brave men and we of Egypt have always heard that among them none is braver than Idernes who gained his advancement through courage and skill in war. Let him therefore come out together with the lord who named me a liar, armed with swords only, and I, who being a liar must also be a coward, together with my servant, a black dwarf, will meet them man to man in the sight of both the armies, and fight them to the death. Or if it pleases Idernes better, let him not come and I will seek him and kill him in the battle, or by him be killed."

The herald, having taken stock of me and of Bes at whom he laughed, returned with the message.

"Will he come, think you, Master?" asked Bes.

"Mayhap," I answered, "since it is a shame for an Eastern to refuse a challenge from any man whom he calls barbarian, and if he did so it might cost him his life afterwards at the hands of the Great King. Also if he should fall there are others to take his command, but none who can wipe away the stain upon his honour."

"Yes," said Bes; "also they will think me a dwarf of no account, which makes the task of killing you easy. Well, they shall see."

Now when I sent this challenge I had more in my mind than a desire to avenge myself upon Idernes and his captain for the public shame they had put upon me. I wished to delay the attack of their host upon our little band and give time for the army of Peroa to come up behind. Moreover, if I fell it did not greatly matter, except as an omen, seeing that I had good officers under me who knew all my plans.

We saw the herald reach the Satrap's army and after a while return towards us again, which made us think my challenge had been refused, especially as with him was an officer who, I took it, was sent to spy out our strength. But this was not so, for the man said,

"The Satrap Idernes has sworn by the Great King to kill the thief of the Signet and send his head to the Great King, and fears that if he waits to meet him in battle, he may slip away. Therefore he is minded to accept your challenge, O Shabaka, and put an end to you, and indeed under the laws of the East he may not refuse. But a noble of the Great King may not fight against a black slave save with a whip, so how can that noble accept the challenge of the dwarf Bes?"

"Quite well," answered Bes, "seeing that I am no slave but a free citizen of Egypt. Moreover, in my own country of Ethiopia I am of royal blood. Lastly, tell the man this, that if he does not come and afterwards falls into my hands or into those of the lord Shabaka, he who talks of whips shall be scourged with them till his life creeps out from between his bare bones."

Thus spoke Bes, rolling his great eyes and looking so terrible that the herald and the officer fell back a step or two. Then I told them that if my offer did not please them, I myself would fight, first Idernes and then the noble. So they returned.

The end of it was that we saw Idernes and his captain advancing, followed by a guard of ten men. Then after I had explained all things to my officers, I also advanced with Bes, followed by a guard of ten picked men. We met between the armies on a little sandy plain at the foot of the rise and there followed talk between the captains of our guards as to arms and so forth, but we four said nothing to each other, since the time for words was past. Only Bes and I sat down upon the sand and spoke a little together of Amada and Karema and of how they would receive the news of our victory or deaths.

"It does not much matter, Master," said Bes at last, "seeing that if we die we shall never know, and if we live we shall learn for ourselves."

At length all was arranged and we stood up to face each other, the four of us being armed in the same way. For as did Idernes and the hawk-eyed lord, Bes and I wore shirts of mail and helms, those that we had brought with us from the East. For weapons we had short and heavy swords, small shields and knives at our girdles.

"Look your last upon the sun, Thieves," mocked Idernes, "for when you see it again, it shall be with blind eyes from the points of spears fastened to the gateway pillars of the Great King's palace."

"Liars you have lived and liars you shall die," shouted Bes, but I said nothing.

Now the agreement was that when the word had been given Idernes and I, and the noble and Bes, should fight together, but if they killed one of us, or we killed one of them, the two who survived might fall together on the remaining man. Remembering this, as he told me afterwards, at the signal Bes leapt forward like a flash with working face and foam upon his lips, and before ever I could come to Idernes, how I know not, had received the blow of the Eastern lord upon his shield and without striking back, had gripped him in his long arms and wrapped him round with his bowed legs. In an instant they were on the ground, Bes uppermost, and I heard the sound of blow upon blow struck with knife or sword, I knew not which, upon the Eastern's mail, followed by a shout of victory from the Egyptians which told me that Bes had slain him.

Now Idernes and I were smiting at each other. He was a taller and a bigger man than myself, but older and one who had lived too well. Therefore I thought it wise to keep him at a distance and tire him, which I did by retreating and catching his sword-cuts on my shield, only smiting back now and again.

"He runs! He runs!" shouted the Easterns. "O Idernes, beware the dwarf!"

"Stand away, Bes," I called; "this is my game," and he obeyed, as often he had done when we were hunting together.

Now a shrewd blow from Idernes cut through my helm and staggered me, and another before I could recover myself, shore the shield from my hand, whereat the Easterns shouted more loudly than before. Then fear of defeat entered into me and made me mad, for this Satrap was a great fighter. With a shout of "Egypt!" I went at him like a wounded lion and soon it was his turn to stagger back. But alas! I struck too hard, for my sword snapped upon his mail.

"The knife!" screamed Bes; "the knife!"

I hurled the sword hilt in the Satrap's face and drew the dagger from my belt. Then I ran in beneath his guard and stabbed and stabbed and stabbed. He gripped me and we went down side by side, rolling over each other. The gods know how it ended, for things were growing dim to me when some thrust of mine found a rent in his mail made when the sword broke and he became weak. His spirit weakened also, for he gasped,

"Spare my life, Egyptian, and my treasure is yours. I swear it by the Fire."

"Not for all the treasure in the world, Slanderer," I panted back and drove the dagger home to the hilt thrice, until he died. Then I staggered to my feet, and when the armies saw that it was I who rose while Idernes lay still a roar of triumph went up from the Egyptians, answered by a roar of rage from the Easterns.

With a cry of "Well done, Master!" Bes leapt upon the dead man and hewed his head from him, as already he had served the hawk-eyed noble. Then gripping one head in each hand he held them up for the Easterns to see.

"Men of the Great King," I said, "bear us witness that we have fought fairly, man to man, when we need not have done so."

The ten of the Satrap's guard stood silent, but my own shouted,

"Back, Shabaka! The Easterns charge!"

I looked and saw them coming like waves of steel, then supported by my men and preceded by Bes who danced in front shaking the severed heads, I ran back to my own ranks where one gave me wine to drink and threw water over my hurts which were but slight. Scarcely was it done when the battle closed in and soon in it I forgot the deaths of Idernes and the Eastern liar.

XIII

AMADA RETURNS TO ISIS

We fought a very terrible fight that evening there by the banks of Nile. Our position was good, but we were outnumbered by four or five to one, and the Easterns and their mercenaries were mad at the death of the Satrap by my hand. Time upon time they came on furiously, charging up the slope like wild bulls. For the most part we relied upon our archers to drive them back, since our half-trained troops could scarcely hope to stand against the onset of veterans disciplined in war. So taking cover behind the rocks we rained arrows on them, shooting the horses in the chariots, and when these were down, pouring our shafts upon the footmen behind. Myself I took my great black bow and drew it thrice, and each time I saw a noble fall, for no mail could withstand the arrows which it sent, and of that art I was a master. None in Egypt could shoot so far or so straight as I did, save perhaps Peroa himself. I had no time to do more since always I must be moving up and down the line encouraging my men.

Three times we drove them back, after which they grew cunning. Ceasing from a direct onslaught and keeping what remained of their chariots in reserve, they sent one body of men to climb along the slope of the hill where the rocks gave them cover from our arrows, and another to creep through the reeds and growing crops upon the bank of the river where we could not see to shoot them well, although the slingers in the ships did them some damage.

Thus they attacked us on either flank, and while we were thus engaged their centre made a charge. Then came the bitterest of the fighting for now the bows were useless, and it was sword against sword and spear against spear. Once we broke and I thought that they were through. But I led a charge against them and drove them back a little way. Still the issue was doubtful till I saw Bes rush past me grinning and leaping, and with him a small body of Greeks whom we held in reserve, and I think that the sight of the terrible dwarf whom they thought a devil, frightened the Easterns more than did the Greeks.

At any rate, shouting out something about an evil spirit whom the Egyptians worshipped, by which I suppose they meant that god after whom Bes was named, they retreated, leaving many dead but taking their wounded with them, for they were unbroken.

At the foot of the slope they reformed and took counsel, then sat down out of bowshot as though to rest. Now I guessed their plan. It was to wait till night closed in, which would be soon for the sun was sinking, and then, when we could not see to shoot, either rush through us by the weight of numbers, or march back to where the cliffs were lower and climb them, thus passing us on the higher open land.

Now we also took counsel, though little came of it, since we did not know what to do. We were too few to attack so great an army, nor if we climbed the cliffs could we hope to withstand them in the desert sands, or to hold our own against them if they charged in the dark. If this happened it seemed that all we could do would be to fight as long as we could, after which the survivors of us must take refuge on our boats. So it came to this, that we should lose the battle and the greater part of the Easterns would win back to Sais, unless indeed the main army under Peroa came to our aid.

Whilst we talked I caused the wounded to be carried to the ships before it grew too dark to move them. Bes went with them. Presently he returned, running swiftly.

"Master," he said, "the evening wind is blowing strong and stirs the sand, but from a mast-head through it I caught sight of Peroa's banners. The army comes round the bend of the river not four furlongs away. Now charge and those Easterns will be caught between the hammer and the stone, for while they are meeting us they will not look behind."

So I went down the lines of our little force telling them the good news and showing them my plan. They listened and understood. We formed up, those who were left of us, not more than a thousand men perhaps, and advanced. The Easterns laughed when they saw us coming down the slope, for they thought that we were mad and that they would kill us every one, believing as they did that Peroa had no other army. When we were within bowshot we began to shoot, though sparingly, for but few arrows were left. Galled by our archery they marshalled their ranks to charge us again. With a shout we leapt forward to meet them, for now from the higher ground I saw the chariots of Peroa rushing to our rescue.

We met, we fought. Surely there had been no such fighting since the days of Thotmes and Rameses the Great. Still they drove us back till unseen and unsuspected the chariots and the footmen of Peroa broke on them from behind, broke on them like a desert storm. They gave, they fled this way and that, some to the banks of the Nile, some to the hills. By the light of the setting sun we finished it and ere the darkness closed in the Great King's army was destroyed, save for the fugitives whom we hunted down next day.

Yes, in that battle perished ten thousand of the Easterns and their mercenaries, and upon its field at dawn we crowned Peroa Pharaoh of Egypt, and he named me the chief general of his army. There, too, fell over a thousand of my men and among them those six hunters whom I had won in the wager with the Great King and brought with me from the East. Throughout the fray they served me as a bodyguard, fighting furiously, who knew that they could hope for no mercy from their own people. One by one they were slain, the last two of them in the charge at sunset. Well, they were brave and faithful to me, so peace be on their spirits. Better to die thus than in the den of lions.

In triumph we returned to Memphis, I bringing in the rearguard and the spoils. Before Pharaoh and I parted a messenger brought me more good news. Sure tidings had come that the King of kings had been driven by revolt in his dominions to embark upon a mighty war with Syria, Greece and Cyprus and other half-conquered countries, in which, doubtless by agreement, the fires of insurrection had suddenly burned up. Also already Peroa's messengers had departed to tell them of what was passing on the Nile.

"If this be true," said Peroa when he had heard all, "the Great King will have no new army to spare for Egypt."

"It is so, Pharaoh," I answered. "Yet I think he will conquer in this great war and that within two years you must be prepared to meet him face to face."

"Two years are long, Shabaka, and in them, by your help, much may be done."

But as it chanced he was destined to be robbed of that help, and this by the work of Woman the destroyer.

It happened thus. Amidst great rejoicings Pharaoh reached Memphis and in the vast temple of Amen laid down our spoils in the presence of the god, thousands of right hands hewn from the fallen, thousands of swords and other weapons and tens of chariots, together with much treasure of which a portion was given to the god. The high priests blessed us in the name of Amen and of the other gods; the people blessed us and threw flowers in our path; all the land rejoiced because once more it was free.

There too that day in the temple with ancient form and ceremonial Peroa was crowned Pharaoh of Egypt. Sceptres and jewels that had been hid for generations were brought out by those who knew the secret of their hiding-places; the crowns that had been worn by old Pharaohs, were set upon his head; yes, the double crown of the Upper and the Lower Land. Thus in a Memphis mad with joy at the casting off of the foreign yoke, he was anointed the first of a new dynasty, and with him his queen.

I too received honours, for the story of the slaying of Idernes at my hands and of how I held the pass had gone abroad, so that next to Pharaoh, I was looked upon as the greatest man in Egypt. Nor was Bes forgotten, since many of the common people thought that he was a spirit in the form of a dwarf whom the gods had sent to aid us with his strength and cunning. Indeed at the close of the ceremony voices cried out in the multitude of watchers, demanding that I who was to marry the Royal Lady of Egypt should be named next in succession to the throne.

The Pharaoh heard and glanced first at his son and then at me, doubtfully, whereon, covered with confusion, I slipped away.

The portico of the temple was deserted, since all, even the guards, had crowded into the vast court to watch the coronation. Only in the shadow, seated against the pedestal of one of the two colossal statues in front of the outer pylon gate and looking very small beneath its greatness, was a man wrapped in a dark cloak whom noting vaguely I took to be a beggar. As I passed him, he plucked at my robe, and I stopped to search for something to give to him but could find naught.

"I have nothing, Father," I said laughing, "except the gold hilt of my sword."

"Do not part with that, Son," answered a deep voice, "for I think you will need it before all is over."

Then while I stared at him he threw back his hood and I saw that beneath was the ancient withered face and the long white beard of my great-uncle, the holy Tanofir, the hermit and magician.

"Great things happen yonder, Shabaka. So great that I have come from my sepulchre to see, or rather, being blind, to listen, who thrice in my life days have known the like before," and he pointed to the glittering throng in the court within. "Yes," he went on, "I have seen

H. RIDER HAGGARD

Pharaohs crowned and Pharaohs die—one of them at the hand of a conqueror. What will happen to this Pharaoh, think you, Shabaka?"

"You should be better able to answer that question than I, who am no prophet, my Uncle."

"How, my Nephew, seeing that your dwarf has borne away my magic Cup? I do not grudge her to him for he is a brave dwarf and clever, who may yet prove a good prop to you, as he has done before, and to Egypt also. But she has gone and the new vessel is not yet shaped to my liking. So how can I answer?"

"Out of the store of wisdom gathered in your breast."

"So! my Nephew. Well, my store of wisdom tells me that feasts are sometimes followed by want and rejoicings by sorrow and victories by defeat, and splendid sins by repentance and slow climbing back to good again. Also that you will soon take a long journey. Where is the Royal Lady Amada? I did not hear her step among those who passed in to the Crowning. But even my hearing has grown somewhat weak of late, except in the silence of the night, Shabaka."

"I do not know, my Uncle, who have only been in Memphis one hour. But what do you mean? Doubtless she prepares herself for the feast where I shall meet her."

"Doubtless. Tell me, what passes at the temple of Isis? As I crept past the pylon feeling my way with my beggar's staff, I thought—but how can you know who have only been in Memphis an hour? Yet surely I heard voices just now calling out that you, Shabaka, should be named as the next successor to the throne of Egypt. Was it so?"

"Yes, holy Tanofir. That is why I have left who was vexed and am sworn to seek no such honour, which indeed I do not desire."

"Just so, Nephew. Yet gifts have a way of coming to those who do not desire them and the last vision that I saw before my Cup left me, or rather that she saw, was of you wearing the Double Crown. She said that you looked very well in it, Shabaka. But now begone, for hark, here comes the procession with the new-anointed Pharaoh whose royal robe you won for him yonder in the pass, when you smote down Idernes and held his legions. Oh! it was well done and my new Cup, though faulty, was good enough to show me all. I felt proud of you, Shabaka, but begone, begone! 'A gift for the poor old beggar! A gift, my lords, for the poor blind beggar who has had none since the last Pharaoh was crowned in Egypt and finds it hard to live on memories!'"

AT OUR HOUSE I FOUND my mother just returned from the Coronation, but Bes I did not find and guessed that he had slipped away to meet his new-made wife, Karema. My mother embraced me and blessed me, making much of me and my deeds in the battle; also she doctored such small hurts as I had. I put the matter by as shortly as I could and asked her if she had seen aught of Amada. She answered that she had neither seen nor heard of her which I was sure she thought strange, as she began to talk quickly of other things. I said to her what I had said to the holy Tanofir, that doubtless she was making ready for the feast since I could not find her at the Crowning.

"Or saying good-bye to the goddess," answered my mother nodding, "since there are some who find it even harder to fall from heaven to earth than to climb from earth to heaven, and after all you are but a man, my son."

Then she slipped away to attire herself, leaving me wondering, because my mother was shrewd and never spoke at random.

There was the holy Tanofir, too, with his talk about the temple of Isis, and he also did not speak at random. Oh! now I felt as I had done when the shadow of the palm-tree fell on me yonder in the palace garden.

The mood passed for my blood still tingled with the glory of that great fight, and my heart shut its doors to sadness, knowing as I did, that I was the most praised man in Memphis that day. Indeed had I not, I should have learned it when with my mother I entered the great banqueting-hall of the palace somewhat late, for she was long in making ready.

The first thing I saw there was Bes gorgeously arrayed in Eastern silks that he had plundered from the Satrap's tent, standing on a table so that all might see and hear him, and holding aloft in one hand the grisly head of Idernes and in the other that of the hawk-eyed noble whom he had slain, while in his thick, guttural voice he told the tale of that great fray. Catching sight of me, he called aloud,

"See! Here comes the man! Here comes the hero to whom Egypt owes its liberty and Pharaoh his crown."

Thereon all the company and the soldiers and servants who were gathered about the door began to shout and acclaim me, till I wished that I could vanish away as the holy Tanofir was said to be able to do. Since this was impossible I rushed at Bes who leapt from the table like a monkey and, still waving the heads and talking, slipped from the hall, I know not how, followed by the loud laughter of the guests.

Then heralds announced the coming of Pharaoh and all grew silent. He and his company entered with pomp and we, his subjects, prostrated ourselves in the ancient fashion.

"Rise, my guests," he cried. "Rise, my people. Above all do you rise, Shabaka, my beloved cousin, to whom Egypt and I owe so much."

So we rose and I took my seat in a place of honour having my mother at my side, and looked about me for Amada, but in vain. There was the carven chair upon which she should have been among those of the princesses, but it was empty. At first I thought that she was late, but when time went by and she did not appear, I asked if she were ill, a question that none seemed able to answer.

The feast went on with all the ancient ceremonies that attended the crowning of a Pharaoh of Egypt, since there were old men who remembered these, also the scribes and priests had them written in their books.

I took no heed of them and will not set them down. At length Pharaoh pledged his subjects, and his subjects pledged Pharaoh. Then the doors were opened and through them came a company of white-robed, shaven priests bearing on a bier the body of a dead man wrapped in his mummy-cloths. At first some laughed for this rite had not been performed in Egypt since she passed into the hands of the Great Kings of the East and therefore was strange to them. Then they grew silent since after all it was solemn to see those death-bearing priests flitting in and out between the great columns, now seen and now lost in the shadows, and to listen to their funeral chants.

In the hush my mother whispered to me that this body was that of the last Pharaoh of Egypt brought from his tomb, but whether this were so I cannot say for certain. At length they brought the mummy which was crowned with a snake-headed circlet of the royal *uræus* and still draped with withered funeral wreaths, and stood it on its feet opposite to Peroa just behind and between my mother and me in such a fashion that it cut off the light from us.

The faint and heavy smell of the embalmer's spices struck upon my nostrils, a dead flower from the chaplets fell upon my head and, glancing over my shoulder, I saw the painted or enamelled eyes in the gilded mask staring at me. The thing filled me with fear, I knew not of what. Not of death, surely, for that I had faced a score of times of late and thought nothing of it. Indeed I am not sure that it was fear I felt, but rather a deep sense of the vanity of all things. It seemed to come home to me—Shabaka or Allan Quatermain, for in my dream the inspiration or whatever it might be, struck through the spirit that animated both of us—as it had never done before, that everything is *nothing*, that victory and love and even life itself have no meaning; that naught really exists save the soul of man and God, of whom perchance that soul is a part sent forth for a while to do His work through good and ill. The thought lifted me up and yet crushed me, since for a moment all that makes a man passed away, and I felt myself standing in utter loneliness, naked before the glory of God, watched only by the flaming stars that light his throne. Yes, and at that moment suddenly I learned that all the gods are but one God, having many shapes and called by many names.

Then I heard the priests saying,

"Pharaoh the Osiris greets Pharaoh the living on the Earth and sends to him this message—'As I am, so shalt thou be, and where I am, there thou shalt dwell through all the ages of Eternity.'"

Then Pharaoh the living rose and bowed to Pharaoh the dead and Pharaoh the dead was taken away back to his Eternal House and I wondered whether his Ka or his spirit, or whatever is the part of him that lives on, were watching us and remembering the feasts whereof he had partaken in his pomp in this pillared hall, as his forefathers had done before him for hundreds or thousands of years.

Not until the mummy had gone and the last sound of the chanting of the priests had died, did the hearts of the feasters grow light again. But soon they forgot, as men alive always forget death and those whom Time has devoured, for the wine was good and strong and the eyes of the women were bright and victory had crowned our spears, and for a while Egypt was once more free.

So it went on till Pharaoh rose and departed, the great gold earrings in his ears jingling as he walked, and the trumpets sounding before and after him. I too rose to go with my mother when a messenger came and bade me wait upon Pharaoh, and with me the dwarf Bes. So we went, leaving an officer to conduct my mother to our home. As I passed her she caught me by the sleeve and whispered in my ear,

"My son, whatever chances to you, be brave and remember that the world holds more than women."

"Yes," I answered, "it holds death and God, or they hold it," though what put the words into my mind I do not know, since I did not understand and had no time to ask her meaning.

H. RIDER HAGGARD

The messenger led us to the door of Peroa's private chamber, the same in which I had seen him on my return from the East. Here he bade me enter, and Bes to wait without. I went in and found two men and a woman in the chamber, all standing very silent. The men were Pharaoh who still wore his glorious robe and Double Crown, and the high priest of Isis clothed in white; the other was the lady Amada also clothed in the snowy robes of Isis.

At the sight of her thus arrayed my heart stopped and I stood silent because I could not speak. She too stood silent and I saw that beneath her thin veil her beautiful face was set and pale as that of an alabaster statue. Indeed she might have been not a lovely living woman, but the goddess Isis herself whose symbols she bore about her.

"Shabaka," said Pharaoh at length, "the Royal Lady of Egypt, Amada, priestess of Isis, has somewhat to say to you."

"Let the Royal Lady of Egypt speak on to her servant and affianced husband," I answered.

"Count Shabaka, General of the armies," she began in a cold clear voice like to that of one who repeats a lesson, "learn that you are no more my affianced husband and that I who am gathered again to Isis the divine, am no more your affianced wife."

"I do not understand. Will it please you to be more plain?" I said faintly.

"I will be more plain, Count Shabaka, more plain than you have been with me. Since we speak together for the last time it is well that I should be plain. Hear me. When first you returned from the East, in yonder hall you told us of certain things that happened to you there. Then the dwarf your servant took up the tale. He said that he gave my name to the Great King. I was wroth as well I might be, but even when I prayed that he should be scourged, you did not deny that it was he who gave my name to the King, although Pharaoh yonder said that if you had spoken the name it would have been another matter."

"I had no time," I answered, "for just then the messengers came from Idernes and afterwards when I sought you you were gone."

"Had you then no time," she asked coldly, "beneath the palms in the garden of the palace when we were affianced? Oh! there was time in plenty but it did not please you to tell me that you had bought safety and great gifts at the price of the honour of the Lady of Egypt whose love you stole."

"You do not understand!" I exclaimed wildly.

"Forgive me, Shabaka, but I understand very well indeed, since from your own words I learned at the feast given to Idernes that 'the name of Amada' slipped your lips by chance and thus came to the ears of the Great King."

"The tale that Idernes and his captain told was false, Lady, and for it Bes and I took their lives with our own hands."

"It had perhaps been better, Shabaka, if you had kept them living that they might confess that it was false. But doubtless you thought them safer dead, since dead men cannot speak, and for this reason challenged them to single combat."

I gasped and could not answer for my mind seemed to leave me, and she went on in a gentler voice,

"I do not wish to speak angrily to you, my cousin Shabaka, especially when you have just wrought such great deeds for Egypt. Moreover by the law I serve I may speak angrily to no man. Know then that on learning the truth, since I could love none but you according to the flesh and therefore can never give myself in marriage to another, I sought refuge in the arms of the goddess whom for your sake I had deserted. She was pleased to receive me, forgetting my treason. On this very day for the second time I took the oaths which may no more be broken, and that I may dwell where I shall never see you more, Pharaoh here has been pleased, at my request to name me high priestess and prophetess of Isis and to appoint me as a dwelling-place her temple at Amada where I was born far away in Upper Egypt. Now all is said and done, so farewell."

"All is not said and done," I broke out in fury. "Pharaoh, I ask your leave to tell the full story of this business of the naming of the lady Amada to the King of kings, and that in the presence of the dwarf Bes. Even a slave is allowed to set out his tale before judgment is passed upon him."

Peroa glanced at Amada who made no sign, then said,

"It is granted, General Shabaka."

So Bes was called into the chamber and having looked about him curiously, seated himself upon the ground.

"Bes," I said, "you have heard nothing of what has passed." (Here I was mistaken, for as he told me afterwards he had heard everything through the door which was not quite closed.) "It is needful, Bes, that you should repeat truly all that happened at the court of the King of kings before and after I was brought from the boat."

Bes obeyed, telling the tale very well, so well that all listened earnestly, without error moreover. When he had finished I also told my story and how, shaken by all I had gone through and already weak from the torment of the boat, the name of Amada was surprised from me who never dreamed that the King would at once make demand of her, and who would have perished a thousand times rather than such a thing should happen. I added what I had learned afterwards from our escort, that this name was already well known to the Great King who meant to make use of it as a cause of quarrel with Egypt. Further, that he had let me escape from a death by horrible torments because of some dream that he had dreamed while he rested before the banquet, in which a god appeared and told him that it was an evil thing to slay a man because that man had bested him at a hunting match and one of which heaven would keep an account. Still because of the law of his land he must find a public pretext for loosing one whom he had once condemned, and therefore chose this matter of the lady Amada whom he pretended to send me to bring to him.

When I had finished, as Amada still remained silent, Pharaoh asked of Bes how it came about that he told one story on the night of our return and another on this night.

"Because, O Pharaoh," answered Bes rolling his eyes, "for the first time in my life I have been just a little too clever and shot my arrow just a little too far. Hearken, Pharaoh, and Royal Lady, and High Priest. I knew that my master loves the lady Amada and knew also that she is quick of tongue and temper, one who readily takes offence even if thereby she breaks her own heart and so brings her life to ruin, and with it perchance her country. Therefore, knowing women whom I have studied in my own land, I saw in this matter just such a cause of offence as she would lay hold of, and counselled my master to keep silent as to the story of the naming of her before the King. Some evil spirit made him listen to this bad counsel, so far at least, that when I lied as to what had chanced, for which lie the lady Amada prayed that I might be scourged till my bones broke through the skin, he did not at once tell all the truth. Nor did he do so afterwards because he feared that if he did I should in fact be scourged, for my master and I love each other. Neither of us wishes to see the other scourged, though such is my lot to-night," and he glanced at Amada. "I have said."

Then at last Amada spoke.

"Had I known all this story from the first, perhaps I should not have done what I have done to-day and perhaps I should have forgiven and forgotten, for in truth even if the dwarf still lies, I believe your word, O Shabaka, and understand how all came about. But now it is too late to change. Say, O Priest of the Mother, is it not too late?"

"It is too late," said the priest solemnly, "seeing that if such vows as yours are broken for the second time, O Prophetess, the curse of the goddess will pursue you and him for whom they were broken, yes, through this life and all other lives that perchance may be given to you upon the earth or elsewhere."

"Pharaoh," I cried in despair, "I made a bond with you. It is recorded in writing and sealed. I have kept my part of the bond; my treasure you have spent; your enemies I have slain; your army I have commanded not so ill. Will you not keep yours and bid the priests release this lady from her vow and give her to me to whom she was promised? Or must I believe that you refuse, not because of goddesses and vows, but because yonder is the Royal Lady of Egypt, the true heiress to the throne who might perchance bear children, which as prophetess of Isis she can never do. Yes, because of this and because of certain cries that came to your ears in the hour of your crowning before Amen-ra and all the gods?"

Peroa flushed as he heard me and answered,

"You speak roughly, Cousin, and were you any other man I might be tempted to answer roughly. But I know that you suffer and therefore I forgive. Nay, you must believe no such things. Rather must you remember that in this bond of which you speak, it was set down that I only promised you the lady Amada with her own consent, and this she has withdrawn."

"Then, Pharaoh, hearken! To-morrow I leave Egypt for another land, giving you back your generalship and sheathing the sword that I had hoped to wield in its defence and yours when the last great day of trial by battle comes, as come it will. I tell you that I go to return no more, unless the lady Amada yonder shall summon me back to fight for her and you, promising herself to me in guerdon."

"That can never be," said Amada.

Then I became aware of another presence in the room, though how and when it appeared I do not know, but I suppose that it had crept in while we were lost in talk. At least between me and Pharaoh, crouched upon the ground, was the figure of a man wrapped in a beggar's cloak.

It threw back the hood and there appeared the ashen face and snowy beard of the holy Tanofir.

"You know me, Pharaoh," he said in his deep, solemn voice. "I am Tanofir, the King's son; Tanofir the hermit, Tanofir the seer. I have heard all that passes, it matters not how and I come to you with a message, I who read men's hearts. Of vows and goddesses and women I say nothing. But this I say to you, that if you break the spirit of your bond and suffer yonder Shabaka to go hence with a bitter heart, trouble shall come on you. All the Great King's armies did not die yonder by the banks of Nile, and mayhap one day he will journey to bury the bones of those who fell, and with them *yours*, O Pharaoh. I do not think that you will listen to me to-night, and I am sure that yonder lady, full of the new-fanned flame of the jealous goddess, will not listen. Still let her take counsel and remember my words: In the hour of desperate danger let her send to Shabaka and demand his help, promising in return what he has asked and remembering that if Isis loves her, that goddess was born upon the Nile and loves Egypt more."

"Too late, too late, *too late!*" wailed Amada

Then she burst into tears and turning fled away with the high priest. Pharaoh went also leaving me and Bes alone. I looked for the holy Tanofir to speak with him, but he too was gone.

"It is time to sleep, Master," said Bes, "for all this talk is more wearisome than any battle. Why! what is this that has your name upon it?" and he picked a silk-wrapped package from the floor and opened it.

Within were the priceless rose-hued pearls!

XIV

Shabaka Fights the Crocodile

W here to?" I said to Bes when we were outside the palace, for I was
so broken with grief that I scarcely knew what I did.

"To the house of the lady Tiu, I think, Master, since there you must
make preparations for your start on the morrow, also bid her farewell.
Oh!" he went on in a kind of rapture which afterwards I knew was
feigned though at the time I did not think about it, "Oh! how happy
should you be who now are free from all this woman-coil, with life
new and fresh before you. Reflect, Master, on the hunting we will have
yonder in Ethiopia. No more cares, no more plannings for the welfare
of Egypt, no more persuading of the doubtful to take up arms, no more
desperate battle-ventures with your country's honour on your sword-
point. And if you must see women—well, there are plenty in Ethiopia
who come and go lightly as an evening breeze laden with the odour of
flowers, and never trouble in the morning."

"At any rate *you* are not free from such coils, Bes," I said and in the
moonlight I saw his great face fall in.

"No, Master, I am tying them about my throat. See, such is the way
of the world, or of the gods that rule the world, I know not which.
For years I have been happy and free, I have enjoyed adventures and
visited strange countries and have gathered learning, till I think I am
the wisest man upon the Nile, at the side of one whom I loved and
holding nothing at risk, except my own life which mattered no more
than that of a gnat dancing in the sun. Now all is changed. I have a
wife whom I love also, more than I can tell you," and he sighed, "but
who still must be looked after and obeyed—yes, obeyed. Further, soon
I shall have a people and a crown to wear, and councillors and affairs
of state, and an ancient religion to support and the Grasshopper itself
knows what besides. The burden has rolled from your back to mine,
Master, making my heart which was so light, heavy, and oh! I wish it
had stopped where it was."

Even then I laughed, sad as I was, for truth lived in the philosophy
of Bes.

"Master," he went on in a changed voice, "I have been a fool and my folly has worked you ill. Forgive me since I acted for the best, only until the end no one ever knows what is the best. Now here is the house and I go to meet my wife and to make certain arrangements. By dawn perhaps you will be ready to start to Ethiopia."

"Do you really desire that I should accompany you there, Bes?"

"Certainly, Master. That is unless you should desire that I accompany you somewhere else instead, by sea southward for instance. If so, I do not know that I would refuse, since Ethiopia will not run away and there is much of the world that I should still like to visit. Only then there is Karema to be thought about, who expects, or, when she learns all, soon will expect, to be a queen," he added doubtfully.

"No, Bes, I am too tired to make new plans, so let us go to Ethiopia and not disappoint Karema, who after holding a cup so long naturally would like to try a sceptre."

"I think that is wisest, Master; at any rate the holy Tanofir thinks it wisest, and he is the voice of Fate. Oh! why do we trouble who after all, every one of us, are nothing but pieces upon the board of Fate."

Then he turned and left me and I entered the house where I found my mother sitting, still in her festal robes, like one who waits. She looked at my face, then asked what troubled me. I sat down on a stool at her feet and told her everything.

"Much as I thought," she said when I had finished. "These over-learned women are strange fish to catch and hold, and too much soul is like too much sail upon a boat when the desert wind begins to blow across the Nile. Well, do not let us blame her or Bes, or Peroa who is already anxious for his dynasty and would rather that Amada were a priestess than your wife, or even the goddess Isis, who no doubt is anxious for her votaries. Let us rather blame the Power that is behind the veil, or to it bow our heads, seeing that we know nothing of the end for which it works. So Egypt shuts her doors on you, my Son, and whither away? Not to the East again, I trust, for there you would soon grow shorter by a head."

"I go to Ethiopia, my Mother, where it seems that Bes is a great man and can shelter me."

"So we go to Ethiopia, do we? Well, it is a long journey for an old woman, but I weary of Memphis where I have lived for so many years and doubtless the sands of the south make good burial grounds."

"We!" I exclaimed. "*We?*"

"Surely, my Son, since in losing a wife you have again found a mother and until I die we part no more."

When I heard this my eyes filled with tears. My conscience smote me also because of late, and indeed for years past, I had thought so much of Amada and so little of my mother. And now it was Amada who had cast me out, unjustly, without waiting to learn the truth, because at the worst I, who worshipped her, had saved myself from death in slow torment by speaking her name, while my mother, forgetting all, took me to her bosom again as she had done when I was a babe. I knew not what to say, but remembering the pearls, I drew them out and placed them round my mother's neck.

She looked at the wonderful things and smiled, then said,

"Such gems as these become white locks and withered breasts but ill. Yet, my Son, I will keep them for you till you find a wife, if not Amada, then another."

"If not Amada, I shall never find a wife," I said bitterly, whereat she smiled.

Then she left me to make ready before she slept a while.

WORK AS WE WOULD NOON had passed two hours, on the following day, before we were prepared to start, for there was much to do. Thus the house must be placed in charge of friends and the means of travel collected. Also a messenger came from Pharaoh praying me for his and Egypt's sake to think again before I left them, and an answer sent that go I must, whither the holy Tanofir would know if at any time Pharaoh desired to learn. In reply to this came another messenger who brought me parting gifts from Pharaoh, a chain of honour, a title of higher nobility, a commission as his envoy to whatever land I wandered, and so forth, which I must acknowledge. Lastly as we were leaving the house to seek the boat which Bes had made ready on the Nile, there came yet another messenger at the sight of whom my heart leapt, for he was priest of Isis.

He bowed and handed me a roll. I opened it with a trembling hand and read:

"From the Prophetess of Isis whose house is at Amada, aforetime Royal Lady of Egypt, to the Count Shabaka,

"I learn, O my Cousin, that you depart from Egypt and knowing the reason my heart is sore. Believe me, my Cousin, I love you well, better than any who lives upon the earth, nor will that love ever change, since the goddess who holds my future in her hands, knows of what we are made and is not jealous of the past. Therefore she will not be wroth at the earthly love of one who is gathered to her heavenly arms. Her blessing and mine be on you and if we see each other no more face to face in the world, may we meet again in the halls of Osiris. Farewell, beloved Shabaka. Oh! why did you suffer that black master of lies, the dwarf Bes, to persuade you to hide the truth from me?"

So the writing ended and below it were two stains still wet, which I knew were caused by tears. Moreover, wrapped in a piece of silk and fastened to the scroll was a little gold ring graven with the royal *uræus* that Amada had always worn from childhood. Only on the previous night I had noted it on the first finger of her right hand.

I took my stylus and my waxen tablets and wrote on one of them:

"Had you been a man, Amada, and not a woman, I think you would have judged me differently but, learned priestess and prophetess as you are, a woman you remain. Perchance a time may come when once more you will turn to me in the hour of your need; if so and I am living, I will come. Yea, if I am dead I think that I still shall come, since nothing can really part us. Meanwhile by day and by night I wear your ring and whenever I look on it I think of Amada the woman whose lips have pressed my own, and forget Amada the priestess who for her soul's sake has been pleased to break the heart of the man who loved her and whom she misjudged so sorely in her pride and anger."

This tablet I wrapped up and sealed, using clay and her own ring to make the seal, and gave it for delivery to the priest.

At length we drew near to the river and here, gathered on the open land, I found the most of those who had fought with me in the battle against the Easterns, and with them a great concourse of others from the city. These collected round me, some of them wounded and hobbling upon crutches, praying me not to go, as did the others who foresaw sorrow to Egypt from my loss. But I broke away from them almost in tears and with my mother hid myself beneath the canopy of the boat. Here Bes was waiting, also his beautiful wife who, although she seemed sad at leaving Egypt, smiled a greeting to us while the steersmen and rowers of the boat, tall Ethiopians every one of them, rose and gave me a General's salute. Then, as the wind served, we hoisted the sail and glided away up Nile, till presently the temples and palm-groves of Memphis were lost to sight.

OF THAT LONG, LONG JOURNEY there is no need to tell. Up the Nile we travelled slowly, dragging the boat past the cataracts till Egypt was far behind us. In the end, many days after we had passed the mouth of another river that was blue in colour which flowed from the northern mountain lands down into the Nile, we came to a place where the rapids were so long and steep that we must leave the boat and travel overland. Drawing near to it at sunset I saw a multitude of people gathered on the sand and beyond them a camp in which were set many beautiful pavilions that seemed to be broidered with silk and gold, as were the banners that floated above them whereon appeared the effigy of a grasshopper, also done in gold with silver legs.

"It seems that my messengers travelled in safety," said Bes to me, "for know, that yonder are some of my subjects who have come here to meet us. Now, Master, I must no longer call you master since I fear I am once more a king. And you must no longer call me Bes, but Karoon. Moreover, forgive me, but when you come into my presence you must bow, which I shall like less than you do, but it is the custom of the Ethiopians. Oh! I would that you were the king and that I were your friend, for henceforth good-bye to ease and jollity."

I laughed, but Bes did not laugh at all, only turned to his wife who already ruled him as though he were indeed a slave, and said, "Lady Karema, make yourself as beautiful as you can and forget that you have ever been a Cup or anything useful, since henceforth you must be a queen, that is if you please my people."

"And what happens if I do not please them, Husband?" asked Karema opening her fine eyes.

"I do not quite know, Wife. Perhaps they may refuse to accept me, at which I shall not weep. Or perhaps they may refuse to accept you, at which of course I should weep very much, for you see you are so very white and, heretofore, all the queens of the Ethiopians have been black."

"And if they refuse to accept me because I am white, or rather brown, instead of black like oiled marble, what then, O Husband?"

"Then—oh! then I cannot say, O Wife. Perhaps they will send you back to your own country. Or perhaps they will separate us and place you in a temple where you will live alone in all honour. I remember that once they did that to a white woman, making a goddess of her until she died of weariness. Or perhaps—well, I do not know."

Then Karema grew angry.

"Now I wish I had remained a Cup," she said, "and the servant of the holy Tanofir who at least taught me many secret things, instead of coming to dwell among black barbarians in the company of a dwarf who, even if he be a king, it seems has no power to protect the wife whom he has chosen."

"Why will women always grow wroth before there is need?" asked Bes humbly. "Surely it would be time to rate me when any of these things had happened."

"If any of them do happen, Husband, I shall say much worse things than that," she replied, but the talk went no further, for at this moment our boat grounded and singing a wild song, many of those who waited rushed into the water to drag it to the bank.

Then Bes stood up on the prow, waving his bow and there arose a mighty shout of, "*Karoon! Karoon!* It is he, it is he returned after many years!"

Twice they shouted thus and then, every one of them, threw themselves face downwards in the sand.

"Yes, my people," cried Bes, "it is I, Karoon, who having been miraculously preserved from many dangers in far lands by the help of the Grasshopper in heaven, and, as my messengers will have told you, of my beloved friend, lord Shabaka the Egyptian, who has deigned to come to dwell with us for a while, have at length returned to Ethiopia that I may shed my wisdom on you like the sun and pour it on your heads like melted honey. Moreover, mindful of our laws which aforetime I defied and therefore left you, I have searched the whole world through till I found the most beautiful woman that it contained, and made her my wife. She too has deigned to come to this far country to be your queen. Advance, fair Karema, and show yourself to these my Ethiopians."

So Karema stepped forward and stood on the prow of the boat by the side of Bes, and a strange couple they looked. The Ethiopians who had risen, considered her gravely, then one of them said,

"Karoon called her beautiful, but in truth she is almost white and very ugly."

"At least she is a woman," said another, "for her shape is female."

"Yes, and he has married her," remarked a third, "and even a king may choose his own wife sometimes. For in such matters who can judge another's taste?"

"Cease," said Bes in a lordly way. "If you do not think her beautiful to-night, you will to-morrow. And now let us land and rest."

So we landed and while I did so I took note of these Ethiopians. They were great men, black as charcoal with thick lips, white teeth and flat noses. Their eyes were large and the whites of them somewhat yellow, their hair curled like wool, their beards were short and on their faces they wore a continual smile. Of dress most of them had little, but their elders or leaders wore lion and leopard skins and some were clad in a kind of silken tunic belted about the middle. All were armed for war with long bows, short swords and small shields round in shape and made from the hide of the hippopotamus or of the unicorn. Gold was plentiful amongst them since even the humblest wore bracelets of that metal, while about the necks of the chieftains it was wound in great torques, also sometimes on their ankles. They wore sandals on their feet and some of them had ostrich feathers stuck in their hair, a few also had grasshoppers fashioned of gold bound on the top of their heads, and these I took to be the priests. There were no women in their number.

As the sun was sinking we were led at once to a very beautiful tent made of woven flax and ornamented as I have described, where we found food made ready for us in plenty, milk in bowls and the flesh of sheep and oxen boiled and roasted. Bes, however, was taken to a place apart, which made Karema even more angry than she was before.

Scarcely had we finished eating when a herald rushed into the tent crying, "Prostrate yourselves! Yea, be prostrated, the Grasshopper comes! Karoon comes."

Here I must say that I found that the title of Karoon meant "Great Grasshopper," but Karema who did not know this, asked indignantly why she should prostrate herself to a grasshopper. Indeed she refused to do so even when Bes entered the pavilion wonderfully attired in a gorgeous-coloured robe of which the train was held by two huge men. So absurd did he look that my mother and I must bow very deeply to hide our laughter while Karema said,

"It would be better, Husband, if you found children to carry your robe instead of two giants. Moreover, if it is meant to copy the colours of a grasshopper, 'tis badly done, since grasshoppers are green and you are gold and scarlet. Also they do not wear feathers set awry upon their heads."

Bes rolled his eyes as though in agony, then turning, bade his attendants be gone. They obeyed, though doubtfully as though they did not like to leave him alone with us, whereon he let down the flap of the pavilion, threw off his gorgeous coverings and said,

"You must learn to understand, Wife, that our customs are different from those of Egypt. There I was happy as a slave and you were held to be beautiful as the Cup of the holy Tanofir, also learned. Here I am wretched as a king and you are held to be ugly, also ignorant as a stranger. Oh! do not answer, I pray you, but learn that all goes well. For the time you are accepted as my wife, subject to the decision of a council of matrons, aged relatives of my family, who will decide when we reach the City of the Grasshopper whether or not you shall be acknowledged as the Queen of the Ethiopians. No, no, I pray you say nothing since I must go away at once, as according to the law of the Ethiopians the time has come for the Grasshopper to sleep, alone, Karema, as you are not yet acknowledged as my wife. You also can sleep with the lady Tiu and for Shabaka a tent is provided. Rest sweetly, Wife. Hark! They fetch me."

"Now, if I had my way," said Karema, "I would rest in that boat going back to Egypt. What say you, lord Shabaka?"

But I made no answer who followed Bes out of the tent, leaving her to talk the matter over with my mother. Here I found a crowd of his people waiting to convey him to sleep and watching, saw them place him in another tent round which they ranged themselves, playing upon musical instruments. After this someone came and led me to my own place where was a good bed in which I lay down to sleep. This however I could not do for a long while because of my own laughter and the noise of the drums and horns that were soothing Bes to his rest. For now I understood why he had preferred to be a slave in Egypt rather than a king in Ethiopia.

In the morning I rose before the dawn and went out to the river-bank to bathe. While I was making ready to wash myself, who should appear but Bes, followed, but at a distance, by a number of his people.

"Never have I spent such a night, Master," he said, "at least not since you took me prisoner years ago, since by law I may not stop those horns and musical instruments. Now, however, also according to the law of the Ethiopians, I am my own lord until the sun rises. So I have come here to gather some of those blue lilies which she loves as a present for Karema, because I fear that she is angry and must be appeased."

"Certainly she is very angry," I said, "or at least was so when I left her last night. Oh! Bes, why did you let your people tell her that she was ugly?"

"How can I help it, Master? Have you not always heard that the Ethiopians are chiefly famous for one thing, namely that they speak nothing but the truth. To them she, being different, seems to be ugly. Therefore when they say that she is ugly, they speak the truth."

"If so, it is a truth that she does not like, Bes, as I have no doubt she will tell you by and by. Do they think me ugly also?"

"Yes, they do, Master; but they think also that you look like a man who can draw a bow and use a sword, and that goes far with the Ethiopians. Of your mother they say nothing because she is old and they venerate the aged whom the Grasshopper is waiting to carry away."

Now I began to laugh again and went with Bes to gather the lilies. These grew at the end of a mass of reeds woven together by the pressure of the current and floating on the water. Bes lay down upon his stomach while his people watched from a distance on the bank amazed into silence, and stretched out his long arms to reach the blue lotus flowers. Suddenly the reeds gave way beneath him just as he had grasped two of the flowers and was dragging at them, so that he fell into the river.

Next instant I saw a swirl in the brown water and perceived a huge crocodile. It rushed at Bes open-mouthed. Being a good swimmer he twisted his body in order to avoid it, but I heard the great teeth close with a snap on the short leathern garment which he wore about his middle.

"The devil has me! Farewell!" he cried and vanished beneath the water.

Now, as I have said, I was almost stripped for bathing, but had not yet taken off my short sword which was girded round me by a belt. In an instant I drew it and amidst the yells of horror of the Ethiopians who had seen all from the bank, I plunged into the river. There are few able to swim as I could and I had the art of diving with my eyes open and remaining long beneath the surface without drawing breath, for this I had practised from a child.

Immediately I saw the great reptile sinking to the mud and dragging Bes with him to drown him there. But here the river was very deep and with a few swift strokes I was able to get under the crocodile. Then with all my strength I stabbed upwards, driving the sword far into the soft part of the throat. Feeling the pain of the sharp iron the beast let go of Bes and turned on me. How it happened I do not know but presently I found myself upon its back and was striking at its eyes. One thrust at least went home, for the blinded brute rose to the surface, bearing me with him, and oh! the sweetness of the air as I breathed again.

Thus we appeared, I riding the crocodile like a horse and stabbing furiously, while close by was Bes rolling his yellow eyes but helpless, for he had no weapon. Still the devil was not dead although blood streamed from him, only mad with pain and rage. Nor could the shouting Ethiopians help me since they had only bows and dared not shoot lest their shafts should pierce me. The crocodile began to sink again, snapping furiously at my legs. Then I bethought me of a trick I had seen practised by natives on the Nile.

Waiting till its huge jaws were open I thrust my arm between them, grasping the short sword in such fashion that the hilt rested on its tongue and the point against the roof of its mouth. It tried to close its jaws and lo! the good iron was fixed between them, holding them wide open. Then I withdrew my hand and floated upwards with nothing worse than a cut upon the wrist from one of its sharp fangs. I appeared upon the surface and after me the crocodile spouting blood and wallowing in its death agonies. I remembered no more till I found myself lying on the bank surrounded by a multitude with Bes standing over me. Also in the shallow water was the crocodile dead, my sword still fixed between its jaws.

"Are you harmed, Master" cried Bes in a voice of agony.

"Very little I think," I answered, sitting up with the blood pouring from my arm.

Bes thrust aside Karema who had come lightly clothed from her tent, saying,

"All is well, Wife. I will bring you the lilies presently."

Then he flung his arms about me, kissed my hands and my brow and turning to the crowd, shouted,

"Last night you were disputing as to whether this Egyptian lord should be allowed to dwell with me in the land of Ethiopia. Which of you disputes it now?"

"No one!" they answered with a roar. "He is not a man but a god. No man could have done such a deed."

"So it seems," answered Bes quietly. "At least none of you even tried to do it. Yet he is not a god but only that kind of man who is called a hero. Also he is my brother, and while I reign in Ethiopia either he shall reign at my side, or I go away with him."

"It shall be so, Karoon!" they shouted with one voice. And after this I was carried back to the tent.

In front of it my mother waited and kissed me proudly before them all, whereat they shouted again.

So ended this adventure of the crocodile, except that presently Bes went back and recovered the two lilies for Karema, this time from a boat, which caused the Ethiopians to call out that he must love her very much, though not as much as he did me.

That afternoon, borne in litters, we set out for the City of the Grasshopper, which we reached on the fourth day. As we drew near the place regiments of men to the number of twelve thousand or more, came out to meet us, so that at last we arrived escorted by an army who sang their songs of triumph and played upon their musical instruments until my head ached with the noise.

This city was a great place whereof the houses were built of mud and thatched with reeds. It stood upon a wide plain and in its centre rose a natural, rocky hill upon the crest of which, fashioned of blocks of gleaming marble and roofed with a metal that shone as gold, was the temple of the Grasshopper, a columned building very like to those of Egypt. Round it also were other public buildings, among them the palace of the Karoon, the whole being surrounded by triple marble walls as a protection from attack by foes. Never had I seen anything so beautiful as that hill with its edifices of shining white roofed with gold or copper and gleaming in the sun.

Descending from my litter I walked to those of my mother and Karema, for Bes in his majesty might not be approached, and said as much to them.

"Yes, Son," answered my mother, "it is worth while to have travelled so far to see such a sight. I shall have a fine sepulchre, Son."

"I have seen it all before," broke in Karema.

"When?" I asked.

"I do not know. I suppose it must have been when I was the Cup of the holy Tanofir. At least it is familiar to me. Already I weary of it, for who can care for a land or a city where they think white people hideous and scarcely allow a wife to go near her husband, save between midnight and dawn when they cease from their horrible music?"

"It will be your part to change these customs, Karema."

"Yes," she exclaimed, "certainly that will be my part," after which I went back to my litter.

XV

The Summons

Now at the gates of the City of the Grasshopper we were royally received. The priests came out to meet us, pushing a colossal image of their god before them on a kind of flat chariot, and I remember wondering what would be the value of that huge golden locust, if it were melted down. Also the Council came, very ancient men all of them, since the Ethiopians for the most part lived more than a hundred years. Perhaps that is why they were so glad to welcome Bes since they were too old to care about retaining power in their own hands as they had done during his long absence. For save Bes there was no other man living of the true royal blood who could take the throne.

Then there were thousands of women, broad-faced and smiling whose black skins shone with scented oils, for they wore little except a girdle about their waists and many ornaments of gold. Thus their earrings were sometimes a palm in breadth and many of them had great gold rings through their noses, such as in Egypt are put in those of bulls. My mother laughed at them, but Karema said that she thought them hideous and hateful.

They were a strange people, these Ethiopians, like children, most of them, being merry and kind and never thinking of one thing for more than a minute. Thus one would see them weep and laugh almost in the same breath. But among them was an upper class who had great learning and much ancient knowledge. These men made their laws wherein there was always sense under what seemed to be folly, designed the temples, managed the mines of gold and other metals and followed the arts. They were the real masters of the land, the rest were but slaves content to live in plenty, for in that fertile soil want never came near them, and to do as they were bid.

Thus they passed from the cradle to the grave amidst song and flowers, carrying out their light, allotted tasks, and for the rest, living as they would and loving those they would, especially their children, of whom they had many. By nature and tradition the men were warriors and hunters, being skilled in the use of the bow and always at war when they could find anyone to fight. Indeed when we came among them their trouble was that they had no enemies left, and at once they implored Bes to lead them out to battle since they were weary of herding kine and tilling fields.

All of these things I found out by degrees, also that they were a great people who could send out an army of seventy thousand men and yet leave enough behind them to defend their land. Of the world beyond their borders the most of them knew little, but the learned men of whom I have spoken, a great deal, since they travelled to Egypt and elsewhere to study the customs of other countries. For the rest their only god was the Grasshopper and like that insect they skipped and chirruped through life and when the winter of death came sprang away to another of which they knew nothing, leaving their young behind them to bask in the sun of unborn summers. Such were the Ethiopians.

Now of all the ceremonies of the reception of Bes and his re-crowning as Karoon, I knew little, for the reason that the tooth of the crocodile poisoned my blood and made me very ill, so that I remained for a moon or more lying in a fine room in the palace where gold seemed to be as plentiful as earthen pots are in Egypt, and all the vessels were of crystal. Had it not been for the skill of the Ethiopian leeches and above all for the nursing of my mother, I think that I must have died. She it was who withstood them when they wished to cut off my arm, and wisely, for it recovered and was as strong as it had ever been. In the end I grew well again and from the platform in front of the temple was presented to the people by Bes as his saviour and the next greatest to him in the kingdom, nor shall I ever forget the shoutings with which I was received.

Karema also was presented as his wife, having passed the Ordeal of the Matrons, but only, I think, because it was found that she was in the way to give an heir to the throne. For to them her beauty was ugliness, nor could they understand how it came about that their king, who contrary to the general customs of the land, was only allowed one wife lest the children should quarrel, could have chosen a lady who was not black. So they received her in silence with many whisperings which made Karema very angry.

When in due course, however, the child came and proved to be a son black as the best of them and of perfect shape, they relented towards her and after the birth of a second, grew to love her. But she never forgave and loved them not at all. Nor was she over-fond of these children of hers because they were so black which, she said, showed how poisonous

H. RIDER HAGGARD

was the blood of the Ethiopians. And indeed this is so, for often I have noticed that if an Ethiopian weds with one of another colour, their offspring is black down to the third or fourth generation. Therefore Karema longed for Egypt notwithstanding the splendour in which she dwelt.

So greatly did she long that she had recourse to the magic lore which she had learned from the holy Tanofir, and would sit for hours gazing into water in a crystal bowl, or sometimes into a ball of crystal without the water, trying to see visions therein that had to do with what passed in Egypt. Moreover in time much of her gift returned to her and she did see many things which she repeated to me, for she would tell no one else of them, not even her husband.

Thus she saw Amada kneeling in a shrine before the statue of Isis and weeping: a picture that made me sad. Also she saw the holy Tanofir brooding in the darkness of the Cave of the Bulls, and read in his mind that he was thinking of us, though what he thought she could not read. Again she saw Eastern messengers delivering letters to Pharaoh and knew from his face that he was disturbed and that Egypt was threatened with calamities. And so forth.

Soon the news of her powers of divination spread abroad, so that all the Ethiopians grew to fear her as a seeress and thenceforth, whatever they may have thought, none of them dared to say that she was ugly. Further, her gift was real, since if she told me of a certain thing such as that messengers were approaching, in due course they would arrive and make clear much that she had not been able to understand in her visions.

Now from the time that I grew strong again and as soon as Bes was firmly seated on his throne, he and I set to work to train and drill the army of the Ethiopians, which hitherto had been little more than a mob of men carrying bows and swords. We divided it into phalanxes after the Greek fashion, and armed these bodies with long lances, swords, and large shields in the place of the small ones they had carried before. Also we trained the archers, teaching them to advance in open order and shoot from cover, and lastly chose the best soldiers to be captains and generals. So it came about that at the end of the two years that I spent in Ethiopia there was a force of sixty thousand men or more whom I should not have been afraid to match against any troops in the world, since they were of great strength and courage, and, as I have said, by nature lovers of war. Also their bows being longer and more powerful, they could shoot arrows farther than the Easterns or the Egyptians.

The Ethiopian lords wondered why their King and I did these things, since they saw no enemy against which so great an army could be led to battle. On that matter Bes and I kept our own counsel, telling them only that it was good for the men to be trained to war, since, hearing of their wealth, one day the King of kings might attempt to invade their country. So month by month I laboured at this task, leading armies into distant regions to accustom them to travelling far afield, carrying with them what was necessary for their sustenance.

So it went on until a sad thing happened, since on returning from one of these forays in which I had punished a tribe that had murdered some Ethiopian hunters and we had taken many thousands of their cattle, I found my mother dying. She had been smitten by a fever which was common at that season of the year, and being old and weak had no strength to throw it off.

As medicine did not help her, the priests of the Grasshopper prayed day and night in their temple for her recovery. Yes, there they prayed to a golden locust standing on an altar in a sanctuary that was surrounded by crystal coffins wherein rested the flesh of former kings of the land. To me the sight was pitiful, but Bes asked me what was the difference between praying to a locust and praying to images with the heads of beasts, or to a dwarf shaped as he was like we did in Egypt, and I could not answer him.

"The truth is, Brother," he said, for so he called me now, "that all peoples in the world do not offer petitions to what they see and have been taught to revere, but to something beyond of which to them it is a sign. But why the Ethiopians should have chosen a grasshopper as a symbol of God who is everywhere, is more than I can tell. Still they have done so for thousands of years."

When I came to my mother's bedside she was wandering and I saw that she could not live long. In a little while, however, her mind cleared so that she knew me and tears of joy ran down her pale cheeks because I had returned before she died. She reminded me that she had always said that she would find a grave in Ethiopia, and asked to be buried and not kept above ground in crystal, as was the custom there. Then she said that she had been dreaming of my father and of me; also that she did not think that I need fret myself overmuch about Amada, since she was sure that before long I should kiss her on the lips.

I asked if she meant that I should marry her and that we should be happy and fortunate. She replied that she supposed that I should marry her, but of the rest would say nothing. Indeed her face grew troubled, as though some thought hurt her, and leaving the matter of Amada she bade Karema bring me the rose-hued pearls, blessed me, prayed for our reunion in the halls of Osiris, and straightway died.

So I caused her to be embalmed after the Egyptian fashion and enclosed in a coffin of crystal with a scarab on her heart that Karema had discovered somewhere in the city, for always she was searching for things that reminded her of Egypt, whereof many were to be found brought from time to time by travellers or strangers. Then with such ceremony as we could without the services of the priests of Osiris, Karema and I buried her in a tomb that Bes had caused to be made near to the steps of the temple of the Grasshopper, while Bes and his nobles watched from a distance.

And so farewell to my beloved mother, the lady Tiu.

AFTER SHE WAS GONE I grew very sad and lonely. While she lived I had a home, but now I was an exile, a stranger in a strange land with no one of my own people to talk to except Karema, with whom, as there were gossips even in Ethiopia, I thought it well not to talk too much. There was Bes it was true, but now he was a great king and the time of kings is not their own. Moreover Bes was Bes and an Ethiopian and I was I and an Egyptian, and therefore notwithstanding our love and brotherhood, we could never be like men of the same blood and country.

I grew weary of Ethiopia with its useless gold and damp eternal green and heat, and longed for the sand and the keen desert air. Bes noted it and offered me wives, but I shrank from these black women however buxom and kindly, and wished for no offspring of their race whom afterwards I could never leave. To Egypt I had sworn not to return unless one voice called me and it remained silent. What then was I to do, being no longer content to discipline and command an army that I might not lead into battle?

At length I made up my mind. By nature I was a hunter as much as a soldier; I would beg from Bes a band of brave men whom I knew, lovers of adventure who sought new things, and with them strike down south, following the path of the elephants to wherever the gods might lead us. Doubtless in the end it would be to death, but what matter when there is nothing for which one cares to live?

While I was brooding over these plans Karema read my mind, perhaps because it was her own, perhaps by help of her strange arts, which I do not know. At least one day when I was sitting alone looking at the city beneath from one of the palace window-places, she came to me looking very beautiful and very mystic in the white robes she always loved to wear, and said,

"My lord Shabaka, you tire of this land of honey and sweetness and soft airs and flowers and gold and crystal and black people who grin and chatter and are not pleasant to be near, is it not so?"

"Yes, Queen," I answered.

"Do not call me queen, my lord Shabaka, for I weary of that name, as we both do of the rest. Call me Karema the Arab, or Karema the Cup, which you will, but by the name of Thoth, god of learning, do *not* call me queen."

"Karema then," I said. "Well, how do you know that I tire of all this, Karema?"

"How could you do otherwise who are not a barbarian and who have Egypt in your heart, and Egypt's fate and——" here she looked me straight in the eye's, "Egypt's Lady. Besides, I measure you by myself."

"You at least should be happy, Karema, who are great and rich and beloved, and the wife of a King who is one of the best of men, and the mother of children."

"Yes, Shabaka, I should be but I am not, for who can live on sweetmeats only, especially when they like what is sour? See now how strangely we are made. When I was a girl, the daughter of an Arab chief, well bred and well taught as it chanced, I tired of the hard life of the desert and the narrow minds about me, I who longed for wisdom and to know great men. Then I became the Cup of the holy Tanofir and wisdom was all about me, strange wisdom from another world, rough, sharp wisdom from Tanofir, and the quiet wisdom of the dead among whom I dwelt. I wearied of that also, Shabaka. I was beautiful and knew it and I longed to shine in a Court, to be admired among men, to be envied of women, to rule. My husband came my way. He was clever with a great heart. He was your friend and therefore I was sure that he must be loyal and true. He was, or might be, a king, as I knew, though he thought that I did not. I married him and the holy Tanofir laughed but he did not say me nay, and I became a queen. And now I wish sometimes that I were dead, or back holding the cup of the holy Tanofir with the wisdom of the heavens flowing round me and the soft darkness of the tombs about me. It seems that in this world we never can be content, Shabaka."

"No, Karema, we only think that we should be if things were otherwise than they are. But how can I help you, Karema?"

"Least of all by going away and leaving me alone," she answered with the tears starting to her eyes.

Looking at her, I began to think that the best thing I could do would be to go away and at once, but as ever she read my thought, shook her head and laughed.

"No, no, I have put on my yoke and will carry it to the end. Have I not two black children and a husband who is a hero, a wit and a mountebank in one, and a throne and more gold and crystal than I ever wish to see again even in a dream, and shall I not cling to these good things? If you went I should only be a little more unhappy than before, that is all. Not for my sake do I ask you to stay, but for your own."

"How for my own, Karema? I have done all that I can do here. I have built the army afresh from cook-boys to generals. Bes needs me no longer who has you, his children and his country, and I die of weariness."

"You can stop to make use of that army you have built afresh, Shabaka."

"Against whom? There are none to fight."

"Against the Great King of the East. Listen. My gift of vision has grown strong and clear of late. Only to-day I have seen a meeting between Pharaoh, the holy Tanofir and the lady Amada. They were all disturbed, I know not at what, and the end of it was that Amada wrote in a roll and gave the writing to messengers, who I think even now are speeding southward—to you, Shabaka. Nay, do not look doubtfully on me, it is true."

"Then you did well to tell me, Karema, for within a moon of this day I should have been where perhaps no messengers would have found me. Now I will wait and let it be your part to prepare the mind of Bes. Do you think that he would give me an army to lead to Egypt, if there were need?"

She nodded and answered,

"He would do so for three reasons. The first is because he loves you, the second because he too wearies of Ethiopia and this rich, fat life of peace, and the third, because I shall tell him that he must."

"Then why trouble to speak of the other two?" I said laughing.

So I stayed on in the City of the Grasshopper, and busied myself with the questions of how to transport and feed a great army that must hold the field for six months or a year; also with the setting of hundreds of skilled men to the making of bows, arrows, swords and shields. Nor did Bes say me no in these matters. Indeed he helped them forward by issuing the orders as his own, wherein I saw the hand of Karema.

Three months went by and I began to think that Karema's power had been at fault, or that her vision was one that came from her lips and not from her heart, to keep me in Ethiopia. But again she read my mind and smiled.

"Not so, Shabaka," she said. "Those messengers have come to trouble and are detained by a petty tribe beyond our borders over some matter of a woman. Ten days ago the frontier guards marched to set them free."

So again I waited and at length the messengers came, three of them Egyptians and three men of Ethiopia who dwelt in Egypt to learn its wisdom, reporting that as Karema had said, through the foolishness of a servant they had been held prisoner by an Arab chief and thus delayed. Then they delivered the writings which they had kept safe. One was from Pharaoh to the Karoon of Ethiopia; one from the holy Tanofir to Karema; and one from the lady Amada to myself.

With a trembling hand I broke the silk and seals and read. It ran thus:

Shabaka, my Cousin,
   "You departed from Egypt saying that never would you return unless I, Amada the priestess, called you, and I told you that I should never call. You said, moreover, that if you came at my call you would demand me in guerdon, and I told you that never would I give myself to you who was doubly sworn to Isis. Yet now I call and now I say that if you come and conquer and I yet live, then, if you still will it, I am yours. Thus stands the case: The Great King advances upon Egypt with an army countless as the sands, nor can Egypt hope to battle against him unaided and alone. He comes to make of her a slave, to kill her children, to burn her temples, to sack her cities and to defile her gods with blasphemies. Moreover he comes to seize me and to drag me away to shame in his House of Women.
   "Therefore for the sake of the gods, for Egypt's sake and for my own, I pray you come and save us. Moreover I still love you, Shabaka, yes, more a thousand times, then ever I did, though whether you still love me I know not. For that love's sake, therefore, I am ready to break my vows to Isis

and to dare her vengeance, if she should desire to be avenged upon me who would save her and her worship, praying that it may fall on my head and not on yours. This will I do by the counsel of the holy Tanofir, by command of Pharaoh, and with the consent of the high priests of Egypt.

"Now I, Amada, have written. Choose, Shabaka, beloved of my heart."

Such was the letter that caused my head to swim and set my soul on fire. Still I said nothing, but thrust it into my robe and waited. Presently Bes, who had been reading in his roll, looked up and spoke, saying,

"Are you minded to see arrows fly and swords shine in war, Brother? If so, here is opportunity. Pharaoh writes to me above his own seal, seeking an alliance between Egypt and Ethiopia. He says that the King of kings invades him and that if he conquers Egypt he has sworn to travel on and conquer Ethiopia also, since he learns that it is now ruled by a certain dwarf who once stole his White Signet, and by a certain Egyptian who once killed his Satrap, Idernes."

"What says the Karoon?" I asked.

Bes rolled his eyes and turning to Karema, asked,

"What says the Karoon's wife?"

Karema laid down the roll she had been studying and answered,

"She says that she has received a command from her master the holy Tanofir to wait upon him forthwith, for reasons that he will explain when she arrives, or to brave his curse upon her, her children, her country and her husband, and not only his but that of the spirits who serve him."

"The curse of the holy Tanofir is not a thing to mock at," said Bes, "as I who revere him, know as well as any man."

"No, Husband, and therefore I leave for Egypt as soon as may be. It seems that my sister is dead, this year past, and the holy Tanofir has no one to hold his cup."

"And what shall I do?" asked Bes.

"That is for you to say, Husband. But if you will, you can stay here and guard our children, giving the command of your army to the lord Shabaka."

Now, for we were alone, Bes twisted himself about, rolling his eyes and laughing as he used to do before he became Karoon of Ethiopia.

"O-ho-ho! Wife," he said, "so you are to go to Egypt, leaving me to play the nurse to babes, and my brother here is to command my armies, leaving me to look after the old men and the women. Nay, I think otherwise. I think that I shall come also, that is if my brother wishes it. Did he not save my life and is it not his and with it all I have? Oh! have done. Once more we will stand side by side in the battle, Brother, and afterwards let Fate do as it will with us. Tell me now, what is the tale of archers and of swordsmen with which we can march against the Great King with whom, like you, I have a score to settle?"

"Seventy and five thousand," I answered.

"Good! On the fifth day from now the army marches for Egypt."

XVI

Tanofir Finds His Broken Cup

March we did, but on the fifteenth day, not the fifth, since there was much to make ready. First the Council of the Ethiopians must be consulted and through them the people. In the beginning there was trouble over the matter, since many were against a distant war, and this even after Bes had urged that it was better to attack than wait to be attacked. For they answered, and justly, that here in Ethiopia distance and the desert were their shields, since the King of kings, however great his strength, would be weary and famished before he set foot within their borders.

In the end the knot was cut with a sword, for when the army came to learn of the dispute, from the generals down to the common soldiers, every man clamoured to be led to war, since, as I have said, these Ethiopians were fighters all of them, and near at hand there were none left with whom they could fight. So when the Council came to see that they must choose between war abroad and revolt at home, they gave way, bargaining only that the children of the Karoon should not leave the land so that if aught befell him, there would be some of the true blood left to succeed.

Also the Grasshopper was consulted by the priests who found the omens favourable. Indeed I was told that this great golden locust sat up upon its hind legs upon the altar and waved its feelers in the air, which only happened when wonderful fortune was about to bless the land. The tale reminded me of the nodding of the statues of our own gods in Egypt when a new Pharaoh was presented to them, and of that of Isis when Amada put up her prayer to the divine Mother. To tell the truth, I suspected Karema of having some hand in the business. However, so it happened.

At length we set forth, a mighty host, Bes commanding the swordsmen and I, under him, the archers, of whom there were more than thirty thousand men, and glad was I when all the farewells were said and we were free of the weeping crowds of women. At first Bes and Karema were somewhat sad at parting from their children, but in a little while they grew gay again since the one longed for battle and the other for the sands of Egypt.

Now of our advance I need say little, except that it was slow, though none dared to bar the road of so mighty an array. Since we must go on foot, we were not able to cover more than five leagues a day, for even after we reached the river boats could not be found for so many, though Karema travelled in one with her ladies. Also cattle and corn must always be sent forward for food. Still we crept on to Egypt without sickness, accident, or revolt.

When we drew near to its frontiers messengers met us from Pharaoh bearing letters in answer to those which we had sent with the tidings of our coming. These contained little but ill news. It seemed that the Great King with a countless host had taken all the cities of the Delta and, after a long siege, had captured Memphis and put it to the sack, and that the army of Egypt, fighting desperately by land and upon the Nile was being driven southwards towards Thebes. Pharaoh added that he proposed to make his last stand at the strong city of Amada, since he doubted whether the troops from Lower Egypt would not rather surrender to the Easterns than retreat further up the Nile. He thanked and blessed us for our promised aid and prayed that it might come in time to save Egypt from slavery and himself from death.

Also there was a letter for me from Amada in which she said,

"Oh! come quickly. Come quickly, beloved Shabaka, lest
of me you should find but bones for never will I fall living
into the hands of the Great King. We are sore pressed and
although Amada has been made very strong, it can stand but
a little while against such a countless multitude armed with
all the engines of war."

For Karema, too, there were messages from the holy Tanofir of the same meaning, saying that unless we appeared within a moon of their receipt, all was lost.

We read and took counsel. Then we pressed forward by double marches, sending swift runners forward to bid Pharaoh and his army hold on to the last spear and arrow.

On the twenty-fifth day from the receipt of this news we came to the great frontier city which we found in tumult for its citizens were mad with fear. Here we rested one night and ate of the food that was gathered there in plenty. Then leaving a small rear-guard of five thousand men who were tired out, to hold the place, we pressed onwards, for Amada was still four days' march away. On the morning of the fourth day we were told that it was falling, or had fallen, and when at length we came in sight of the place we saw that it was beleaguered by an innumerable host of Easterns, while on the Nile was a great fleet of Grecian and Cyprian mercenaries. Moreover, heralds from the King of kings reached us, saying:

"Surrender, Barbarians, or before the second day dawns you shall sleep sound, every one of you."

To these we answered that we would take counsel on the matter and that perhaps on the morrow we would surrender, since when we had marched from Ethiopia, we did not know how great was the King's strength, having been deceived as to it by the letters of the Pharaoh. Meanwhile that the King of kings would do well to let us alone, since we were brave men and meant to die hard, and it would be better for him to leave us to march back to Ethiopia, rather than lose an army in trying to kill us.

With these words which were spoken by Bes himself, the messengers departed. One of them however, who seemed to be a great lord, called in a loud voice to his companions, saying it was hard that nobles should have to do the errands, not of a man but of an ape who would look better hanging to a pole. Bes made no answer, only rolled his yellow eyes and said when the lord was out of hearing,

"Now by the Grasshopper and all the gods of Egypt I swear that in payment for this insult I will choke the Nile with the army of the Great King, and hang that knave to a pole from the prow of the royal ship." Which last thing I hope he did.

WHEN THE EMBASSY HAD GONE Bes gave orders that the whole army should eat and lie down to sleep.

"I am sure," said he, "that the Great King will not attack us at once, since he will hope that we shall flee away during the night, having seen his strength."

So the Ethiopians filled themselves and then lay down to sleep, which these people can do at any time, even if not tired as they were. But while they rested Bes and I and Karema, with some of the generals consulted together long and earnestly. For in truth we knew not what to do. But a league away lay the town of Amada beset by hundreds of thousands of the Easterns so that none could come in or out, and within its walls were the remains of Pharaoh's army, not more than twenty thousand men, all told, if what we heard were true. On the Nile also was the great Grecian and Cyprian fleet, two hundred vessels and more, though as we could see by the light of the setting sun the most of these were made fast to the western bank where the Egyptians could not come at them.

For the rest our position was good, being on high desert beyond the cultivated land which bordered the eastern bank. But in front of us, separating us from the southern army of the King, stretched a swamp hard to cross, so that we could not hope to make an attack by night as there was no moon. Lastly, the main Eastern strength, to the number of two hundred thousand or more, lay to the north beyond Amada.

All these things we considered, talking low and earnestly there in the tent, till it grew so dark that we could not see each other's faces while behind us slumbered our army that now numbered some seventy thousand men.

"We are in a trap," said Bes at length. "If we await attack they will weigh us down with numbers. If we flee they have camels and horses and will overtake us; also ships of which we have none. If we attack it must be without cover through swamp where we shall be bogged.

"Meanwhile Pharaoh is perishing within yonder walls of Amada which the engines batter down. By the Grasshopper! I know not what to do. It seems that our journey is vain and that few of us will see Ethiopia more; also that Egypt is sped."

I made no answer, for here my generalship failed me and I had nothing to say. The captains, too, were silent, only woman-like, Karema wept a little, and I too went near to weeping who thought of Amada penned in yonder temple like a lamb that awaits the butcher's knife.

Suddenly, coming from the door of the tent which I thought was closed, I heard a deep voice say,

"I have ever noted that those of Ethiopian blood are melancholy after sundown, though of Egyptians I had thought better things."

Now about this voice there was something familiar to me, still I said nothing, nor did the others, for to speak the truth, all of us were frightened and thought that we must dream. For how could any thing that breathed approach this tent through a triple line of sentries? So we sat still, staring at the darkness, till presently in that darkness appeared a glow of light, such as comes from the fire-flies of Ethiopia. It grew and grew while we gasped with fear, till presently it took shape, and the shape it took was that of the ancient withered face, the sightless eyes, and the white beard of the holy Tanofir. Yes, there not two feet from the ground seemed to float the head of the holy Tanofir, limned in faint flame, which I suppose must have been reflected on to it from the light of some camp-fire without.

"O my beloved master!" cried Karema, and threw herself towards him.

"O my beloved Cup!" answered Tanofir. "Glad am I to know you well and unshattered."

Then a torch was lit and lo! there before us, wrapped in his dark cloak sat the holy Tanofir.

"Whence come you, my Great-uncle?" I asked amazed.

"From less far than you do, Nephew," he answered. "Namely out of Amada yonder. Oh! ask me not how. It is easy if you are a blind old beggar who knows the path. And by the way, if you have aught to eat I should be glad of a bite and a sup, since in Amada food has been scarce for this last month, and to-night there is little left."

Karema sped from the tent and presently returned with bread and wine of which Tanofir partook almost greedily.

"This is the first strong drink that I have tasted for many a year," he said as he drained the goblet; "but better a broken vow than broken wits when one has much to plan and do. At least I hope the gods will think so when I meet them presently. There—I am strong again. Now, say, what is your force?"

We told him.

"Good. And what is your plan?"

We shook our heads, having none.

"Bes," he said sternly, "I think you grow dull since you became a king—or perhaps it is marriage that makes you so. Why, in bygone years schemes would have come so fast that they would have choked each other between those thick lips of yours. And Shabaka, tell me, have you lost all your generalship whereof once you had plenty, in the soft air of Ethiopia? Or is it that even the shadow of marriage makes *you* dull? Well, I must turn to the woman, for that is always the lot of man. Your plan, Karema, and quickly for there is no time to lose."

Now the face of Karema grew fixed and her eyes dreamy as she spoke in a slow, measured voice like one who knows not what she says.

"My plan is to destroy the armies of the Great King and to relieve the city of Amada."

"A very good plan," said holy Tanofir, "but the question is, how?"

"I think," went on Karema, "that about a league above this place there is a spot where at this season the Nile can be forded by tall men without the wetting of their shoulders. First then, I would send five thousand swordsmen across that ford and let them creep down on the navy of the Great King where the sailors revel in safety, or sleep sound, and fire the ships. The wind blows strongly from the south and the flames will leap fast from one of them to the other. Most of their crews will be burned and the rest can be slain by our five thousand."

"Good, very good," said the holy Tanofir, "but not enough, seeing that on the eastern bank is gathered the host of over two hundred thousand men. Now how will you deal with *them*, Karema?"

"I seem to see a road yonder beyond the swamp. It runs on the edge of the desert but behind the sand-hills. I would send the archers of whom there are more than thirty thousand, under the command of Shabaka along that road which leads them past Amada. On its farther side are low hills strewn with rocks. Here I would let the archers take cover and wait for the breaking of the dawn. Then beneath them they will see the most of the Eastern host and with such bows as ours they can sweep the plain from the hills almost to the Nile, and having a hundred arrows to a man, should slaughter the Easterns by the ten thousand, for when these turn to charge a shaft should pierce through two together."

"Good again," said Tanofir. "But what of the army of the Great King which lies upon this side of Amada?"

"I think that before the dawn, believing us so few, it will advance and with the first light begin to thread the swamp, and therefore we must keep five thousand archers to gall it as it comes. Still it will win through, though with loss, and find us waiting for it here shoulder to shoulder, rank upon rank with locked shields, against which horse and foot shall break in vain, for who shall drive a wedge through the Ethiopian squares that Shabaka has trained and that Bes, the Karoon, commands? I say that they shall roll back like waves from a cliff; yes, again and again, growing ever fewer till the clamour of battle and the shouts of fear and agony reach their ears from beyond Amada where Shabaka and the archers do their work and the sight of the burning ships strikes terror in them and they fly."

"Good again," said the holy Tanofir. "But still many on both fronts will be left, for this army of Easterns is very vast. And how will you deal with these, O Karema?"

"On these I would have Pharaoh with all his remaining strength pour from the northern and the southern gates of Amada, for so shall they be caught like wounded lions between two wild bulls and torn and trampled and utterly destroyed. Only I know not how to tell Pharaoh what he must do, and when."

"Good again," said the holy Tanofir, "very good. And as for the telling of Pharaoh, well, I shall see him presently. It is strange, my chipped Cup which I had almost thrown away as useless, that although broken, you still hold so much wisdom. For know, wonderful though it may seem, that just such plans as you have spoken have grown up in my own mind, only I wished to learn if you thought them wise."

Then he laughed a little and Karema stretched her arms as one does who awakes from sleep, rubbed her eyes and asked if he would not eat more food.

In an instant Tanofir was speaking again in a quick, clear voice.

"Bes, or King," he said, "doubtless you will do your wife's will. Therefore let the host be aroused and stand to its arms. As it chances I have four men without who can be trusted. Two of these will guide the five thousand to the ford and across it; also down upon the ships. The other two will guide Shabaka and the archers along the road which Karema remembers so well; perhaps she trod it as a child. For my part I return to Amada to make sure that Pharaoh does his share and at the right time. For mark, unless all this is carried through to-night Amada will fall to-morrow, a certain priestess will die, and you, Bes, and your soldiers will never look on Ethiopia again. Is it agreed?"

I nodded who did not wish to waste time in words, and Bes rolled his eyes and answered,

"When one can think of nothing, it is best to follow the counsel of those who can think of something; also to hunt rather than to be hunted. Especially is this so if that something comes from the holy Tanofir or his broken Cup. Generals, you have heard. Rouse the host and bid them stand to their arms company by company!"

The generals leapt away into the darkness like arrows from a bow, and presently we heard the noise of gathering men.

"Where are these guides of yours, holy Tanofir?" asked Bes.

Tanofir beckoned over his shoulder, and out of the gloom, one by one, four men stole into the tent. They were strange, quiet men, but I can say no more of them since their faces were veiled, nor as it chances, did I ever see any of them after the battle, in which I suppose that they were killed. Or perhaps they appeared after—well, never mind!

"You have heard," said Tanofir, whereupon all four of them bowed their mysterious veiled heads.

"Now, my Brother," whispered Bes into my ear, "tell me, I pray you, how did four men who were not in the tent, hear what was said in this tent, and how did they come through the guards who have orders to kill anyone who does not know the countersign, especially men whose faces are wrapped in napkins?"

"I do not know," I answered, whereon Bes groaned, only Karema smiled a little as though to herself.

"Then, having heard, obey," said the holy Tanofir, whereon the four veiled ones bowed again.

"Will you not give them their orders, O most Venerable?" inquired Bes doubtfully.

"I think it is needless," said Tanofir in a dry voice. "Why try to teach those who know?"

"Will you not offer them something to eat, since they also must be hungry?" I asked of Karema.

"Fool, be silent," she replied, looking on me with contempt. "Do the—friends—of Tanofir need to eat?"

"I should have thought so after being beleaguered for a month in a starving town. If the master wants to eat, why should not his men?" I murmured.

Then a thought struck me and I was silent.

A general returned and reported that the orders had been executed and that all the army was afoot.

"Good," said Bes. "Then start forthwith with five thousand men, and burn those ships, according to the plan laid down by the Queen Karema, which you heard her speak but now," and he named certain regiments that he should take with him, those of the general's own command, adding: "Save some of the ships if you can, and afterwards cross the Nile in them with your men, and join yourself either to my force or to that of the lord Shabaka, according to what you see. May the Grasshopper give you victory and wisdom."

The general saluted and asked,

"Who guides us to and across the ford of the great river?"

Two of the veiled men stepped forward whereon the general muttered into my ear,

"I like not the look of them. I pray the Grasshopper they do not guide us across the River of Death."

"Have no fear, General," said the holy Tanofir from the other end of the tent. "If you and your men play their parts as well as the guides will play theirs, the ships are already burned together with their companies. Only take fire with you."

So that general departed with the two guides, looking somewhat frightened, and soon was marching up Nile at the head of five thousand swordsmen.

Now Bes looked at me and said,

"It seems that you had better be gone also, my Brother, with the archers. Perchance the holy Tanofir will show you whither."

"No, no," answered Tanofir, "my guides will show him. Look not so doubtful, Shabaka. Did I fail you when you were in the grip of the King of kings in the East, and only your own life and that of Bes were at stake?"

"I do not know," I answered.

"You do not know, but I know, as I think do Bes and Karema, since the one received the messages which the other sent. Well, if I did not fail you then, shall I fail you now when Egypt is at stake? Follow these guides I give you, and——" here he took hold of the quiver of arrows that lay beside me on the ground, and as certainly as though he could see it with his blind eyes, touched one of them, on the shaft of which were two black and a white feather, "remember my words after you have loosed this arrow from your great black bow and noted where it strikes."

Then I turned to Bes and asked,

"Where do we meet again?"

"I cannot say, Brother," he answered. "In Amada if that may be. If not, at the Table of Osiris, or in the fields of the Grasshopper, or in the blackness which swallows all, gods and men together."

"Does Karema come with me or bide with you?" I asked again.

"She does neither," interrupted Tanofir, "she accompanies me to Amada, where I have need of her and she will be more safe. Oh! fear nothing, for every hermit however poor, still carries his staff and his cup, even if it be cracked."

Then I shook Bes by the hand and went my way, wondering if I were awake or dreaming, and the last thing I saw in that tent was the beautiful face of Karema smiling at me. This I took to be a good omen, since I knew that it was the heart of the holy Tanofir which smiled, and that her eyes were but its mirror.

Already my thirty thousand archers were marshalling, and having made sure that there was ample store of arrows and that all their gourds were filled with water, I set myself at their head while in front of me walked the two veiled guides. I looked upon them doubtfully, since it seemed dangerous to trust an army to unknown men who for aught I knew, might lead us into the midst of our foes. Then I remembered that they were vouched for by the holy Tanofir, my own great-uncle whom I trusted above any man on earth, and took heart again.

How had he come into our tent, I wondered, and how, blind as he was, would he get back into Amada with Karema, if he took her? Well, who could account for the goings or the comings of the holy Tanofir, who was more of a spirit than a man? Perhaps it was not really he whom we had seen, but what we Egyptians called his *Ka* or Double which can pass to and fro at will. Only do *Kas* eat? Of this matter I knew only that offerings of food and drink are made to them in tombs. So leaving the holy Tanofir to guard himself, I turned my mind to our own business, which was to surprise the army of the Great King.

Skirting the swamp we came to rough and higher ground and though I could see little in that darkness, I knew that we were walking up a hill. Presently we crossed its crest and descending for three bowshots or so, I felt that my feet were on a road. Now the guides turned to the left and after them in a long line came my army of thirty thousand archers. In utter silence we went since we had no beasts with us and our sandalled feet made little noise; moreover orders had been passed down the line that the man who made a sound should die.

For two hours or more we marched thus, then bore to the left again and climbed a slope, by which time I judged we must be well past the town of Amada. Here suddenly the guides halted and we after them at whispered words of command. One of them took me by the cloak, led me forward a little way to the crest of the ridge, and pointed with his white-sleeved arm. I looked and there beneath me, well within bowshot, were thousands of the watchfires of the King's army, flaring, some of them, in the strong wind. For a full league those fires burned and we were opposite to the midmost of them.

"See now, General Shabaka," said the guide, speaking for the first time in a curious hissing whisper such as might come from a man who had no lips, "beneath you sleeps the Eastern host, which being so great, has not thought it needful to guard this ridge. Now marshal your archers in a fourfold line in such fashion that at the first break of dawn they can take cover behind the rocks and shoot, every man of them without piercing his fellow. Do you bide here with the centre where your standard can be seen by all to north and south. I and my companion will lead your vanguard farther on to where the ridge draws nearer to the Nile, so that with their arrows they can hold back and slay any who strive to escape down stream. The rest is in your hands, for we are guides, not generals. Summon your captains and issue your commands."

So we went back again and I called the officers together and told them what they were to do, then despatched them to their regiments.

Presently the vanguard of ten thousand men drew away and vanished, and with them the white-robed guides on whom I never looked again. Then I marshalled my centre as well as I could in the gloom, and bade them lie down to rest and sleep if they were able; also, within thirty minutes of the sunrise, to eat and drink a little of the food they carried, to see that every bow was ready and that the arrows were loosened in every quiver. This done, with a few whom I trusted to serve me as messengers and guard, I crept up to the brow of the hill or slope, and there we laid us down and watched.

XVII

The Battle—And After

Two hours went by and I knew by the stars that the dawn could not be far away. My eyes were fixed upon the Nile and on the lights that hung to the prows of the Great King's ships. Where were those who had been sent to fire them, I wondered, for of them I saw nothing. Well, their journey would be long as they must wade the river. Perhaps they had not yet arrived, or perhaps they had miscarried. At least the fleet seemed very quiet. None were alarmed there and no sentry challenged.

At length it grew near to dawn and behind me I heard the gentle stir of the Ethiopians arising and eating as they had been bidden, whereon I too ate and drank a little, though never had I less wished for food. The East brightened and far up the Nile of a sudden there appeared what at first I took to be a meteor or a lantern waving in the wind that now was blowing its strongest, as it does at this season of the year just at the time of dawn. Yet that lantern seemed to travel fast and lo! now I saw that it was fire running up the rigging of a ship.

It leapt from rope to rope and from sail to sail till they blazed fiercely, and in other ships also nearer to us, flame appeared that grew to a great red sheet. Our men had not failed; the navy of the King of kings was burning! Oh! how it burned fanned by the breath of that strong wind. From vessel to vessel leapt the fire like a thing alive, for all of them were drawn up on the bank with prows fastened in such fashion that they could not readily be made loose. Some broke away indeed, but they were aflame and only served to spread the fire more quickly. Before the rim of the sun appeared for a league or more there was nothing but blazing ships from which rose a hideous crying, and still more and more took fire lower down the line.

I had no time to watch for now I must be up and doing. The sky grew grey, there was light enough to see though faintly. I cast my eyes about me and perceived that no place in the world could have been better for archery. In front the hill was steep for a hundred paces or more and scattered over with thousands of large stones behind which bowmen might take shelter. Then came a gentle slope of loose sand up which attackers would find it hard to climb. Then the long flat plain whereon the Easterns were camped, and beyond it, scarce two furlongs away, the banks of Nile.

Indeed the place was ill-chosen for so great an army, nor could it have held them all, had not the camping ground been a full league in length, and even so they were crowded. Out of the mist their tents appeared, thousands of them, farther than my eye could reach, and almost opposite to me, near to the banks of the river, was a great pavilion of silk and gold that I guessed must shelter the majesty of the King of kings. Indeed this was certain since now I saw that over it floated his royal banner which I knew so well, I who had stolen the little White Signet of signets from which it was taken. Truly the holy Tanofir, or his Cup, Karema, or his messengers, or the spirits with whom he dwelt, I know not which, had a general's eye and knew how to plan an ambuscade.

So, thought I to myself as I ran back to my army to meet the gathered captains and set all things in order. It was soon done for they were ready, as were the fierce Ethiopians fresh from their rest and food, and stringing their bows, every one of them, or loosening the arrows in their quivers. As I came they lifted their hands in salute, for speak they dared not and I sent a whisper down their ranks, that this day they must fight and conquer, or fall for the glory of Ethiopia and their king. Then I gave my orders and before the sun rose and revealed them they crept forward in a fourfold line and took shelter behind the stones, lying there invisible on their bellies until the moment came.

The red rim of Ra appeared glorious in the East, and I, from behind the rocks that I had chosen, sat down and watched. Oh! truly Tanofir or the gods of Egypt were ordering things aright for us. The huge camp was awake now and aware of what was happening on the Nile. They could not see well because of the tall reeds upon the river's rim and therefore, without order or discipline, by the thousand and the ten thousand, for their numbers were countless, some with arms and some without, they ran to the slope of sand beneath our station and began to climb it to have a better view of the burning ships.

The sun leapt up swiftly as it does in Egypt. His glowing edge appeared over the crest of the hill though the hollows beneath were still filled with shadow. The moment was at hand. I waited till I had counted ten, glancing to the right and left of me to see that all were ready and to suffer the crowd to thicken on the slope, but not to reach the lowest rocks, whither they were climbing. Then I gave the double signal that had been agreed.

Behind me the banner of the golden Grasshopper was raised upon a tall pole and broke upon the breeze. That was the first signal whereat every man rose to his knees and set shaft on string. Next I lifted my bow, the black bow, the ancient bow that few save I could bend, and drew it to my ear.

Far away, out of arrow-reach as most would have said, floated the Great King's standard over his pavilion. At this I aimed, making allowance for the wind, and shot. The shaft leapt forward, seen in the sunlight, lost in the shadow, seen in the sunlight again and lastly seen once more, pinning that golden standard against its pole!

At the sight of the omen a roar went up that rolled to right and left of us, a roar from thirty thousand throats. Now it was lost in a sound like to the hissing of thunder rain in Ethiopia, the sound of thirty thousand arrows rushing through the wind. Oh! they were well aimed, those arrows for I had not taught the Ethiopians archery in vain.

How many went down before them? The gods of Egypt know alone. I do not. All I know is that the long slope of sand which had been crowded with standing men, was now thick with fallen men, many of whom lay as though they were asleep. For what mail could resist the iron-pointed shafts driven by the strong bows of the Ethiopians?

And this was but a beginning, for, flight after flight, those arrows sped till the air grew dark with them. Soon there were no more to shoot at on the slope, for these were down, and the order went to lift the bows and draw upon the camp, and especially upon the parks of baggage beasts. Presently these were down also, or rushing maddened to and fro.

At last the Eastern generals saw and understood. Orders were shouted and in a mad confusion the scores of thousands who were unharmed, rushed back towards the banks of Nile where our shafts could not reach them. Here they formed up in their companies and took counsel. It was soon ended, for all the vast mass of them, preceded by a cloud of archers, began to advance upon the hill.

Now I passed a command to the Ethiopians, of whom so far not one had fallen, to lie low and wait. On came the glittering multitude of Easterns, gay with purple and gold, their mail and swords shining in the risen sun. On they came by squadron and by company, more than the eye could number. They reached the sand slope thick with their own dead and wounded and paused a little because they could see no man, since the black bodies of the Ethiopians were hid behind the black stones and the black bows did not catch the light.

Then from a gorgeous group that I guessed hid the person of the Great King surrounded by his regiment of guards, ten thousand of them who were called Immortals, messengers sprang forth screaming the order to charge. The host began to climb the slippery sand slope but still I held my hand till their endless lines were within fifty paces of us and their arrows rattled harmlessly against our stones. Then I caused the banner of the Grasshopper that had been lowered, to be lifted thrice, and at the third lifting once more thirty thousand arrows rushed forth to kill.

They went down, they went down in lines and heaps, riddled through and through. But still others came on for they fought under the eye of the Great King, and to fly meant death with shame and torture. We could not kill them all, they were too many. We could not kill the half of them. Now their foremost were within ten paces of us and since we must stand up to shoot, our men began to fall, also pierced with arrows. I caused the blast of retreat to be sounded on the ivory horn and step by step we drew back to the crest of the ridge, shooting as we went. On the crest we re-formed rapidly in a double line standing as close as we could together and my example was followed all down the ranks to right and left. Then I bethought me of a plan that I had taught these archers again and again in Ethiopia.

With the flag I signalled a command to stop shooting and also passed the word down the line, so that presently no more arrows flew. The Easterns hesitated, wondering whether this were a trap, or if we lacked shafts, and meanwhile I sent messengers with certain orders to the vanguard, who sped away at speed behind the hill, running as they never ran before. Presently I heard a voice below cry out,

"The Great King commands that the barbarians be destroyed. Let the barbarians be destroyed!"

Now with a roar they came on like a flood. I waited till they were within twenty paces of us, and shouted, "Shoot and fall!"

The first line shot and oh! fearful was its work, for not a shaft missed those crowded hosts and many pinned two together. My archers shot and fell down, setting new arrows to the string as they fell, whereon the second line also shot over them. Then up we sprang and loosed again, and again fell down, whereon the second line once more poured in its deadly hail.

Now the Easterns stayed their advance, for their front ranks lay prone, and those behind must climb over them if they could. Yes, standing there in glittering groups they rocked and hesitated although their officers struck them with swords and lances to drive them forward. Once more our front rank rose and loosed, and once more we dropped and let the shafts of the second speed over us. It was too much, flesh and blood could not bear more of those arrows. Thousands upon thousands were down and the rest began to flee in confusion.

Then at my command the ivory horns sounded the charge. Every man slung his bow upon his back and drew his short sword.

"On to them!" I cried and leapt forward.

Like a black torrent we rushed down the hill, leaping over the dead and wounded. The retreat became a rout since before these ebon, great-eyed warriors the soft Easterns did not care to stand. They fled screaming,

"These are devils! These are devils!"

We were among them now, hacking and stabbing with the short swords upon their heads and backs. There was no need to aim the blow, they were so many. Like a huddled mob of cattle they turned and fled down Nile. But my orders had reached the vanguard and these, hidden in the growing crops on the narrow neck of swampy land between the hills and the Nile, met them with arrows as they came, also raked them from the steep cliff side. Their chariot wheels sank into the mud till the horses were slain; their footmen were piled in heaps about them, till soon there was a mighty wall of dead and dying. And our centre and rearguard came up behind. Oh! we slew and slew, till before the sun was an hour high over half the army of the Great King was no more. Then we re-formed, having suffered but little loss, and drank of the water of the Nile.

"All is not done," I cried.

For the Immortals still remained behind us, gathered in massed ranks about their king. Also there were many thousands of others between these and the walls of Amada, and to the south of the city yet a second army, that with which Bes had been left to deal, with what success I knew not.

"Ethiopians," I shouted, "cease crying Victory, since the battle is about to begin. Strike, and at once before the Easterns find their heart again."

So we advanced upon the Immortals, all of us, for now the vanguard had joined our strength.

In long lines we advanced over that blood-soaked plain, and as we came the Great King loosed his remaining chariots against us. It availed him nothing, since the horses could not face our arrows whereof, thanks be to the gods! I had prepared so ample a store, carried in bundles by lads. Scarce a chariot reached our lines, and those that did were destroyed, leaving us unbroken.

The chariots were done with and their drivers dead, but there still frowned the squares of the Immortals. We shot at them till nearly all our shafts were spent, and, galled to madness, they charged. We did not wait for the points of those long spears, but ran in beneath them striking with our short swords, and oh! grim and desperate was that battle, since the Easterns were clad in mail and the Ethiopians had but short jerkins of bull's hide.

Fight as we would we were driven back. The fray turned against us and we fell by hundreds. I bethought me of flight to the hills, since now we were outnumbered and very weary. But behold! when all seemed lost a great shouting rose from Amada and through her opened gates poured forth all that remained of the army of Pharaoh, perhaps eighteen or twenty thousand men. I saw, and my heart rose again.

"Stand firm!" I cried. "Stand firm!" and lo! we stood.

The Egyptians were on them now and in their midst I saw Pharaoh's banner. By degrees the battle swayed towards the banks of Nile, we to the north, the Egyptians to the south and the Easterns between us. They were trying to turn our flank; yes, and would have done it, had there not suddenly appeared upon the Nile a fleet of ships. At first I thought that we were lost, for these ships were from Greece and Cyprus, till I saw the banner of the Grasshopper wave from a prow, and knew that they were manned by our five thousand who had gone out to burn the fleet, and had saved these vessels. They beached and from their crowded holds poured the five thousand, or those that were left of them, and ranging themselves upon the bank, raised their war-shout and attacked the ends of the Easterns' lines.

Now we charged for the last time and the Egyptians charged from the south. Ha-ha! the ranks of the Immortals were broken at length. We were among them. I saw Pharaoh, his *uræus* circlet on his helm. He was wounded and sore beset. A tall Immortal rushed at him with a spear and drove it home.

Pharaoh fell.

I leapt over him and killed that Eastern with a blow upon the neck, but my sword shattered on his armour. The tide of battle rolled up and swept us apart and I saw Pharaoh being carried away. Look! yonder was the Great King himself standing in a golden chariot, the Great King in all his glory whom last I had seen far away in the East. He knew me and shot at me with a bow, the bow he thought my own, shouting, "Die, dog of an Egyptian!"

His arrow pierced my helm but missed my head. I strove to come at him but could not.

The real rout began. The Immortals were broken like an earthen jar. They retreated in groups fighting desperately and of these the thickest was around the Great King. He whom I hated was about to escape me. He still had horses; he would fly down Nile, gain his reserves and so away back to the East, where he would gather new and yet larger armies, since men in millions were at his command. Then he would return and destroy Egypt when perchance there were no Ethiopians to help her, and perhaps after all drag Amada to his House of Women. See, they were breaking through and already I was far away with a wound in my breast, a hurt leg and a shattered sword.

What could I do? My arrows were spent and the bearers had none left to give me. No, there was one still in the quiver. I drew it out. On its shaft were two black feathers and one white. Who had spoken of that arrow? I remembered, Tanofir. I was to think of certain things that he had said when I noted what it pierced. I unslung my bow, strung it and set that arrow on the string.

By now the Great King was far away, out of reach for most archers. His chariot forging ahead amidst the remnant of his guards and the nobles who attended on his sacred person, travelled over a little rise where doubtless once there had been a village, long since rotted down to its parent clay. The sunlight glinted on his shining armour and silken robe, whereof the back was toward me.

I aimed, I drew, I loosed! Swift and far the shaft sped forward. By Osiris! it struck him full between the shoulders, and lo! the King of kings, the Monarch of the World, lurched forward, fell on to the rail of his chariot, and rolled to the ground. Next instant there arose a roar of, "The King is dead! The Great King is dead! *Fly, fly, fly!*"

So they fled and after them thundered the pursuers slaying and slaying till they could lift their arms no more. Oh! yes, some escaped though the men of Thebes and country folk murdered many of them and but a few ever won back to the East to tell the tale of the blotting out of the mighty army of the King of kings and of the doom dealt to him by the great black bow of Shabaka the Egyptian.

I stood there gasping, when suddenly I heard a voice at my side. It said,

"You seem to have done very well, Brother, even better than we did yonder on the other side of the town, though some might think that fray a thing whereof to make a song. Also that last shot of yours was worthy of a good archer, for I marked it, I marked it. A great lord was laid low thereby. Let us go and see who it was."

I threw my arm round the bull neck of Bes and leaning on him, advanced to where the King lay alone save for the fallen about him.

"This man is not yet sped," said Bes. "Let us look upon his face," and he turned him over, and stretched him there upon the sand with the arrow standing two spans beyond his corselet.

"Why," said Bes, "this is a certain High one with whom we had dealings in the East!" and he laughed thickly.

Then the Great King opened his eyes and knew us and on his dying features came a look of hate.

"So you have conquered, Egyptian," he said. "Oh! if only I had you again in the East, whence in my folly I let you go——"

"You would set me in your boat, would you not, whence by the wisdom of Bes I escaped."

"More than that," he gasped.

"I shall not serve you so," I went on. "I shall leave you to die as a warrior should upon a fair fought field. But learn, tyrant and murderer, that the shaft which overthrew you came from the black bow you coveted and thought you had received, and that this hand loosed it—not at hazard."

"I guessed it," he whispered.

"Know, too, King, that the lady Amada whom you also coveted, waits to be my wife; that your mighty army is destroyed, and that Egypt is free by the hands of Shabaka the Egyptian and Bes the dwarf."

"Shabaka the Egyptian," he muttered, "whom I held and let go because of a dream and for policy. So, Shabaka, you will wed Amada whom I desired because I could not take her, and doubtless you will rule in Egypt, for Pharaoh, I think, is as I am to-day. O Shabaka, you are strong and a great warrior, but there is something stronger than you in the world—that which men call Fate. Such success as yours offends the gods. Look on me, Shabaka, look on the King of kings, the Ruler of the earth, lying shamed in the dust before you, and, accursed Shabaka! do not call yourself happy until you see death as near as I do now."

Then he threw his arms wide and died.

WE CALLED TO SOLDIERS TO bear his body and having set the pursuit, with that royal clay entered into Amada in triumph. It was not a very great town and the temple was its finest building and thither we wended. In the outer court we found Pharaoh lying at the point of death, for from many wounds his life drained out with his flowing blood, nor could the leeches help him.

"Greeting, Shabaka," he said, "you and the Ethiopians have saved Egypt. My son is slain in the battle and I too am slain, and who remains to rule her save you, you and Amada? Would that you had married her at once, and never left my side. But she was foolish and headstrong and I—was jealous of you, Shabaka. Forgive me, and farewell."

He spoke no more although he lived a little while.

Karema came from the inner court. She greeted her husband, then turned and said,

"Lord Shabaka, one waits to welcome you."

I rested myself upon her shoulder, for I could not walk alone.

"What happened to the army of the Karoon?" I asked as we went slowly.

"That happened, Lord, which the holy Tanofir foretold. The Easterns attacked across the swamp, thinking to bear us down by numbers. But the paths were too narrow and their columns were bogged in the mud. Still they struggled on against the arrows to its edge and there the Ethiopians fell on them and being lighter-footed and without armour, had the mastery of them, who were encumbered by their very multitude. Oh! I saw it all from the temple top. Bes did well and I am proud of him, as I am proud of you."

"It is of the Ethiopians that you should be proud, Karema, since with one to five they have won a great battle."

We came to the end of the second court where was a sanctuary.

"Enter," said Karema and fell back.

I did so and though the cedar door was left a little ajar, at first could see nothing because of the gloom of the place. By degrees my eyes grew accustomed to the darkness and I perceived an alabaster statue of the goddess Isis of the size of life, who held in her arms an ivory child, also lifesize. Then I heard a sigh and, looking down, saw a woman clad in white kneeling at the feet of the statue, lost in prayer. Suddenly she rose and turned and the ray of light from the door ajar fell upon her. It was Amada draped only in the transparent robe of a priestess, and oh! she was beautiful beyond imagining, so beautiful that my heart stood still.

She saw me in my battered mail and the blood flowed up to her breast and brow and in her eyes there came a light such as I had never known in them before, the light that is lit only by the torch of woman's love. Yes, no longer were hers the eyes of a priestess; they were the eyes of a woman who burns with mortal passion.

"Amada," I whispered, "Amada found at last."

"Shabaka," she whispered back, "returned at last, to me, your home," and she stretched out her arms toward me.

But before I could take her into mine, she uttered a little cry and shrank away.

"Oh! not here," she said, "not here in the presence of this Holy One who watches all that passes in heaven and earth."

"Then perchance, Amada, she has watched the freeing of Egypt on yonder field to-day, and knows for whose sake it was done."

"Hearken, Shabaka. I am your guerdon. Moreover as a woman I am yours. There is naught I desire so much as to feel your kiss upon me. For it and it alone I am ready to risk my spirit's death and torment. But for you I fear. Twice have I sworn myself to this goddess and she is very jealous of those who rob her of her votaries. I fear that her curse will fall not only on me, but on you also, and not only for this life but for all lives that may be given to us. For your own sake, I pray you leave me. I hear that Pharaoh my uncle is dead or dying, and doubtless they will offer you the throne. Take it, Shabaka, for in it I ask no share. Take it and leave me to serve the goddess till my death."

"I too serve a goddess," I answered hoarsely, "and she is named Love, and you are her priestess. Little I care for Isis who serve the goddess Love. Come, kiss me here and now, ere perchance I die. Kiss me who have waited long enough, and so let us be wed."

One moment she paused, swaying in the wind of passion, like a tall reed on the banks of Nile, and then, ah! then she sank upon my breast and pressed her lips against my own.

And After

FOR A FEW MOMENTS I, Shabaka, seemed to be lost in a kind of delirium and surrounded by a rose-hued mist. Then I, Allan Quatermain, heard a sharp quick sound as of a clock striking, and looked up. It was a lock, a beautiful old clock on a mantelpiece opposite to me and the hands showed that it had just struck the hour of ten.

Now I remembered that centuries ago, as I was dropping asleep, I did not know why, I had seen that clock and those hands in the same position and known that it was striking the second stroke of ten. Oh! what did it all mean? Had thousands of years gone by or—only eight seconds?

There was a weight upon my shoulder. I glanced round to see what it was and discovered the beautiful head of Lady Ragnall who was sweetly sleeping there. Lady Ragnall! and in that very strange dream which I had dreamed she was the priestess called Amada. Look, there was the mark of the new moon above her breast. And not a second ago I had been in a shrine with Amada dressed as Lady Ragnall was to-night, in circumstances so intimate that it made me blush to think of them. Lady Ragnall! Amada!—Amada! Lady Ragnall! A shrine! A boudoir! Oh! I must be going mad!

I could not disturb her, it would have been—well, unseemly. So I, Shabaka, or Allan Quatermain, just sat still feeling curiously comfortable, and tried to piece things together, when suddenly Amada—I mean Lady Ragnall woke.

"I wonder," she said without lifting her head from my shoulder, "what happened to the holy Tanofir. I think that I heard him outside the shine giving directions for the digging of Pharaoh's grave at that spot, and saying that he must do so at once as his time was very short. Yes, and I wished that he would go away. Oh! my goodness!" she exclaimed, and suddenly sprang up.

I too rose and we stood facing each other.

Between us, in front of the fire stood the tripod and the bowl of black stone at the bottom of which lay a pinch of white ashes, the remains of the *Taduki*. We stared at it and at each other.

"Oh! where have we been, Shaba—I mean, Mr. Quatermain?" she gasped, looking at me round-eyed.

"I don't know," I answered confusedly. "To the East I suppose. That is—it was all a dream."

"A dream!" she said. "What nonsense! Tell me, were you or were you not in a sanctuary just now with me before the statue of Isis, the same that fell on George two years ago and killed him, and did you or did you not give me a necklace of wonderful rosy pearls which we put upon the neck of the statue as a peace-offering because I had broken my vows to the goddess—those that you won from the Great King?"

"No," I answered triumphantly, "I did nothing of the sort. Is it likely that I should have taken those priceless pearls into battle? I gave them to Karema to keep after my mother returned them to me on her death-bed; I remember it distinctly."

"Yes, and Karema handed them to me again as your love-token when she appeared in the city with the holy Tanofir, and what was more welcome at the moment—something to eat. For we were near starving, you know. Well, I threw them over your neck and my own in the shrine to be the symbol of our eternal union. But afterwards we thought that it might be wise to offer them to the goddess—to appease her, you know. Oh! how dared we plight our mortal troth there in her very shrine and presence, and I her twice-sworn servant? It was insult heaped on sacrilege."

"At a guess, because love is stronger than fear," I replied. "But it seems that you dreamed a little longer than I did. So perhaps you can tell me what happened afterwards. I only got as far as—well, I forget how far I got," I added, for at that moment full memory returned and I could not go on.

She blushed to her eyes and grew disturbed.

"It is all mixed up in my mind too," she exclaimed. "I can only remember something rather absurd—and affectionate. You know what strange things dreams are."

"I thought you said it wasn't a dream."

"Really I don't know what it was. But—your wound doesn't hurt you, does it? You were bleeding a good deal. It stained me here," and she touched her breast and looked down wonderingly at her sacred, ancient robe as though she expected to see that it was red.

"As there is no stain now it *must* have been a dream. But my word! that was a battle," I answered.

"Yes, I watched it from the pylon top, and oh! it was glorious. Do you remember the charge of the Ethiopians against the Immortals? Why of course you must as you led it. And then the fall of Pharaoh Peroa—he was George, you know. And the death of the Great King, killed by your black bow; you were a wonderful shot even then, you see. And the burning of the ships, how they blazed! And—a hundred other things."

"Yes," I said, "it came off. The holy Tanofir was a good strategist—or his Cup was, I don't know which."

"And you were a good general, and so for the matter of that was Bes. Oh! what agonies I went through while the fight hung doubtful. My heart was on fire, yes, I seemed to burn for——" and she stopped.

"For whom?" I asked.

"For Egypt of course, and when, reflected in the alabaster, I saw you enter that shrine, where you remember I was praying for your success—and safety, I nearly died of joy. For you know I had been, well, attached to you—to Shabaka, I mean—all the time—that's my part of the story which I daresay you did not see. Although I seemed so cold and wayward I could love, yes, in that life I knew how to love. And Shabaka looked, oh! a hero with his rent mail and the glory of triumph in his eyes. He was very handsome, too, in his way. But what nonsense I am talking."

"Yes, great nonsense. Still, I wish we were sure how it ended. It is a pity that you forget, for I am crazed with curiosity. I suppose there is no more *Taduki*, is there?"

"Not a scrap," she answered firmly, "and if there were it would be fatal to take it twice on the same day. We have learned all there is to learn. Perhaps it is as well, though I should like to know what happened after our—our marriage."

"So we *were* married, were we?"

"I mean," she went on ignoring my remark, "whether you ruled long in Egypt. For you, or rather Shabaka, did rule. Also whether the Easterns returned and drove us out, or what. You see the Ivory Child went away somehow, for we found it again in Kendah Land only a few years ago."

"Perhaps we retired to Ethiopia," I suggested, "and the worship of the Child continued in some part of that country after the Ethiopian kingdom passed away."

"Perhaps, only I don't think Karema would ever have gone back to Ethiopia unless she was obliged. You remember how she hated the place. No, not even to see those black children of hers. Well, as we can never tell, it is no use speculating."

"I thought there *was* more *Taduki*," I remarked sadly. "I am sure I saw some in the coffer."

"Not one bit," she answered still more firmly than before, and, stretching out her hand, she shut down the lid of the coffer before I could look into it. "It may be best so, for as it stands the story had a happy ending and I don't want to learn, oh! I don't want to learn how the curse of Isis fell on you and me."

"So you believe in that?"

"Yes, I do," she answered with passion, "and what is more, I believe it is working still, which perhaps is why we have all come down in the world, you and I and George and Hans, yes, and even old Harût whom we knew in Kendah Land, who, I think, was the holy Tanofir. For as surely as I live I *know* beyond possibility of doubt that whatever we may be called to-day, you were the General Shabaka and I was the priestess Amada, Royal Lady of Egypt, and between us and about us the curse of Isis wavers like a sword. That is why George was killed and that is why—but I feel very tired, I think I had better go to bed."

As I recall that I have explained, I was obliged to leave Ragnall Castle early the next morning to keep a shooting engagement. O heavens! to keep a shooting engagement!

But whatever Amada, I mean Lady Ragnall, said, there *was* plenty more *Taduki*, as I have good reason to know.

Allan Quatermain

A Note About the Author

Sir Henry Rider Haggard, (1856–1925) commonly known as H. Rider Haggard was an English author active during the Victorian era. Considered a pioneer of the lost world genre, Haggard was known for his adventure fiction. His work often depicted African settings inspired by the seven years he lived in South Africa with his family. In 1880, Haggard married Marianna Louisa Margitson and together they had four children, one of which followed her father's footsteps and became an author. Haggard is still widely read today, and is celebrated for his imaginative wit and impact on 19th century adventure literature.

A Note from the Publisher

Spanning many genres, from non-fiction essays to literature classics to children's books and lyric poetry, Mint Edition books showcase the master works of our time in a modern new package. The text is freshly typeset, is clean and easy to read, and features a new note about the author in each volume. Many books also include exclusive new introductory material. Every book boasts a striking new cover, which makes it as appropriate for collecting as it is for gift giving. Mint Edition books are only printed when a reader orders them, so natural resources are not wasted. We're proud that our books are never manufactured in excess and exist only in the exact quantity they need to be read and enjoyed. To learn more and view our library, go to minteditionbooks.com

bookfinity & MINT EDITIONS

Enjoy more of your favorite classics with Bookfinity,
a new search and discovery experience for readers.
With Bookfinity, you can discover more vintage
literature for your collection, find your Reader Type,
track books you've read or want to read,
and add reviews to your favorite books.
Visit www.bookfinity.com, and click on
Take the Quiz to get started.

Don't forget to follow us
@bookfinityofficial and @mint_editions